Heart's Compass

FLIGHT OF THE HAWK

ALIYAH BURKE

Keeper of the Stars
Part One
Part Two
Part Three
Part Four
Part Five

Astral Guardians
Chasing the Storm
Highlands at Dawn
Fields of Thunder
Branded by Frost
Driven by Night
Moon of Fire

Family Forever
Don't You Wanna Stay?
Love and Moonshine
First You Dream

What's her Secret?
Preconception

A Little Bit Cupid
This Ain't No Love Story

My Bloody Valentine
Perfect Duet

With Taige Crenshaw

Single Title
Unbreakable Bonds

Kemet Uncovered
Talios
Devi
Linc
Saffron
Taber
Ashia

FLIGHT OF THE HAWK

Chapter One

Blood soaked the field where the battle had taken its toll on all involved. Black, white, pro, con, it didn't matter the reason you fought, for in the end everyone's blood had run the same. Red. Dark, rich red.

Lots of it.

Too much of it.

The men's boots sank into the mix of snow, mud and blood and made an awful sucking noise when they tried to walk on it. A noise that pulled at your soul, if you still had one in your body, after surviving the battle.

Very few men were left alive. Most of the dead and dying had been picked clean of both clothes and any articles that the scavengers had believed to be worth something. Many items had been lost — watches, trinkets from wives and anything that could bring a bit of food to hungry mouths.

Trace Morgan was such a man. A man that was barely alive. Only the presence of extreme pain allowed him to know that he was not yet dead. He could feel the survivors as they picked the last remaining bits of undamaged clothing from his body while he lay unable to defend himself. They turned him over to lie face down in the red slush.

They didn't care who he was. Not anymore. All that mattered was that he was injured and prey for their desperation. A craze that set in among even some of the most stalwart of men during wartime. War—it seemed to bring out the best and of course the worst in everyone. The wintry air shot straight through to his bones as he felt his boots being removed, exposing horridly blistered feet to the bitter cold, for his socks had long since fallen apart.

The darkness swarmed over him as he realized that he no longer felt cold. Just an overwhelming sadness that he would never see his wife or child again. He didn't want to die like this. It wasn't fair.

* * * *

Finally, the noises from the battle stopped. Leona emerged from her home. It was built into the side of one of the smaller mountains, most spacious and well-hidden. People could walk right past it and not even see the entrance.

She had only known one other home. That was the plantation she had been born on. Leona was the daughter of a slave who had been impregnated by her master. Apparently, his wife had found out and so he'd sold her mother up the river and she had been born on a different plantation than she had been conceived on. Leona had never known her real father. But she didn't miss what she didn't know.

Leona had grown up with the youngest son of the plantation master. They had played together during the day and comforted each other when necessary, completely ignoring the fact that they were slave and owner. He had been her one true friend, up until his betrayal. He'd taught her to read and write in secret, even knowing that they would both be severely punished for it if they were ever discovered. They'd discovered and explored their intimate feelings for each other.

For Leona, there had never been another, for her mother had taken her and escaped just before she turned fourteen, after she'd overheard that the master was talking of breeding her daughter to some other slave. That and of course the punishment she had endured because of her so-called 'friend'. She had never seen her friend again.

Years later, as her mother had been dying slowly from some strange disease, a disease that was unknown to them both, she'd taken her daughter and shown her what it was like to be free. Her mother had taken herself and her child to a place that didn't allow slavery, but still being scared for a time she'd hidden them from most people. That had changed, however, since by the end of her mother's time, Leona had met most of the people in the town.

Before she had died, Ellie, Leona's mom, had shared her knowledge of herbal medicines and cooking with the only child she had seen grow up to be an adult. The only child that had not been taken from her and sold.

Now Leona was alone. Well, she had animals around to keep her company, but not much human contact. That being the main reason why she had stayed hidden when the battle had begun. Men were to be considered dangerous normally, but a battle brought out the worst in them. Brought out the worst in *everyone*.

As she crept cautiously to the edge of the bloody meadow, her breath left her in a gasp. The view was horrible. Dead bodies lay scattered out in the cold. Most were barefoot and without coats or even shirts on their bodies as their blood congealed with the snow and began to freeze, leaving behind a red ice-slushy mess.

Gritting her teeth, she listened for any noise of live humans before she dared venture forth. Once she confirmed that silence was all she heard, she began to skirt the edge of the destruction on the field. The battle for slavery had come back to her. These men, these intruders, believed that they could come to this island, what they called Saba, and take what they wanted. They had not counted on finding any opposition, much less the organized resistance the islanders had put up.

This island was a profitable one and had attracted many people. Slavery was not allowed, otherwise anyone was welcome to stay. There were people from all walks of life living here, and they had brought their own special talents along with them. There was knowledge of warfare, weapons, the most advanced healing methods and even the latest fashions for women.

About halfway around the field, Leona heard the moan. In less time than it took for the sound to fade from the air she had made herself invisible to the naked eye as she sought out the source of the noise. She knew the noise came from a human. Seeing no new threat, she focused on the field. The sound came again. There was a live person out there. When she'd looked before, none of the islanders had been there, only the interlopers.

Do I dare?

Her heartbeat sped up as her breath quickened. Leona never liked to expose herself this way. It was a large field and if anyone came along, they would be able to see her. On the other hand, if someone was still alive, maybe she could help them. It could be one of the islanders, her friends. Perhaps she'd not seen them.

With nerves running scared, she chewed on her full lower lip. Her eyes searching for the exact place the noise had come from. It came again and she locked on to the position. Her decision was made. She had to go.

Cautiously she stepped from her hiding place and made her way to the edge of the trees. Still no sign of any danger. As she began to creep out into the field, a herd of deer surrounded her. They stayed next to her as she ventured into the middle of the field. Protected her. Shielded her from unwanted gazes. Most importantly, they covered her tracks with their own.

Leona silently thanked her friends as she found the man who had emitted the noise. He had no shoes, which exposed blistered, raw feet to the cold, and he bled from many wounds. His thick brown hair, the color of walnuts, was matted with blood, plastering it to his head. His skin was pale from loss of blood. He lay there dying. She had to help him, and so without further thought she knelt beside him.

Gently she reached out to turn him over. The sight that met her froze her solid as the ground she was upon, for a moment. Emotions believed long dead rushed to the surface and washed over her like a tidal wave. When she regained her composure, she moved quickly. She could do nothing less.

Concern for her own safety had faded and she hastily formed a travois to move him with. Leona picked up the ends, headed away from the battle scene and back to her house. The deer followed behind and they walked very deliberately over her tracks. Erasing them. Keeping her anonymous even still.

Leona made good speed back to her home. Once there she moved the man to a bed, clumsily, for he was a large man and stood about a head taller than she and was full of hardened muscle. That done, she stripped him of his clothes and swiftly but thoroughly bathed and cleansed his wounds. She built up the fire then piled blankets upon him to warm him.

His body was perfectly browned by the sun. His wide shoulders tapered into a narrow waist. Brown hair covered his chest. There was not an ounce of fat on him.

As she gazed upon his body, Leona felt a rush of longing and trembling in her own. Staring upon such beauty made her want to touch and taste him. She shook her head to regain her focus as she made sure that he was warming up.

She made him drink down some tea to help him heal and she wondered about the head wound. Should she risk taking him to town? They had a doctor there and she wouldn't be keeping a man alone in her home. No, the risk was too great. With all the outsiders here, she didn't want to run into any of them. Any *more* of them. After making sure he swallowed at least one cup she let him sleep. Warm and safe at last. For now.

* * * *

Trace experienced a strong presence bring him back from the light that he headed toward. He felt himself being moved and felt someone giving him something warm to drink. It made his head feel better but made him even drowsier. The touch seemed familiar to him, but from where he couldn't recall.

Weeks passed and he continued to lie as still as death. Trace woke only to take healing drinks and broth. Although his body mended, still he did not rise from the bed. Somewhere along the days, he'd lost track of how many had passed.

Pain laced through his dream state. Trace fought to remember where he was and what had happened. His memories were fuzzy and flashed across his mind in a dizzying whirl. "Hello?" His voice, scratchy from lack of use, penetrated the air. "Is anyone there?"

He tried to open his eyes, but it hurt too much. He had begun to panic when a low, melodious voice broke through his rising dread and chased it away.

"I am here. You are not alone. Stay still." A cool hand brushed his face in a motherly or wifely gesture. At once Trace knew that this was the very person who had tended to him. The touch from her fingers, so familiar. Comfort flowed from her body and encircled him with warmth that kept the hounds of pain at bay.

Where am I? He didn't even have the energy to ask the question out loud. *Why can't I see?*

"Don't try to open your eyes. I have bandaged your head. You are safe here, that is all I can tell you. Rest now, we will talk more later. After you have rested."

Trace could do nothing but what she commanded him to. Her soft pleasant-sounding voice flowed over his senses and took away any thought of disobeying her words. Into a world of happiness and joy he spiraled, with only a faint wonderment as to where he knew that touch from.

* * * *

A few days later he woke to the soft voice, whosever it was, humming. His world nevertheless remained dark. Head still throbbed. He barely remembered sitting up and taking in food and water. "Water, please. May I have some water?"

Silently, the unknown woman helped him to a sitting position, placed the cup to his lips. He took gulps, feeling refreshed as the cool liquid poured life back into him.

"Not too much. Drink slowly." Her voice brought him back to the here and now.

"Where am I? Who are you? Where is the rest of my unit?" Memories of men lying bleeding to death came to him in flashes. With them they brought sharp pains that lanced his body.

"I found you in a field. You were the only one left alive. You have been here for over a month."

Chapter Two

"Why are my eyes covered?"

His pain flowed through Leona's body and made her realize where his thoughts were. She had tried to offer comfort. Leona gulped as she understood that hadn't worked so well. Now was the time when she answered that part. "You had a severe head injury. To be honest, I do not know if there was any damage to your eyes or not."

"Are you a doctor?" Cold anger clipped his words, shoving icy daggers into her soul.

"No, I am not a doctor. But — "

"But nothing. If you are not a doctor, then what right do you have to keep me in the dark like this? This comes off now!"

With the rage erupting from him, Leona blinked a few times, reminding herself that he was scared and that was making him scarier than she'd known he would be. She rose from his side. She carried the cup away and came back to sit beside him.

Dampening her lips, she willed her hands to stop shaking. "Hold still while I unwrap your head. I know I am not a doctor, but at least keep your eyes closed until I get all the bandaging off. Then just open them slowly. You do not want to burn them since they have been in the dark for so long."

"Just get on with it. I am not stupid, you know." His voice cut her to the quick and brought a wave of involuntary tears to her eyes.

"Of course."

Her voice held no hint of the tears that clouded her vision, but Trace could feel them in his own eyes. He knew that he had hurt her, could feel her pain at his words, and had no way of explaining it to himself.

Could this be his wife? No, Bethany did not take care of other people. She was more concerned with herself. She rarely dealt with their child.

Bethany, the epitome of grace and beauty. A petite brown-haired, blue-eyed woman, she appeared to be sweet and kind. That was a farce. She was a spoiled rich girl. A vindictive woman who took what she wanted without concern of who might be hurt. She was very mean to the slaves and even mean to the people that she associated with.

Trace had slaves because his father had had them. He didn't agree with the idea of owning a person, owning slaves, and for that reason he had not been at all ready to go to war to get more slaves. But Bethany would not be seen to have a husband who didn't wish to keep slavery around.

They should be able to get slaves from wherever they wanted to. After all, those people were inferior. At least, that's what Bethany believed. Not Trace. But he had secrets that he'd never told anyone. Well, not since he was sixteen.

Regardless, he knew the woman tending him wasn't his wife. She smelled like a mix of the outdoors — a fresh scent, and a hint of a flower, a familiar one but one he couldn't identify right now — instead of an overly rich, bottled smell. A soft gentle scent. Comforting. Calming. He had never thought of the outdoors as having a sensual smell, but with her it worked.

He felt the bandages coming off. Her movements were steady yet very gentle as she unwound the layers of material that surrounded his head and removed the soft squares from over his eyes. Her arms encircled his head, making her subtle scent tantalize his nose even more. Trace focused on her smell and not the fact that he would soon find out if he could see again.

"They are off."

Trace began to open his eyes slowly. Nothing but dark. When he had his eyes open all the way it was still just as dark. He couldn't see.

He couldn't see. Damn it, he was blind. Rage welled up inside of him. It built up like a volcano needing to explode. He was useless. He was blind.

"I cannot see. Damn it! I cannot see. What did you do to me? If you had taken me to a doctor, I wouldn't be blind right now. This is your fault. Do you understand that? You... You are to blame for this." Trace shoved blindly and connected with something soft, her arm maybe, what did he know, he was blind. "Get away from me. This is your fault."

Trace heard her walk off. His blood raged. It burned from deep within his soul. He lost himself to the anger. Gave himself over to the rage. He ranted and raved, his voice getting louder and louder as his anger and disbelief came to the surface. It was like a large explosion and he was going to blow for quite a while.

He tore at the blankets and threw anything within his reach. Pillows flew and the fact that they were not his belongings did not matter. He lurched from the bed and fell flat on his face. His muscles had grown so weak during his time in bed, with their lack of use, that they couldn't support him at all.

Head splitting, Trace pounded on the cold floor as he emitted deep gut-wrenching cries. Cries of disbelief and despair for his situation.

Grief of never seeing his child again. Fear of living the rest of his life in the dark.

In part of his mind, Trace waited for her to try to calm him down. When she did not, he grew angry again, and perhaps more scared, as he imagined himself alone. It was one thing to be blindfolded and in the dark alone, and something completely different to know you couldn't see and believe yourself to be alone. He struggled to a sitting position.

"Are you still here?" His voice rang rough and gravely. "Or did you leave because of your guilt? Do you just not like me because I am white? Is that why you let me go blind?"

There was so much venom in his voice it chilled Leona to the bone. Trace's face was nothing more than a glowering mask of rage.

Leona sat frozen to her seat and so did not move when he lashed out. He caught her on the face with jagged nails and drew blood. Somehow, she still held on to her calm, rose silently and walked away from him with blood welling up to drip down her face.

Leona's temper had begun to rise as his continued snipes at her wore down the edges of her control. Even as she struggled to contain it, his harsh words fell on her like blocks of ice. They shattered her heart and her foolish childhood dreams and fantasies. "I risked my own life to get you out of that field. You had been picked clean by men believing you to be dead. Or rather by men who didn't care what your state was but knew were you too weak to defend yourself against them. I brought you to my house because you had lost so much blood I didn't think you would last going anywhere else.

"Apparently my decision to save your worthless spoiled hide was a mistake, and I apologize for not ignoring your bleeding body and taking you all the way into town to see the doctor. I did the best I could, and I am sorry that my attempts to nurse you for over a month were nothing but a waste of time. I will get ready to take you to the doctor in the morning."

He rounded on her. "Do you know who you're talking to? Do you? You are insolent. What is your name?"

She didn't respond, just stared at the shell of a man she'd thought about often.

Without waiting for an answer from her, he continued his tirade. "I am Colonel Morgan. I demand you take me to the nearest town."

She gave short bark of laughter. "You demand? You? *Demand*? Me?" Her voice was no longer caring, but scornful and harsh. "I am no slave for you to order around, nor am I one of your soldiers. I have already said that if you wished to go to town I would take you, but you do *not* give me orders. Do we understand each other, *Colonel Morgan*? I am not yours to order around. If I didn't like you because of your skin color then why would I have rescued you? Don't be stupid."

She knew she'd shocked him, for he stared in her direction in silence. She supposed it was because as a colonel in the army he was used to instant obedience, could not even fathom that a woman, a mere woman, would defy him. Plus of course, how he had been raised.

Leona flattened her lips as she strove to locate her lost control. "Perhaps you would like to get off the floor now?"

"What do you think? That I like to be down here? Of course I want to get up." He fumbled with his arms and found the edge of the bed and pulled himself up clumsily.

Leona remained silent as he regained the sleeping pallet. After he sat back, she rose and began to pick up the things that he had thrown in his fit of rage. Her body trembled with exhaustion and her face stung. The scratch would leave a scar. This man had left *another* mark on her for all time.

"Who are you?" The question came after they had been in silence for a while.

"My name is of no concern, especially since you are leaving tomorrow."

"What are you doing?"

"Cleaning up your mess and making dinner." There was no censure in her words. *See, I can do this without letting him know that he affects me in any way at all. He won't know this from me, and I will continue to carry all our secrets with me to the grave.*

"Dinner? How am I supposed to eat? I am *blind*, or have you forgotten?" His voice rose with resentment again and he spoke with reckless anger. Strong fists grabbed and scrunched the blankets.

"The same way you have been eating, with some help. Why is this any different than eating with the blindfold on? You couldn't see then and you managed. Why is now different?"

He muttered some unflattering words beneath his breath and she didn't respond to them, not going to be drawn into another senseless argument.

Dinner was horrible. Trace made a huge mess, finally forgoing utensils and eating like a wild animal. Leona didn't say one word to him. She made three attempts to have a conversation but he growled at her and so she finally fell silent.

After dinner she assisted him as he stumbled very weakly back to his bed and lay down with his face inches from the cold stone wall.

He just couldn't figure out where he was at. His world, once bright, had gone black and he didn't know how to fix it. His sleep, after it was obtained, was full of old memories — long-forgotten memories — or so he had believed.

* * * *

Trace, aged twelve

"What do you think? Do you think it is possible?"

"Of course it is. That is, if you aren't scared." There was a hint of teasing in that soft voice, and a lot of challenge.

"Be quiet, girl. You know I am not scared. I am older than you and don't know how to be scared."

"By three years, that is not much older. Besides, I have already done it so I have no reason to be scared."

"When did you do this?" The boy grabbed her by her skinny arm and shook her until her vision blurred. "Not last night, did you? Tell me it wasn't at night." He was scared for her safety and she knew it and he knew she did and that it made her happy.

"Stop shaking me. Yes, I did it last night. I am not scared of the dark." She smiled up into his eyes.

The young boy couldn't help but smile back into those mischievous tawny eyes. She was so full of life. The only one who could keep up with him. The only one that looked at him like he had just handed her the moon. Something moved inside him that made him stiffen, and he wondered what that feeling had been. "Promise me you won't do anything like this again, at least not without me around."

"Okay. I promise. But I have to go home now. See you later." With a quick grin and a jaunty wave, she headed off.

Not able to let her go, he grabbed her arm and pulled her back to him. One hand cupped her face and the stark difference in their skin color made him feel all the more possessive toward her. Their relationship was about to change. He was about to end their friendship. Made him want to protect her. Her beauty astounded him. She was his. He was hers. His lips touched hers for the first time and both of them felt the entwining of their souls.

She pulled free and ran off without a second look. He knew she never realized that he had marked her for all eternity.

Chapter Three

Trace woke up sweating, alone and surrounded by the dark. He lay there and listened to the sounds of the night. Just listened.

The sound of water running somewhere, like a pool or waterfall, reached his ears. The smell that his nose picked up on did not have the odor of salt water, so it had to be fresh. Then he located her scent.

She was not far. He could hear her breathing and smell her. She smelled a lot more like that flower than the outdoors. He still couldn't place the flower but it was very familiar to him, that much he knew. Her breathing hitched and he heard her turn over.

"What are you doing awake?" Her honeyed voice reached out to stroke him. His eyes closed and he felt himself lean into her words as they caressed his face and bathed him in a warm glow. Her words alone made him feel safe even in his darkened world.

"I am listening. Is there water nearby?"

"Yes. There is fresh water and a hot spring nearby."

"I can hear the water, and I could smell that it was fresh water."

There was the rustle of material followed by the soft padding of feet crossing the floor. He could feel her warmth surround him as she came closer. "That's wonderful. You will soon learn to utilize your other senses." She touched his arm, sending waves of heat through his body. "How do you feel? Do you have a fever or anything like it?"

He had a fever all right. Trace cleared his throat as he shook his head. "No, I am fine. Just not tired. I guess I slept so much I am not sleepy any longer. What time is it?"

"Near dawn. Can you not hear the birds beginning to wake? Can you not smell the freshness of the dawn, the crispness that only comes with the morning?" There was pure joy in her voice as she spoke of the wonders to him.

Instead of snapping at her, Trace focused on her words and found he could hear what she spoke of. His anger was gone just by hearing her voice. He could smell the morning – it had a very unique smell. A smile broke across his face. She brought joy to him. A beacon of light in his darkened world.

"How is it you know so much about being blind? Are you blind?"

"My mother lost her sight about three years before she died."

"My apologies."

"Thank you. Look, I am offering to help you learn how to cope with your blindness. Or I can take you to town. But my offer is there."

Trace thought about her words. By all rights he should go to town. But then he might be captured as the enemy. And be at a serious disadvantage with his blindness. Perhaps she was on his side and could provide useful information for the war. On the other hand, she could be a spy for the other side.

He would take her up on it. He would learn what he needed to then if she did turn out to be a spy he would capture her. "I would like to stay and learn what I can from you."

Trace heard her breathing change and wondered if he was right about the spy thing. No, he had to be wrong. His gut told him that she wasn't a spy.

"Very well. I will help you as much as I can."

"Thank you. Does this mean you will tell me your name? How did your mother learn to cope?"

"She learned to use her ears and her other senses. You can call me Elle." She pronounced it just like the letter 'L' in the alphabet.

"How did she die?"

"She had some disease that we couldn't cure. I still don't know what it was." She cleared her throat. "So, tell me about you, Colonel Morgan. What are you doing here? Where are you from?"

There was compulsion in her voice. Trace found he did not want to ignore her questions. He wanted to answer them all. So, against his better judgment, he did. With that voice of hers she would make an incredible interrogator.

"I am from a large plantation. I came from across the sea. Obviously, I came here to fight in the war. I have a wife…"

Trace stopped because of a sharp pain that lanced his body. When it finally diminished, he continued. "I have a son who is nine years old."

"What is your plantation called? What do you raise on it?" Her question fell casually.

"Hawk's Cove. It is beautiful there. By the water. We raise tobacco and cotton."

"This means you have slaves." The voice was harsh and accusing.

"Yes, but they are treated quite well."

"That would mean you are fighting to take people from this island to use as slaves." The heartbroken sound of her voice struck a chord in him.

"Yes. Look, I do not agree with slavery. I would just as soon let mine go, but then someone would take them up and perhaps not treat them as well."

Leona thought about his words and the fact he was going to be here for a while with her. No one else, just him and her. It was part of why she'd given him just Elle for her name—in case he recalled much like she did.

"You may not agree with it, but in your own way you support it. Enough. What you do is your business, not mine." Leona dropped the conversation. She didn't want to go through this. She just couldn't. Not with him.

Leona rose and changed into her buckskins then went back over to where he still sat on the bed. "Ready to begin your lessons? I think we should start small and allow you to build up your strength, as well."

"Lead on, little one." A shiver of desire ran through her body at his words.

They spent the day working on the interior of her home. Since her mother had been blind, most of the furniture was along the walls. Trace learned to count his steps. Most of the day, they were touching, side by side, as she tried not to forget he was the representation of all she despised and was married. Her heart wasn't in agreement.

* * * *

As the days passed, they fell into a routine. Trace grew more and more confident as his other senses increased. He and Leona walked around the home, and she took him farther and farther into the mountains.

They soaked in the hot spring and bathed in the running water pool. Trace's body filled out and he got life back into him.

Leona put more and more things in his path, and with the help of a walking stick he learned to circumvent them all with ease and dexterity. He could pass for a man that had his vision intact. *At least here in and around my home.*

The night was a different story. That was when memories and desires could run free.

"What do you look like, Elle?" Trace asked her one day.

Leona stopped in her tracks. *How am I going to answer this one?* She countered with a question of her own. "What do you think I look like?"

Trace laughed. "I imagine you come to about my shoulder. Long hair, straight. Beautiful smile. Kind eyes. Come on, tell me," his deep voice coaxed.

"Pretty close. In fact, close enough."

He reached out an arm and caught her in his strong grip. Leona ignored the feeling he invoked in her, but from his expression he had already felt her response. There was something between them even though he had never even seen what she looked like. As an adult. He pulled her to stand between his legs. Trace put his hands on her face.

He closed his eyes like he was memorizing her face with his hands. She tried to imagine what he felt when he did. Then she listened to him muttering to himself as his touch moved over her.

"Skin as soft as silk. Long eyelashes. A somewhat flat button nose, leading to full lips. Graceful neck that leads down to a full chest."

His hands lingered over her full breasts as he committed them to memory. Her waist was tiny and her hips flared before he found her firm legs.

Leona didn't move, just allowed his touch to send her to heaven. Her eyes fell closed and her head lolled back as he continued his perusal of her. When he buried his face into her stomach she just about lost control of her legs.

"Beautiful. You are beautiful. I know that much. What color are your eyes? Your hair?"

"My hair is black. My eyes are light brown, tan." Leona stepped back, needing to get some space from him in order to regain her control.

Trace felt her separation from him deep within his heart. But he let her go, angry at himself for his lack of control. He had a wife. He had a son. With her words though, he put together a picture in his mind. To his surprise, it looked vaguely familiar. Not at all what he expected.

Leona spoke again. "I am going to lie down for a nap. I don't feel all that well."

"I will take one also." Trace knew exactly where her bed was. It was twenty steps from his own. He waited until he heard her lie down before he lay back himself.

* * * *

Trace, aged sixteen

Their lips met for the umpteenth time. Now whenever they were together they were exploring their bodies. The same jolt speared both of them, jerking them apart. She didn't doubt her eyes were wild with fear, uncertainty and a rising passion. His full of desire and the knowledge of what they were doing. At sixteen, he was aware of his sexuality and she was beginning to understand hers.

With one step he reduced the distance between them. His touch was extremely gentle as he stroked her cheek with his callused hand. Letting her know he would never hurt her. "You are beautiful, little one. I am not even supposed to be interested in you. My father says I am to marry someone from up the road. But I can't get you out of my head. My heart. Tell me you feel it as well. Tell me you feel the same way about me as I do about you. Tell me!" It was a command.

The young girl answered, "You know I do, even if I am not supposed to. I think about you all the time."

If possible, he stepped closer to her. Encircled her with his arms, holding her snugly in his embrace, already showing the strength Trace's arms would have when he was fully grown. She had seen him in fights delivering out punishing blows with those arms and fists of iron. But now they held her as if she were the most delicate piece of lace.

Their trembling bodies touched as he lowered his mouth to hers yet again. At the same time his hand found her budding breast, causing a rush of wetness and pleasure to course through her body.

Suddenly they were jerked apart. Angry brown eyes glared at them both as they were dragged away. Away from each other. A gunny sack dropped over her head, blocking out all daylight, leaving her to smell the stale scent of the grain that had been in the sack.

The young girl heard the voices saying that she had done this before. With him, and that he had confirmed it. Her heart shattered at the news of his betrayal.

Before the night was over she received fifteen lashes on her virgin skin.

She stayed proud and silent as the whip fell again and again on her back as she hung by her wrists, marking her forever. Never had she felt such pain. Only when she was back with her mother did she allow the tears to fall. Not tears from the pain of the whip, but from the pain of his treachery.

She grew up fast that day, not that it mattered. He was never there to see it. In fact, he never saw her again.

* * * *

Leona awoke feeling sick. Silently she rose and headed for the hot springs. She groaned as she sank into the water, let the steam and warmth work its magic on her.

Her calm was broken by the shuffle of steps that heralded his arrival. "Would you like some company? Or is this time just for you?"

"I am just soaking, feel free to join me." Her tongue peeked out to wet her lips and she was for a second, glad he couldn't see her, knowing full well he would be witness to the raging lust in her eyes.

"You know, if we were back home this would be highly improper. Then again, maybe not, since I am blind and can't see your body anyway."

Leona smiled at his words. "If you could see you wouldn't be here anyway. So it really doesn't matter. Come in."

Trace dropped his clothes and carefully made his way into the pool of warmth. He smiled and she realized he'd heard her sharp intake of breath.

"Is it fair that you can look upon mine and I can't see yours?" he teased.

Leona sensed his joyful mood and ran with it. "Probably not. But you won't hear any arguments from me. If you wish, I can close my eyes as well."

"If you think that will make it easier for you."

"Sure, I can picture whatever I want."

A low, primitive growl emerged from his throat.

Leona smiled. He wanted her. She could hear him, and she felt his jealousy as he tried to control it. It made her toes curl to imagine this type of power. Revenge would be so sweet.

After a bit, Leona stood. "I am going to get something ready to eat then later maybe we can go outside for a bit. It is time for you to start navigating out in the open."

Trace nodded, and when he spoke, his words were clear. "Fine, I will go with you." He too rose from the water. Baring all to Leona's hungry gaze.

What the hell did I get myself into? How will I control my longings? Leona asked herself as she followed the naked and very beautiful man up to the main part of her home.

As she got food ready, Trace wandered and counted as he prepared himself for the outdoors. He had a pair of boots that Leona gave to him to wear. They were fur-lined and very warm.

She watched him deliberately place himself on her bed, wanting or needing to touch a part of her, she wasn't sure, but she liked him there.

"How is it you have a hot spring in your home? Where are we?"

"It is not in my home as much as connected to my home."

"It's like the healing waters of Bath, a place in England people go to get healed. Supposedly."

"Have you been to England?"

31

She wasn't able to hide the longing in her voice.

"Yes. I have been. Bunch of arrogant rich people."

Not much different from the plantation owners, Leona thought. "I would love to go. To have a small cabin by the sea. A piece of land to call my own. I think it would be wonderful."

"I will keep my plantation, thanks. I like where I live. That is, if we don't have to give everything up because of the war. Then I don't know what I would do."

Leona's eyes narrowed and her teeth bared a silent snarl. "Perhaps we should go outside for now."

Trace rose and put out his arm for her to take. Leona took it after putting on her coat. His touch still affected her even through both their coats.

She took him outside and let him enjoy the fresh air before they began to walk. Even though she knew he counted, she made sure that there were no tracks left behind. The snow had vanished and spring was well on its way.

Leona's senses were all alert. Tuned to pick up the slightest sound. They were all good sounds for her to hear. Nothing new or strange approached.

They spent the afternoon and evening outside. Together they headed back in when they were hungry for dinner. Trace attempted to help by trying to set the table. Dinner was a strained affair. Leona couldn't forget his comment and while she understood Trace had no way of reading her expression, it didn't make things any easier.

"Is there anyone you would like to contact? I have to go to town, so I could send a note for you."

"Can I go into town with you?"

"No. I don't wish it to be known that there is a man staying with me."

"Why? Are you married? Is your husband in this war?"

"No, unlike you, I am not married. But I do have a reputation. And I don't want it ruined."

"I can respect that."

"I will go in the morning. If you change your mind about a note let me know. I am going to bed. Good night, Colonel Morgan."

"Good night, Elle. Please call me Trace. Everyone does."

Everyone but your slaves. "Very well. Good night, Trace." Her voice dropped an octave as she said his name.

* * * *

Trace, aged fifteen

He knew she was young. *She* knew she was, but some of the other girls had already lain with guys at her age. Some were going to have children. He knew she loved him despite her not having said the words. Was she scared? Should he say them first?

Moaning with pleasure, he pulled out of her tight warmth and spilled his seed on her stomach. He always took care so she wouldn't end up pregnant. It was amazing with her. Almost spiritual. Something that felt so wonderful, so perfect couldn't be wrong. Could it?

They lay entwined. Naked in the sun. His hand wrapped in her thick soft hair. As their breathing slowed, he whispered to her how he felt.

"I love you. I know I am not supposed to, but I do. I will always protect you. Do you believe me? Do you?"

"I know how you feel. I can feel it inside me. Your happiness and sorrow, I feel it all. What *you* feel, *I* feel.

I don't know how, but I can. I love you too. And yes, I believe that you will always protect me."

"Good, sleep now. I will keep watch." He pressed her face against his chest and smiled contentedly when she fell asleep. She was his. He would not marry that other woman. He wanted her.

"*Liar*! You were supposed to protect me. You lied to me. You are a *liar*!" The voice, so filled with hatred and venom, blared to life inside his head, shattering the peace he had found.

Trace bolted up in bed. Sweat poured down his face. The voice was right—he hadn't protected her. He had let her down.

His anguish was too intense to keep quiet and he moaned softly to the night air.

"Trace? What is it? What is wrong?" Elle sank on the bed beside him, hand on his shoulder.

His hands groped blindly for her and he pulled her down beside him as he fell back. "I failed. I couldn't keep her safe."

Elle slid her arm around him and rubbed his back. "I am sure she is all right. Don't worry so."

"No, you don't understand. I failed. I failed her. I failed her!"

"When you get home, you can make it up to her. I'm sure."

"No, it's too late for that." His voice was so full of despair.

She sat with him in silence for a while.

"Get some sleep. Maybe it won't seem so bad in the morning. Just so you know I'll be gone for most of the day. I will leave food out for you on the table. Good night." Elle gave him a quick hug and rose to head back to her own bed.

Trace fell back to sleep. Only to have his dreams invaded by of pictures of his brothers laughing about how much blood there had been. Explaining it all to him in detail as they untied him from where they had kept him prisoner.

* * * *

Leona awoke early. She dressed quickly then headed out to town. She walked fast and stayed hidden until she was on the outskirts. Then and only then did she walk on the trail.

Her first stop was the general store. She entered the store and was immediately surrounded by people who were overly exuberant.

"Did you hear the good news?" the general store owner, Paul, asked.

"I was worried about you, lass, out there all alone. None of the soldiers found you though, I see. That's wonderful. Isn't it great?" That was from Jackson O'Neill.

"What?" Leona was thoroughly confused. "What's so wonderful?"

Jackson, a big burly Irishman who had somehow found his way to this island, picked her up and spun her around. "We've won! The war is over here. We won. They are gone!"

Jackson stood about five inches over six feet and had raven-black hair that he kept cropped close to his head. He had tan skin from his daily schedule of working outside and his eyes were a vibrant blue-green, like the clear ocean waters that surrounded the island. He looked very good for his age. In fact, he looked much younger than his actual age.

Trace bolted upright in the bed. Someone was touching her. A *man* touched her. Jealousy reared its ugly head and roared to life inside him. His low growl was one of danger — danger to the one who dared touch what was his.

Leona felt the rumble deep within her. A smile crossed her face. He knew where she was and what was going on. She opened her mind and feelings to him even more. Time for him to feel what it was like.

She'd discovered this connection with Trace when they were young. Neither could explain it but she could always feel his emotions, even when they weren't together, and he'd relayed he could with hers as well.

The bond between them was unique and special.

With a laugh, Leona hugged Jackson back. They had done it. They had won. "What about causalities? How many did we lose?"

"Not as bad as it could have been. The battle in Rainbow's Field was the battle turning point. Their whole unit was wiped out." Jackson still had his arm around her.

"Their colonel was supposedly killed there as well. But we have a person who is claiming to be Colonel Morgan. They were just not ready for all the opposition that we gave them. They are gone. We are free of them and their twisted ideas." At his message her heart skipped a beat. Someone claiming to be Trace? Who could it be?

Leona asked questions about the prisoners. Who would be posing as Trace? Could it be someone else who could recognize her and take her back? "What is this Colonel Morgan like?"

Jackson smiled down at her. "You are just too full of questions. He is over in the jail. If you want, I will take you there." Jackson had fallen in love with Leona's mother and knew of the name Morgan and what it meant to her and her mother.

"Yes. I would like to go and look at him."

"Very well, lass. Let's go." He rose and took her arm. They made a quiet march through the town that celebrated their victory.

As they approached the jail, Leona looked at Jackson. Such a dear man. As close to a father as she had ever known, she truly loved him. Her love for him was transmitted to Trace, who answered with another low rumble of jealousy.

Chapter Four

As she entered into the darkened building, Leona unconsciously stepped closer to the large man beside her. She closed down her link with Trace as much as she could, as she didn't want him to be exposed to the full extent of her emotions anymore. Jackson spoke to the sergeant in charge. When the man opened the door for them to walk back to the prisoners, Leona's breath became short.

Jackson walked beside her as they went down the aisle toward where the supposed colonel was being kept. In a solitary cell sat a man.

The man was large and had wide shoulders. He had Trace's narrow waist, but that was where the similarities ended. The man had blond hair, unkempt and dirty so it appeared brown. His eyes were an angry nondescript blue.

He sneered at her. "Oh look, a darkie bitch."

Jackson responded immediately, lunging forward clearly with the full intent of ripping the insolent man to pieces. Leona's touch on his arm stopped him, but only barely.

"I would like to have a private word with the colonel, please."

"What could I possibly have to say to a Ni— Darkie?" The man spat in her direction.

Leona struggled to hold on to her temper. "I have news about your wife." The man posing as Colonel Morgan fell silent and waited for her to continue. Leona turned to Jackson and said, "I will be all right. I do not think he will hurt me. Leave us, please."

"I don't like this at all, Leo..." He stopped at her pleading look. "Very well. I will wait over here." As Jackson turned his deadly gaze at the prisoner he vowed, "You hurt a single hair on her head, and I will personally see to your long and painful death." The Irishman turned and walked off to leave them in a relatively private situation.

The imposter came to the bars and glared at her. "Well, what is it? What do you know of my wife?"

Leona stepped closer, until she could have reached out and touched the man. Close enough that his ripe stench didn't miss her nose and made her gag. "I know you are not Colonel Morgan. You are an imposter. What would they do if they knew what you had done to your commanding officer? Why, you would probably wish to remain here in the prison."

At her admission, the man's eyes bulged and he looked panicked. "What do you know? You are making this up. All darkies lie." Even though the man's eyes showed fear, his voice still contained enough venom to make her shiver and wish to be anywhere but there.

Leona narrowed her eyes in response. Over the years her experiences had taught her she didn't like to be scared and threatened. "I know exactly who and what you are, Steven. I know all about you, your secret obsession with the colonel's wife. Everything."

Paling, the filthy man reached for her but stopped as he saw Jackson step forward with a menacing glare. "How do you know who I am? Bethany said no one should know me here." As soon as he said it, he saw his mistake.

Realization dawned. Trace's wife had set him up in order to be with his older brother. The thought left her cold. Rage began to rise within her. She realized she was unconsciously transmitting her feelings to Trace. First the fear and now the rage, for their link could never be completely closed.

"You are a disgrace. You are his *older* brother. He should have been able to trust you. It must have been so hard for you to take orders from your younger brother. You always were dumber than him." She taunted him recklessly.

"You're a liar. I don't know this Steven person."

"Ballocks. We both know you're Steven Morgan. I know because, you asshole, you have blond hair and blue eyes. No amount of mud will cover your hair color. And even though you keep your eyes downcast, they are still blue. Your brother, on the other hand, has thick brown hair and chocolate-brown eyes. Not to mention that I would know him from a mile away. No, I am sure, you are Steven. There is no way you're Trace, and when he finds out what you did... Well, if I cared what happened to you, I would feel sorry for you. But I don't, so I won't."

Leona stepped back. Reaching into her pocket, she pulled out a chain with two rings. One was Trace's academy ring. The second ring had been a gift to Trace from his father. "I hope you know what these are. Something he would never part with, not while he was alive. If you are Colonel Morgan, then where is your ring? Goodbye, Steven."

She left without another word. They had set him up to be killed. Leona could feel the stare of the phony colonel boring holes into her back as she walked away. Shoulders straight, she never let him know how much he scared her.

Back at the darkened home, Trace shook with anger that she was so frightened and he could do nothing to help her. He had no way of finding the town even if he could see. Being blind didn't do anything but complicate the situation even more.

He was so angry at his helplessness that he struck out at anything in his way. Again. Within moments her home was like a storm had blown through.

He knew when she returned and could hear her sharp intake of disbelief. She dropped her purchases on the floor in shock. "What the hell happened here?"

Trace stumbled over to her. He was furious as his gaze sightlessly sought out her face.

"Who was the man that you let paw you all over? Is that why you didn't want me to come with you? Were you scared that he might not want you, seeing you with a man from 'the other side of the war'?"

"What did you do to my house?"

"How the hell should I know? I'm blind, remember?" he sneered at her.

"My *house*. What did you do to my *house*?" She took a deep, shuddering breath. "Blind, yes, but I didn't think that you would be this disrespectful. What makes you think that I let a man paw all over me?"

"I felt it." Even to his anger-clouded mind, that didn't seem like a logical reason. "I just... I just know. You smell like a man was touching you. And you smell like you were around a man that was very dirty."

"Impressive." He wasn't sure what to make of the change in her tone. She gripped his arm and cleared her throat. "The war is over. Apparently you are alive and in prison. I spoke with you today. Funny thing, though. You have blond hair and blue eyes."

Trace sat down heavily on the bed. The war was over? The war was over! He was in the prison? The only person who would be able to pull off passing as him would be...

"The bastard," he seethed. "It was planned all along." All the pieces fell into place and the veil of fog that had been over his eyes was lifted.

"I should have known when I saw them together, whispering, and they said it was about my birthday. Damn her. Damn him." Trace didn't even acknowledge that there were tears falling from his eyes. His brain was working out the problem and coming up with a suitable punishment for his brother and his wife.

Elle sat silently through the whole tirade. After a while she asked, "So who are you really? If that man is who you say you are, then who are you?"

He faced the direction her voice had come from. "I am the true Colonel Morgan. He is an imposter."

"Why should I believe you? It's not like you have anything on you to prove who you are."

"I'm blind. Why would I lie about who I am? I never said anything different about who I was. Do you believe me?" He pleaded for her to believe his words.

"Well, if you were trying to plant yourself as a spy, getting a head injury wasn't the best way to go about doing it. And your story hasn't changed about who you are, so very well, I'll take your word for it."

"What can you tell me about the man who calls himself me? Does he have anything that you remember that sticks out in your mind?"

"Besides his smell?"

A small chuckle. "Yes, besides that." She could make him laugh even in the midst of all this bad news. Again in the back of his mind came a small yet persistent tingle of recognition, but he just couldn't put a face he should remember with the feeling.

"Let me see... He was about as tall as you, but even under that dirt in his hair it was easy to tell that he was blond. His shoulders weren't as broad as yours. He didn't move with the same effortless grace that you do."

Elle didn't have any idea what her description was doing to Trace. He had completely focused on her words and was imagining how he looked through her eyes. It was very erotic for him, to find out how she pictured him.

It wasn't just her words alone. They created a misty or hazy image in his mind and he could almost see what her words described. To her Trace was a tall, proud man. Handsome.

"I guess the one thing about him that stood out... Well, there were two things. One, a scar on his left cheek, down toward his chin."

Trace knew that scar. He had given it to his brother Steven in a fight when he had been sixteen and Steven had been twenty. He had been ganged up on by his brothers for the last time and soundly beaten the tar out of his older brother.

"And the second thing?" His voice was hard with painful memories.

"His eyes." Elle spoke slowly, as if unsure how her words would be accepted. "While they were blue they were scary in some way. It's like...well, like..." She searched for the right word. "Soulless. They were soulless. It was like looking into the eyes of the devil himself."

'Soulless. It was like looking into the eyes of the devil himself.' Trace had heard that description of his brother once before. But where? Who'd said that to him?

Why was this an important memory for him to remember? *Why can't I remember?* Fists clenched as he searched for those lost memories that seemed always just out of reach.

It was his brother Steven. He knew that. Their eldest brother had been killed years earlier by a jealous husband who had found his wife and their brother David in bed together. After that, it was just Steven and Trace. Steven was the worst by far.

Steven was very hard on his slaves. He beat his wife for no reason and would kill a slave after blaming them for touching her. He was pure evil. So much more evil than David had ever been. Growing up with him had taught Trace how to defend himself at a young age.

But to plan his own brother's murder... Was Steven really capable of that? Of course he was. He had always resented the fact that Trace had made colonel and he had to salute him. Hated that he was just a private in the army. Steven even thought that Bethany should have been his. Well, apparently, she really was.

Curiously, though, Trace wasn't all that saddened about losing her. His son would be another story. If he *was* even his own son. He did love Garrett Hawkins

Morgan with all his heart and always would, no matter if he was his flesh and blood or not.

Trace swallowed down his rage. Now was not the time for fury. It was the time for decisions. He waited for Elle to continue with her account of her day. When there were no more words forthcoming, he used his nose to find her scent and faced the direction where he believed her to be. And prodded.

"Is that it? What else did you do?" Why was he more concerned about the fact she had spent time with another male in town? It was like he was at the edge of a cliff waiting for her answer.

"I ate with a friend and went to the jail. Nothing more, besides getting some needed supplies."

Trace barely suppressed the growl of rage at the thought of her eating with another male. Laughing for another man.

Chapter Five

Elle began to make them something to dine on. Trace was content to stay quiet and think on what she had told him. His blood still boiled at the thought of his brother's and his wife's betrayal.

But as he sat there and listened to the now familiar sounds of Elle in the kitchen, his blood slowly cooled. He could do nothing now, but soon.

When he was better, he would take care of things. Steven would wish he had never even sustained the notion of betraying his brother again.

Trace's head fell back against the cool wall as he listened to Elle hum softly to herself as she cooked.

He lost himself in more memories of the past. Ones he'd thought he'd buried long ago.

* * * *

Trace, aged sixteen

Maybe, just maybe, it was a lie. He hoped so.

The door had opened slowly and with caution, however, and two blond heads had blocked out the little bit of light as they'd peeked in at their brother sitting in there trussed up tighter than a Christmas pig.

Their faces had been full of demonic joy as they'd sneered at him. An unholy light had filled their gazes as they'd told him the details.

"There was so much blood. Can you believe how much there was? Fifteen lashes. Fifteen! It was amazing to watch." This had been from his oldest brother, David.

Steven had spoken then. *"Don't forget how it was to watch the whip breaking across her skin. It was a work of art to see the skin, her tender skin, separating under the force of each stroke of the lash."*

Tied up, he'd strained against his ropes, his face becoming mottled with rage combined with the exertion of pulling on the ropes. He'd spat around the filthy gag that had been in his mouth as he'd ranted and raved, and Trace knew his eyes had burned with vehemence. His struggles had been futile however, and the two older boys had wickedly egged him on.

David, the eldest, had continued telling his story. *"We all got to see her naked. For a slave, she was pretty cute all stripped down. If I had known what she looked like I would have had her like you did."*

"Me too. I would have liked to sample that one. I bet she was a nice fuck." That had been from Steven, the middle child.

"Not that it matters now, for Dad says he's going to breed her to Big Jake. I bet he'll tear her up good when he takes her to bed," David had said, laughing at the prospect of causing the slave more pain.

The boys had jerked up their younger brother and dragged him out of the closet. Ripping off his gag, they'd begun to beat him. It had been as if witnessing the whipping had made them excited and this was the only way they knew to expend their bloodlust.

So, tied up and completely unable to defend himself, the youngest brother had taken hit after hit, kick after kick, until his body had been covered in bruises and blood had streamed from open cuts. After his brothers had beaten him into unconsciousness, they'd untied him and put him in his bed.

He'd stayed in his bed for two weeks, until he'd been healed completely. He never forgave his brothers, and had spent the much of his time trying to find out what had happened to the girl, without his father's knowledge. She and her mom had escaped. He had never seen her again since the day they'd been yanked out of each other's arms by his angry father.

Now, despite owning slaves and being married, he still had never forgotten about that young girl. The one who had befriended him, the one who had been a *true* friend, the one he hadn't been able to protect. *Couldn't protect her. I couldn't protect her.*

Her memory lived on in the back of his mind, far enough back that he could say to himself that he had gotten over her, over his shame of failure, and that she was forgotten. Although he knew that was a lie, for no matter how fast or hard he ran, she was always there behind him, blaming him, accusing him.

Leona knew he had awoken from whatever thoughts had taken him. She could feel the direction of his thoughts. It was comforting to her to sense that he wished he could have protected her more when they were younger. It made her feel special.

"You *are* special." His voice broke through the path she wandered down in her mind.

Leona almost dropped the bowl of potatoes that she was carrying to the table. How had he known what she was thinking? Was he testing her? Did he really know who she was?

"Thank you, I think. What made you say that?"

"Not many people would do what you have done for me. That alone makes you special."

With the table filled with food, Leona turned to look at her blind guest, eagerly drinking her fill of his ruggedly handsome and defiantly good looks. His recovery had been amazing. His face was no longer overly gaunt, but healthy. Nicely firm lips sat on a face that spoke of power, and an ageless strength made her weak in the knees.

His eyes, although sightless to him, were a rich warm chocolate-brown to her. They were magnetic, and drew her like a moth to a flame, speaking in volumes. He had thick lashes that framed his eyes like a lover holding onto his woman.

The walking they had done outside had filled him back out. His body had become lean with a sinewy strength. Powerful shoulders, broad chest. He was a beautiful man and she enjoyed looking at his attractive and very tempting male physique.

Her mouth had gone dry as a barren wasteland and her breathing had become hitched. Leona's eyes fluttered as her thoughts began to fill with desire.

Leona realized the second he knew what she had been thinking. His face got a look on it that men get when they know they are desired. His eyes flared with a response to her own desire and one side of his mouth quirked up in an attempt to keep the smirk off his face.

"Are you ready to eat?" Leona asked as she walked over to him. Determined not to let him know that she knew he knew how she felt. Her voice, however, was nothing more than a husky whisper.

He answered in words that held a faint tremor, as if some unknown emotion touched him. Deep and sensual, his timbre sent through her body a ripple of awareness. "I couldn't be more ready."

Somehow she didn't think that it was dinner he spoke of.

His arm reached out for hers. At the contact of skin on skin, both of them felt the current of energy. He rose smoothly beside her and waited for her to lead him to the table.

Dinner was eaten in silence as each was lost in their own personal thoughts. Over the time they had been together, Trace had gotten better at eating. Leona was careful to place things in the same spots, just as she had done for her mother. She learned that for her mother it was to make sure she didn't feel so helpless, and she wanted it to be the same for him. Trace was proven with his quick study and learning of how to function blind. He learned where everything was and didn't seem to fumble as much anymore.

"Will you go on a walk with me after dinner?" Trace interrupted her thoughts as she ate.

"A walk? After dinner? Yes. I think that would be a lovely idea."

With dinner and clean-up over, they got ready to go on a stroll.

Arm in arm, they exited out of her house. Leona instinctively headed up the trail toward the mountains. She was heading to her favorite spot to just sit and think — and where she got her ideas.

They moved in companionable silence up the path. When they finally got to her clearing, she spoke up. Her spoken words were low, soft and clear. "Don't go much past where we'll be sitting. There is an edge. It's about fifty steps forward from where we'll sit."

It was on the tip of Trace's tongue to ask why she would take him to a place where he could hurt himself. Immediately he was angry that she didn't seem to care about him. But then he sensed a feeling of contentment emerge from her that banished his anger back to where it belonged, under control.

Trace sank to the ground by her feet and leaned his back up against the log she sat on, content to just be close to her. She was calm, and he knew that this place held some special meaning for her.

"What is this place?" Trace's murmured voice was hushed.

"My favorite place in the world. We're on the side of the mountain. I come here to watch the sunsets. My mom and I used to come here together. She loved this place. Even after she lost her sight, we still came at least once a week. Mama always said that she could still see the sunsets. She said that their colors smelled beautiful." Leona's statement cracked with emotion. "I still feel close to her when I am here."

Trace sought her hand and picked it up in one of his own, offering silent comfort. Threading their fingers together, he rubbed his thumb back and forth across her thumb and the back of her silken hand. "What do you see right now? Can you explain it to me? Let me see it through your eyes."

Lost in the sensation of his touch, it took her a moment to process his request. When it registered, she opened her eyes and looked out over the magnificent view her mountains presented.

Leona opened herself up to him completely. She allowed him to see the world through her eyes. "Well, the sun is going down between two of the largest mountains. There are about six peaks that you can see from here. Some with snow, some without. There is a river that snakes into the mountains that the sun is reflecting off of. The sky is a multitude of colors, vibrant colors. Beautiful colors. The colors blend together making almost new ones. Blues, purples, reds, oranges, yellows. It is absolutely amazing."

She shifted on the grass, took a deep breath and closed her eyes briefly. "Just sitting here makes one realize what in life is really important. It kind of makes me feel small. There's a pair of eagles flying on the wind currents. Down by the stream is a family of deer drinking water and eating the rich grass. It is perfect harmony. Here and now, the world is perfect. There is no ugliness, only beauty." Leona stopped, unable to continue speaking amidst the beauty.

Hands intertwined, they sat together in silence.

When the sun had almost set, leaving just enough light for the walk back, Leona rose. She pulled on Trace, not wanting to speak, but needing him to rise.

He pulled himself up but did not relinquish his hold on her hand. They headed back down the path in silence, hands joined as if they were really a couple. In a sense they were.

She fit perfectly next to him. Was the right size for him. *Only for me.* That thought gave him a start.

Unable to stand the directions that his thoughts were going, he had to break the silence. "Thank you for that. It was a nice walk."

Trace could feel her trembling and knew that he was the cause. For that single moment in time he had no other life. His soul was content. He had no thought of his former life, his wife or his command. The fact that he had lost his sight held no meaning. The emptiness, longing and yearning for something that had eluded him, that had plagued him for the past fifteen years was gone. He was complete.

Merely holding hands with this woman who he had never seen made Trace view life in a whole new way. With her by his side he could face anything that presented itself. Nothing would be too hard.

Trace stopped and pulled her back. To him. Spun her into his broad and muscular chest. While she was still off balance from being spun he wrapped his strong arms around her possessively. Tenderly, as a lover would do to the one who meant more than anything to them in the world, to make them understand just how much they were cherished. Protectively, to show he would protect her at any cost.

Even though he knew what he was doing was wrong, he didn't care. Couldn't care. Wouldn't care. He had to taste her, had to brand her his.

One arm moved up and his fingers trailed down her face until they cupped her chin.

Leona knew what was going to happen. Knew she should stop it. But, it had been so long, she wanted to feel again. Just once more, to have that special feeling.

With her chin cradled gently between his callused fingers and his other strong hand at the small of her back, both of them illuminated by the moonlight, he put his lips to hers. Blind or not, he needed no help to find her lips. They were urgent and searching as he pressed her more fully against him. There was no gentleness in this kiss. It only lasted mere moments and when he pulled away she felt lost.

He raised his head an indiscernible distance from hers and he looked upon her as if he had not lost his sight. His words were nothing more than a low mummer as he spoke into her ear. "I am sorry. I just can't help myself. I have to kiss you." His last words spoken in his deep timbre were against her soft lips.

As he reclaimed her lips, she opened herself to him. He ran his tongue around her mouth, seeking entrance and gaining it. Their mouths met hungrily as tongues dueled in a mating dance as old as time.

Time stopped for the two joined as one. Their passions flared as the kiss deepened. Souls became one, halves once separated were rejoined.

Breathlessly they pulled apart. Leona's lips were swollen and tender. Trace pulled her to his chest as she fought to regain control of her runaway emotions.

His warmth surrounded her and their breath was visible in the cool night. The kiss had gone on for much longer than she had thought.

With the moon fully above them, Leona realized that it was much later. She stayed facing his chest as she spoke. "We should go back."

"You're right. It's getting late." Trace made no move to release her from his arms and she didn't try to remove herself.

Leona closed her eyes as she inhaled his masculine scent. Her heart had finally slowed down and she tried to close the link she shared with Trace. She couldn't do it. Her feelings and emotions were wide open to him. As his were to her.

After a few more moments together, they separated and walked down the path in silence. Trace held on to her arm as she carefully chose their path.

Leona's eyes were sore, and she couldn't explain why, just they hurt and she was getting a headache as she struggled to pick a safe path for them. The night silence was only broken by her soft-spoken words of, "Step up. Root. Low branch."

At the door to her house they separated as if by magic. Trace held the door for her as she entered first. Again, more proof he was learning to function without his sight, he was learning.

"Would you like something to drink?" Leona asked as she watched him make his way to the table. His expression twisted like he was in pain as she was.

"Please. Maybe some tea." He sounded nervous.

Leona put on some water and took out some leftover pie, dished it up and set a piece beside Trace. She was a little nervous as well.

"What's the plan for tomorrow?" Trace broke through her concentration.

"I have to go into town, but other than that I don't have any plans."

Jealously flared to life inside him. She was going to see that other man, even after the kiss they had shared? How could she? Of course, he did have a wife, so he really didn't have much room to talk.

But what happened on the mountain path had been like a dream, a memory long past. One he thought about only in private. There was something so right, so familiar about Elle, but he just couldn't figure out from where.

* * * *

"She's gone. Just wait until father finds her and her mother. He'll probably just kill them both outright. Maybe I'll ask if I can have the girl. I'm sure I can break her spirit." The two brothers had spoken to each other, ignoring the fact that their youngest brother could hear them. Or maybe they'd known he could hear them.

Up on the landing, the sixteen-year-old Trace had had tears welling up in his eyes. She was gone. She had been whipped. Yanked cruelly from his arms and savagely beaten, her beautiful skin covered with blood and welts. His love, his soul mate. He hadn't been able to protect her, as he'd promised her he would.

And he had not seen her again.

He would never again get to hold her lovely body in his arms. Never get to kiss her full lips. Never get to be complete again. From the depths of his soul, anger had begun to build.

As he'd watched, his eldest brother, twenty-two-year-old David, had risen and left the room with a very reluctant slave girl. There had not been a single doubt in anyone's mind that the girl was in for a rough time.

His middle brother, Steven, had been twenty. He'd kept speaking, so he'd known that his younger brother was listening to him. His tone had been vicious as he'd tormented his brother with the visions his words would cause. *"That girl of yours was something else. I had a taste of her myself. Should have heard her begging. I ripped into her and it was..."*

Smack!

The fight had commenced. The brothers had tumbled over the furniture, upending Victorian tables and breaking Chippendale chairs. Rare porcelain items had been shattered under the flailing bodies of the destructive brothers. Steven had quickly gotten the upper hand and his fists had pounded into his younger brother. Then he'd made a mistake, while he had been choking Trace.

Spit had flown from Steven's mouth into his brother's face as he'd sneered, "*I made sure she'll never forget me. I told her that you just used her. I told her that the whipping was your fault, that you weren't there because you were busy sleeping with your next one. The next slave girl to be your toy. But that you had wanted all the details of the whipping and the amounts of blood.*"

His brown eyes had bored into blue with a lethal calmness that would have scared a smarter man. Should have scared his brother. Trace, although bleeding and cut, had reached his breaking point and had been about to turn the tables.

With a strength born from resentment, hatred and the loss of a soul he'd thrown his brother off him like he weighed nothing, and jumped up after him, emitting a guttural cry that had stopped everything and everyone that heard it in its tracks.

Before Steven had had a chance to regain his feet, Trace had been on him. Pummeling him to the ground. Smashing his face into the floor. At one point the edge of a table had caught Steven's face, ripping it open and causing the once pretty boy to scream in agony.

Trace had kept beating him, punching everywhere, even the open cut. All the time yelling at him, "*You bastard! I hate you.*" Trace had beat his brother into unconsciousness as he himself had been beaten before.

Rising over his brother, dripping blood, his own and that of his despised rival, Trace had hissed, "*You will never hurt me again. Ever.*"

* * * *

"Trace? Trace? Is everything all right? Your tea is ready."

Hearing her husky voice brought Trace back to the present. His body remained tense and rigid with rage. Trace took a few deep breaths to calm himself down.

"I'm fine. Just getting a headache. Don't worry about me." Trace was touched that she was worried about him and he smiled inwardly with male satisfaction. He reached for his drink and found it without spilling a drop—it was in the same place she always put it. The warmth of the drink helped to dull the pounding in his head and lessen the ache around his eyes.

As he sat there, he found himself wondering how she made her living. What did she do? Was it something she didn't want to? Would she be embarrassed about it? The desire to know, no, the *need* to know, almost made him choke on his tea.

"What do you do, Elle?" Trace asked as he inhaled the smell of fresh mint and berries from where Elle sat.

"I make things to sell in town."

"What do you sell?" His voice stayed modulated as he forced himself not to jump to conclusions.

"Pictures. I paint. I make art and sell it. Well, Jackson handles the selling for me. I really just do the easy part."

His breath left in a rush, making him realize he had been holding it waiting for her response.

Who the hell was Jackson? Was he the man she went to see in town? What did she do for him in return for his handling the sale of her artwork?

He'd known someone from a lifetime ago who had used to love to draw.

Instead of asking the question he really wanted to, Trace asked, "What do you paint?"

"Almost anything. But I'm best at animals and nature. At least I think so."

Trace wondered just how much of a living she could earn. Maybe that was why she was living on the side of a mountain.

She knew by the look on his face that he didn't think she could make much of a living doing this. He would be wrong. She was an extremely talented artist. She had acquired an enormous amount of savings from her sales. In fact, she was downright wealthy, as Jackson had invested her money and it had more than quadrupled. Her paintings were being requested over in England now. She had almost more work than she could handle.

Her dream of going to England was almost ready to come true. She just hadn't been able to leave her mom buried here alone. And she also didn't want to leave Jackson. So here she was as rich as a member of the peerage in England and living on the side of a mountain, close to nature.

What is he thinking? Leona watched as many different emotions passed over Trace's face. How he had changed. How he had grown into the magnificent man she had known he would become. He had filled out so nicely. Even her vivid dreams couldn't have painted him in this model of perfection to her eyes.

* * * *

Trace, aged sixteen

"Come here." The voice was deep. It probably wouldn't get any deeper. If it did, it wouldn't be by much, as it was already a rich baritone.

Trace was tall. Well over six feet, he was a boy who had just about come into his own. And he was used to being obeyed. By almost everyone. But not her. Never her.

"Come here, I said." He was sitting under a tree, leaning on the trunk, one leg pulled up with one strong arm draped over it.

A demand. A demand it seemed going entirely unnoticed by its intended recipient. The one to whom he was speaking continued to ignore him. He shook his head as he realized she was paying no heed to him and would continue to do so until she deemed him worthy of her attentions. Quite a spunky little woman. He passed the time by committing her to his memory.

She was a little thin, but then, she was just a teen. Her body, however, had begun to bud and show the woman she would become. Her hair fell around her shoulders like black silk. Her skin shone with health. A pert but somewhat flat nose and full lips. Her eyes were stunning, by far her most striking feature. They were tawny, lion-like and different, but it only added to her allure.

Her face was a gentle oval accenting her high and well-defined cheekbones. The promise of stunning beauty to come was apparent. She was beautiful now, but in a youthful innocent way, not with the maturity that would come with age.

"Why don't you come to me?" The question was asked breezily. Her voice got to him in the depths of his insides, as it always did. It rendered him weak in the knees and removed his ability to tell her no. She had a very powerful voice.

He alone really ever heard her voice, for she never spoke unless directly ordered to do so. Her silence made her a favorite at his father's dinner parties and functions. She was easy on the eyes and made all the men wonder about her.

Her name was Leona, named for her eyes, which often glowed golden like her namesake's. He called her 'little one' or 'kitten'. She called him 'Trey'. There weren't any secrets between them. What they had was a secret to everyone.

Leona's mother was the most feared of all the slaves. She was the shaman, priestess or medicine woman, and didn't like her people to get out of control and cause trouble, so she ran them more effectively than the overseer ever could. For that reason, Leona was given a little extra leniency.

Trace's father didn't want a slave revolt on his hands for the mistreatment of the shaman or her daughter. The slaves made a big deal over her voodoo and firmly believed in it. There were times that punishment from the priestess could be more severe than from the master.

Growing up with Leona, Trace had a different view of the whole slavery issue. He didn't see her as a slave. She was his love, his other half, and he knew this even at the age of sixteen. He had fallen in love with this young woman currently ignoring him by the river. What had started out as a friendship had grown intensely into something more. They had developed into beings that were two halves of the same whole.

Trace knew that his parents' marriage was a horrible match, as they hated each other. He had heard his father telling the slave woman that he slept with that he loved her. His father would do nothing about it. He would stay married to his bitter wife and continue to sleep with his slave. Not Trace. He was determined not to be in a loveless marriage like his father. Trace was sure he would marry Leona. They belonged together and their love was strong enough to conquer anything.

"Why don't you come to me?" She repeated her question, still not once looking at him, keeping her focus on the paper in her lap.

Rising smoothly, he moved toward her. As he neared her he saw her looking at him with such love and trust in her gaze it nearly broke his heart. "I'll come to you, little one. But you'll regret it, for you should have come to me."

A very unfeminine snort was her response. With a coy look she taunted, "I am not scared of you. You won't hurt me."

His hand causally stroked his chin as he regarded her thoughtfully, as if he were making a momentous decision. The second her guard was down he moved. Like a lightning strike he had her in his possession and her momentary protest faded away to be lost among the chirping and squawking of the animals of the woods.

* * * *

Her eyes aching, Leona rubbed them. She was exhausted. The day's emotions had finally taken their toll on her. Rising, she quickly cleared the table and got herself ready for bed.

"I'm going to go to sleep. I'll talk to you in the morning. Good night, Trace."

As he rubbed his eyes, he answered, "Good night, kitten."

Just hearing those words again made time slip away for her. Taking her back to a different time and place.

Leona shook her head. These were just memories that she couldn't afford to revisit. She waited until he had risen from the table and headed for his sleeping area before she took to her own bed.

* * * *

Trace woke early. He lay there just listening to the sound of her breathing. Maybe it was time for him to move on.

He heard Elle bolt out of bed. Her panic was in full force and he could tell this even without seeing her.

Trace demanded, "What's wrong?"

"Someone's coming."

She was frightened. Her breathing was very irregular as she scrambled around.

"Elle, don't worry, whatever there is we can handle it." He looked in her direction, or what he thought was her direction. As he blinked, he noticed that he could see the outline of a person. He blinked a few more times, but the shadowy figure was still there.

It looked like a woman. A naked woman for all he knew, for he could only see the shape of her body — of course, it was all fuzzy and shady. She had the shape of an hourglass.

"Trace. Trace? What's the matter?" Elle stopped pacing.

"Nothing. I was just wondering why you were so upset."

A knock at the door stopped her answer. Whoever it was had to be known to her for they found the door and knocked. Elle went to open it. He wanted to snatch her back, away from any potential danger.

A sigh of relief poured out of her and Trace bristled.

"Jackson." The gratefulness in her voice was apparent to Trace. "What are you doing here?"

"I was worried about you. And since when do I need a reason to come see you? I never have before. Is something wrong? What are you trying to keep from me? Don't think you can keep any secrets from —"

"I believe the lady asked you a question." Trace's silky voice broke into Jackson's question with more than a hint of challenge. He had moved stealthily to her side. He had slipped into his pants but was not wearing his shirt. The top button of his pants sat undone in a silent message to the man at the door.

"Who are you and what are you doing in this house?"

"I believe Elle was asking you the questions." Trace slipped his arm around Elle possessively.

"I'm here to check on her and get some more of her paintings." The voice thickened with challenge. "What are you doing here? Why is your arm around *Elle*?"

"I'm a friend." Trace's voice was barely controlled. "Where my arm is not your concern."

Jackson's lilt became very pronounced as he took up the unspoken challenge. "Everything about *Elle* is my concern. You're not known here. A stranger. Don't push your luck with me, lad. I know her friends and you, I've never met."

"Stop it. Just stop. Both of you. You're acting like children." Elle stepped between the two of them and placed a hand on each of their chests. Trace did not relinquish his hold on her waist.

Trace could make out the outline of the man standing in the door to her home. He was big. Almost as big as Trace himself. Or would have been if Trace had been at full health. As it was, they were pretty close to the same size.

Suddenly Elle was yanked out of his arms and pulled up close to the one called Jackson. Trace growled his displeasure at this turn of events.

Leona turned to the man who had just pulled on her. "Jackson. A word."

She walked off a little way and expected he would follow. He did.

Trace held himself still as he listened to their whispers, unable to make out more than that. When the man hugged her, he nearly lost his control, but locked it down and forced himself to remain still.

Chapter Six

Jackson gripped Leona's arm and escorted her a bit farther from Trace.

"Aren't you afraid he can recognize you, lass?"

"He can't see." Leona looked in Trace's direction, his scowl in place as he waited away from them both.

"Are you sure about that? Why is he calling you Elle?"

Leona pulled out of his arms and came clean to Jackson. "I told him that was my name. I can't tell him my real name in case he recognizes me from it. I went out after the fighting was over and he was the only one left alive. Once I turned him over and saw who it was, I couldn't do anything but what I did."

She rubbed her bare arms, feeling cold. "I fed him broth for about a month. When the bandages came off he couldn't see and so he has been learning to use his other senses. I couldn't leave him there, Jackson. I just *couldn't*. But, there is nothing going on between us."

Jackson cupped her face in his large hands. "Listen to me, lass. This man is *married*. I don't want you to get hurt." Jackson's thumb skimmed over the healing scar on Leona's face. "Where did this come from?"

"I know he is married. I have known since he *got* married. I can feel him inside me, Jackson. I still love him. The scar was an accident. He didn't mean to do it. Please believe me."

"Are you *sure* he doesn't know who you are?"

She shook her head, determined to ignore how much the realization hurt. One of them had held onto the childhood fantasy while the other had forged his own way and taken up where his father had left off. "No, I'm pretty sure he doesn't have a clue."

Jackson looked down at her face and glanced again at the new scar. "Just a minute, lass. I'm going to have a chat with him. This isn't over between us. You still have some questions to answer." He strode off before she could respond.

Trace stood tall and defiantly in front of the man approaching him. He still felt at a disadvantage for not being able to see anything other than shadows, but that was better than nothing.

Jackson stopped in front of him. "You. You hurt her again and I will kill you." There was no doubt that he meant those very words.

"I haven't hurt her. I'm —"

"Don't speak. I saw the marks on her face. You put them there, for no one else would hurt her. Do it again and I will rip you apart."

He had hurt her? Marked her? When? For the love of God, he didn't remember. She'd never said anything to him about it. *This man must be lying.* "I didn't hurt her."

"Don't lie to me. She wouldn't mark her own face up. You're lucky she told me it was all right. This is your one warning. Touch her again like that and I *will* kill you."

"Who are you to her? What does she do so you'll sell her paintings?" Rage and pain he could hear, laced his voice as he asked Jackson the question he couldn't ask Elle.

"That's none of your business. Just know that I love her and will protect her at all costs." Jackson's non-answer provoked him.

He loves her and she loves him. Why did that statement hurt so much to hear? What right did he have to think that he deserved to be with someone who made him so happy? After all, the one person that Trace was supposed to love and protect had suffered. He had failed at his job to defend her. Maybe this was God evening the score.

An immense sadness filled Trace. Happiness was slipping away for the second time in his life. "I don't want to hurt her. I would never hurt her." His voice was honest and emotional.

"Good. Now, who are you and what are you doing here?"

Elle came over to where they were and stood by Jackson, a slight that dug deep to Trace. She answered that question. "His name is Colonel Morgan, Colonel Trace Morgan. Colonel, this is Jackson O'Neill."

"Are you going to turn me in to the authorities?" he asked. "Now that the war is over and we've lost?"

"You were on the other side?" Jackson was incredulous. "How can this be? You're still for slavery?"

"Obviously, if I came here and there is an imposter with my name behind bars, I was fighting for the other side. Look, I came for a different reason. One I can't really explain. Yes, like I told Elle, I have slaves. Don't want them, but I have them. No, I am not *for* slavery. I just wanted...I wanted..." Trace trailed off, unable to answer what he wanted. There wasn't any way he could make it sound any way other than what it was. He owned people.

"I understand." Jackson sounded sincere, as if he meant it.

Jackson turned to Leona and spoke to her next. "L... Elle, a word with you." Grasping her by the elbow, he led her off a little distance away.

She watched him, waiting for him to speak.

"What are you going to do about him? I don't think he's blind. At least not completely. Let me take him into town and to the doc. I won't turn him in. I just think that it is time for you to let it go. He's married. You can't forget that."

"Jackson, his wife conspired with the man that's posing as him in the jail to kill him. What kind of wife would do that?" Her voice strained with emotion.

"Also not your concern, lass. Let him handle it. You did everything you could. Now, listen to me. It is time for you to go to England."

Leona's mouth opened and shut just like a fish's. "What are you talking about? I can't go to England."

"Lass, you're wealthy. You can and you will. I've already contacted some people over there. There is a home by the water for you to rent, or perhaps to buy if you so desire. There is a marquess and his wife who want to commission your work for a family portrait."

"Will you come with me, Jackson?" She couldn't bear it if she were to lose him as well.

"Of course I will. You didn't think that I would let you go alone, did you?"

"Thank you, Jackson. I don't know what I would do without you."

"Don't worry, lass, that won't ever be an issue. I will never leave you." That last statement was spoken aloud, and she knew it went straight to Trace's ears.

Even as the pain lanced through his heart, Trace fought back the tears. He had no reason to cry. She was better off with a man who could see. Not to mention one who didn't already have a wife.

"Show me the paintings you were going to bring to town, lass. I need to get back. There are also some supplies outside for you. I figured you might be hungry, since you don't seem to be making it into town as often anymore."

Elle and Jackson got the paintings ready, and Trace watched their shadowy figures as he put on his shirt and shoes. Things were becoming clearer to him. He could see the shape of the table and both beds. There were no colors in his world, but at least there were shapes again.

"Are you all right, Trace?" Her voice, cool and soft, reached across the room to him.

"Fine. Just waiting for you two to be done. We still have to have breakfast and our lessons for the day."

"How would you like to go with Jackson back to town and pay a visit to the doctor? I think that I've helped you as much as I could. He won't tell anyone who you are, so you can take care of the business you need to with your wife and brother."

He didn't want to leave her. Ever. But she was right, it was time. He had some unfinished business with Steven and Bethany.

So, keeping his tone as even and unemotional as possible, he responded. "I think that would be wise. I do have some things to attend to. And I need to get home, to my wife."

"Very well." Her own voice was unemotional.

"I was wondering if we could take a walk first. There are some things I would like to say to you before I go." With a pointed look at Jackson's general direction, he added, "Alone."

Elle flicked a glance at Jackson, who was keeping his mouth shut.

"Yes, I would like that. Let's go." Elle walked over to Trace and took his arm before leading them out through the door.

Together they wandered up the mountain. Neither speaking, just enjoying each other's company for the last time. They came to the copse that they had sat at the other night. He knew because the way they came was the opposite of how they'd gotten home.

Trace stared at her blurry shape. In the sunlight it seemed that she glowed golden. He blinked as the sun burned his sensitive eyes. She was exquisite, he knew that, even if he couldn't see it.

"Thank you. For taking me in and healing me. I would be dead now if it wasn't for you. I know that I wasn't the easiest patient in the world, but from the bottom of my heart I thank you." Trace turned so he faced Leona. He blinked as he unknowingly put his intense brown eyes onto her tawny ones.

With one lean finger he reached out and tenderly outlined the curve of her cheekbone and jaw. He skimmed his thumb across her cheek, enabling him to feel the scars there. The ones Jackson had said he put there.

"I am sorry about these. I never meant to hurt you. Can you ever forgive me?" His voice was husky yet thick and unsteady, as if he really cared that she forgave him. His brows were drawn together, creating an agonizing expression across his handsome face.

Leona closed her eyes against the pleasure of his touch. Without conscious thought, she reached up and touched his hand with her own.

"I know you would never hurt me intentionally. Don't worry about it." Her forgiveness was for more than just his current transgression of scarring her face. She was forgiving him for not protecting her like he had promised to do. She forgave him for the lashing that she had endured for the words he'd spoken. "We should get back. I have lots of things to do today and you need to get to town with Jackson."

After he helped her to stand, he held her hand a little longer than necessary before dropping it and taking her arm.

They spoke little on the way back down the mountain. A small distance from her home, he stopped. Leona stopped and looked back at him. "What's wrong, Trace?"

"I can't do it." His voice sounded rough and matter of fact.

Thoroughly confused, Leona asked, "Can't do what? What can't you do?"

"Go. I can't go. Not without...without..."

"Without what, Trace? What's the problem?"

Chapter Seven

"Without this." He grabbed her, his hand strong and sure, and dragged her toward him. His lips covered hers masterfully, dominatingly. The heat that sprang between them was the type that forged metals.

Hot.

Searing.

Molten.

Leona staggered under the forcefulness of his kiss. She had been rendered useless. Her body leaned into his for support. Flames licked up along their skin where they touched. There was no softness in the kiss, or in her response. Her kiss was just as harsh and demanding as his.

At the same time, their kiss spoke volumes. It was passionate, loving and most of all, it bound. Their souls reached out and intertwined with each other.

Trace dragged his lips off her. "I dream about you. You don't love that Jackson, and after I get home and get my affairs in order, I will come for you. Then you won't be just a dream." The words were spoken with the certainty of a man who would never be satisfied with just a dream.

On legs that shook, Leona listened to his words. She couldn't respond, for she had put her faith in him once and look how that had turned out for her. She had her own life now, and nothing would stand in her way.

Her own voice could hardly be lifted above a whisper. "We should get back." She reached for his arm and guided him back down the path.

Trace walked in silence beside her. What he would give to see her face. To gaze upon her beauty, into her eyes, which she'd said were light brown. He would someday glimpse her face and be able to look into her eyes when he kissed her. For he would be kissing her again. Someday he would kiss her perfect lips once again.

Jackson waited for them outside. Impatiently, he paced back and forth. He appeared almost ready to come out looking for her. He had his horse waiting, and on the sides were big canvas pieces which Leona knew held her paintings.

She smiled at Jackson as his warm, yet concerned gaze fell on her. Leona walked Trace over to Jackson and stopped in front of him. Letting go of Trace's arm, she stepped up to Jackson, her eyes upon him as she spoke.

"Take care of him, Jackson. Let me know when you're ready." She patted his arm and turned back to Trace. "Godspeed, Trace. I hope you find what you are looking for. Goodbye, Colonel Morgan."

Leona reached up pressed her lips to his bearded cheek. "Don't worry, Trace Morgan. She has forgiven you. Don't be afraid of her memory anymore." She blinked back tears as she entered her house without looking back. She stayed in there until she heard Jackson's horse leave. "Goodbye, Trey," she said to her empty house as she began to clean and pack.

* * * *

Trace and Jackson headed back to town. After some moments of silence Jackson asked the man who was riding his horse some questions. "Why did you tell her you were blind?"

How had he known? "What are you talking about? When the bandages were removed, I had no sight. That was not a lie."

"Aye. I believe that, but now you can see something. I know. You were watching her. Can you see completely?"

Trace decided to tell the truth. "No. I can see shadows. It only happened this morning. I can see your shadow down there beside the horse, but I can't tell what you look like."

"Curious to know what type of man she favors?" Jackson goaded. "Fine, I'll tell you. I am about five inches over six feet. I have dark black hair and blue-green eyes. Which for your information, she thinks are the same color as her beloved ocean. I am very handsome, which she also tells me over and over."

Trace shook with rage. That was not what he'd wanted to hear. Not at all. Elle would be his. Maybe not today, maybe not tomorrow. However, someday she *would* be his.

His mind went to what Elle had said to him before she'd left him alone with this man. "*She has forgiven you.*

Don't be afraid of her memory anymore." How had she known what he had been afraid of? He had secrets that he had only shared with one person.

* * * *

The rest of the way into town passed in silence. Jackson dropped Trace off at the doctor's office. As the door closed behind Colonel Morgan, Jackson headed for his store, where he unloaded the pictures he'd gotten from Leona.

His little girl had grown up. He was so proud of her, and her artwork was amazing. This most recent request from the Marquess of Heartstone to come to paint a portrait of his family was amazing. The man was one of the most influential and wealthy in all of England. It was an honor just to be acknowledged by him.

Jackson loved Leona with all his heart. She was the daughter that he'd never had, and he would do anything in his power to protect her from being hurt again. He was the only person on the island, other than her mother, who had seen the marks on her back. They still made him incensed.

He just wasn't sure that Colonel Morgan man was right for her. It was time to get her out of his reach. England would be a good place for her to start a new life. She'd needed a change since her mother had died.

He headed for the bank to make sure their affairs were all in order.

* * * *

As he sat in the doctor's office Trace told the doctor all he could remember. When he finished the doctor didn't say much. His main response was, "You couldn't have been in better hands. She is, next to her mother, the person I would want to have taking care of me. You know, I am not much for women healers, but there isn't anyone I would trust more. If she thought it was best to keep you at her place, then that was the smartest thing. To be honest, I wouldn't have thought that your sight would have come back at all with the extensive injuries you say that you had sustained.

"Her mom was like a shaman, a medicine woman. She taught me some things. Amazing woman, her mother. We all miss her."

"*Shaman. Medicine woman.*" Leona's mom had been that on the plantation. *Stop it! Stop thinking of her. It is time to move on. Finally.*

"Tell me what you see."

The doctor preformed all sorts of tests. He put Trace up in a room and kept him there for another two weeks of observation.

Over those two weeks, Trace slowly regained the entirety of his vision. He got color back in his life. And his memories of being called a liar in his dreams had vanished. It was as if Elle's parting words had given him the peace he had been seeking.

What he didn't get back in his life was Elle. He never saw her. He didn't go looking for her, but he'd hoped to run into her, to finally see her. One day he found himself passing Jackson's shop and entered.

It was a large shop with brightly polished wood floors. There were large paintings on the wall that took his breath away. They were amazing.

They were wildlife paintings and scenic paintings. The animals looked like they were ready to jump off the canvas. The detail was so intricate. In his heart he knew who had done them.

There were people in the store looking at and placing orders for paintings. Jackson saw him and came over. The man had been conservative with his own personal description. He was a very good-looking man. One any woman would be happy with. A thought which made Trace grumble with jealousy as did the picture of Elle with him.

"Good to see you out and around. How are you doing?" Jackson was very professional toward him.

"I am well, thanks."

"Looks like you got your sight back."

"Yes. I leave tomorrow to go home and take care of some unfinished business. Will Elle be coming in today?" The question slipped out against his better judgment.

"No. She was in town yesterday." Jackson didn't embellish on that.

Trace didn't know what to say. So he nodded his farewell and turned around and left the shop. He went back to the doctor's office and packed his meager belongings. As he was packing, the doc came to the door and knocked.

"Come in."

The doctor opened the door. "Do you have a minute?"

"Of course. Please." Trace waved him in. The doc took a chair and looked at Trace. He was holding a small package. "What can I do for you?"

"I was just wondering how you were doing. Any soreness in your eyes?"

"No. I feel great."

"That's wonderful. I'm glad you made a full recovery."

"I have a question for you."

"Shoot." The doc leaned forward in his chair.

"What happened to Elle's mom? How did she die?"

There was a surprised and confused look on Doc's face. Like he wasn't sure what he was talking about. "Elle? Who's Elle?"

"The woman who took care of me."

The doctor shook his head. "Son, maybe you aren't as well as you thought. Her mom died of some unknown disease. But her name isn't Elle. Where did you get that idea?"

Now it was Trace's turn to be confused. *Her name isn't Elle?* "Of course her name is Elle. Why would she have lied?"

"Son, I don't know about that. But I know two things. One, she left this for you." Doc handed him the package. "Two, her name is not Elle. Her name is Leona. Good luck, son." He left the room and shut the door behind him.

Trace fell to the bed as his legs gave out on him. *Leona.* She was *his* woman. It was the love of his life and she had to have known who he was the whole time and never told him.

He had to find her. No, he had to go home and deal with the traitors. But to leave her again… Could he do it?

He opened the package and what was inside brought tears to his eyes. It was a portrait of him in his dress uniform. She had captured him perfectly, except his eyes. They were happy, which his weren't. They couldn't be, for she wasn't there with him.

He found two rings contained in the wrapped piece of cloth that he opened next. One was a very familiar academy ring and the other... The other was the one good thing he'd gotten from his father and had he had given to someone long ago, a slave girl who had stolen his heart. It really *had* been Leona who had helped him. Had kissed him. Had made him whole again.

Bringing the cloth up to his nose, he inhaled deeply. It smelled faintly of her flowery scent. Slipping the rings on his fingers, he rose quickly. He had to get to Jackson's.

Trace ran up the street, ignoring the stares of those he barely managed to miss running into. Sliding to a halt in front of the store, he entered. Breathing hard, he walked up to the counter, hoping that Jackson was still there.

"Can I help you, sir?" A young woman stood on the other side of the counter. She was a cute little thing with a pleasant face and kind eyes. Not the woman he was looking for.

"Where is Jackson? I need to speak to him on an important matter."

Regret slipped across her features. "I am sorry, sir. He's gone."

"When will he be in tomorrow?" Maybe he could talk to him before Trace's ship left.

"Perhaps I wasn't clear enough, sir. He is *gone*. My pa and I are watching his store for him while he's gone. He's leaving the island, or rather, *has* left the island."

Gone. He is gone? "Can you tell me where he went?"

"Sorry, sir. My pa would know, but he won't be in until the day after tomorrow."

Trace's eyes closed in agony. Perhaps they just weren't destined to be together. He reached for the link that he had with Elle, or rather Leona, and sought out her feelings. They were apprehensive and yet excited. Possibly she didn't feel the same way he did. They were from two different worlds.

He wanted to be a part of the same world with her. "Do you know Leona? Do you know where I can find her?"

The girl's eyes grew shuttered. She clearly thought carefully about her answer before it left her mouth. "Of course I know Leona. Everyone in town does. These are her paintings she sells here. She's gone though. She left with Jackson."

That answer hurt, causing misery so acute it became an actual physical pain. Trace stumbled to the counter and leaned on it for support. His body shook with pain and loss. Intense sickness and desolation swept over him as he gasped for breath.

"Sir, sir, are you all right?"

Blankly he looked at her. Not a word did he speak.

"Sir? Please, sir, answer me. Are you all right?"

"I will be. Thanks for your help." Trace turned and slowly rose to his full height before walking out of the shop. For the second time in his life Trace felt lost. The one thing that meant more than anything to him was gone. Again. And again, he had been powerless to stop it from happening.

So, silently Colonel Morgan boarded on the ship that would take him home to his former life. His life and his son.

Chapter Eight

Hawk's Cove Plantation, five months later

Colonel Morgan and his commanding officer, General Harrington, headed toward the main house. Both men were in military dress, riding horses that were decked out as well. They were followed by more soldiers.

His house was a huge stone mausoleum. Large marble pillars graced the front and a veranda ran the entirety of the house. At four stories high, it screamed wealth and power. It wasn't a happy place for him, never had been.

Dismounting at the house, Trace walked with the general, both bearing stoic faces up the stairs. The door opened by a silent black man dressed impeccably in the burgundy and royal blue colors of Hawk's Cove. It was obvious that the colonel was recognized by the man, but he made no noise.

Inside there were more men waiting to take their coats and open doors. The inside was even more spectacular than the outside. The floors were marble, and they sparkled with cleanliness. The wood banisters gleamed and the smell of lemon and beeswax filled the air.

The men took no notice but walked down the hall toward the office, where Colonel Morgan opened the door without knocking. Behind the desk was a blond man with his hand up a young slave girl's dress. He was laughing cruelly at the pain he was causing her.

Without missing a step, the general addressed the man. "Sergeant Morgan."

The man paled then, if at all possible, did so even more when his eyes fell on the man next to the general. The scared girl shrank back and tried to hide from the view of the men in the room.

"Sergeant Morgan." This time there was a warning in his voice. "You are hereby placed under military arrest for the false impersonation of an officer. For the conspiracy to commit murder of a superior officer, you are also being charged."

"Trace. You're alive. I thought you were dead." Steven rose and made like he was going to hug his brother.

"Don't come near me. Your plan failed, brother." Trace stalked up to him leaned into him so only he could hear. "While I doubt you remember what I told you long ago because I'd just beaten you into unconsciousness, I'll remind you. I said you would never hurt me again. You and that bitch of a woman I married, tried to have me killed, accept your punishment."

"You can't let them take me. I'm your brother. Damn it, Trace. Don't let them take me." Steven's voice strained with fear as two men positioned themselves on either side of him.

"You are not my brother. I don't have a brother." His voice was harsh and emotionless as he watched the men take his brother from the house and put him in the back of a wagon with chains on his hands and feet.

After his brother had been removed, Trace sat down behind the desk. The only one left in the room were the general and the girl who huddled, scared, in the corner.

Trace turned to her. "What's your name?"

"Sandy, Master, sir."

"Go on, Sandy. Go to wherever you should be right now."

"That would be here, Master, sir. Master Steven keeps me here for three hours a day." Her voice trembled at that admission.

"Then go home, Sandy. Go on."

"Yes, sir, Master, sir." She backed out of the room, looking at them like they were going to jump on her any second.

After the door shut behind her, the general looked him. "What are you going to do now?"

"I'm done. I'm going to do something for myself now. I'm going to get my son, then I will be going to track down the woman who's left her mark on me. I think I am going to England."

"You don't know where she is? Who is she? What about Bethany? Done with what?"

"*She* is Leona. She is the other half of my soul. I am going to divorce Bethany and go find her. I'm done with the army. I am resigning my commission."

The general eyed his man with renewed interest.

"Is there nothing I can say to keep you in the army? You're too good an officer to lose. Why not just take some time and find this woman then come back?"

Trace turned serious eyes to the general. "She and I wouldn't be welcome here. I have lived too long conforming to this island's beliefs. Eden may be changing but not fast enough for me. I need to be happy and she makes me happy. The color of her skin should have no bearing on that, but here it does. I will die before I inflict more pain on her. Never again."

Jonas Harrington stared at him. "Who is she? The girl who just left?" There was no condemnation in his voice, just fatherly concern.

"No, she is not a slave. Not anymore. She is my best friend, or was at one time. The one I told everything to. But now she has some man in her life named Jackson O'Neill."

"Jackson O'Neill. Jackson O'Neill? Tall, dark hair, blue-green eyes? From Ireland? Sells things, deals with monetary matters? That Jackson O'Neill?" Jonas asked, surprised.

"You've heard of him?"

"Oh yes. His knowledge of financial matters is legendary. Even here on this island. He is considered to have the Midas touch. His fighting skills are also legendary. I have never had the opportunity to meet him but those who have speak highly of his abilities, and women speak highly of his appearance. He's supposed to know some of the higher-ups in England. You know, members of the *ton* and all that.

"The last I heard he had left England and was hidden on an island and had taken up with a…a woman of color. It is said that their love was so strong they still speak of it on that island. I didn't know that it was the island you were sent to."

Trace knew Jonas wished for his friend Trace to be happy, but if Leona were truly in love with this Jackson fellow he would never stand a chance.

"Look, General, I have served well. I have to get on with my own life now. I'm going to deal with Bethany first then head back to the island and see if I can track her down." He would not, he vowed, dwell on the fact that it was well known that Jackson was with a woman of color. Leona would be his.

"I won't argue that you have served well. Don't hesitate to call upon me if you ever need anything. Anything at all. For what it's worth, I hope you find her, Trace. Really, I do. There is only one person out there who will complete your soul and when you find them, one must do whatever necessary to keep them. Keep in touch, Colonel, and let me know how it turns out."

Jonas rose and stuck out his hand, which Trace took. The two men shook hands and the general nodded once more. He did an about-face then marched out of the door without looking back. Trace watched from the window as he rose into his saddle and led the men down the drive with Steven chained in the back of the wagon.

Sitting back down at his desk, Trace began making a list of all the things he had to do. Find Bethany and deal with her issue in his attempted murder. Divorce her. Find the papers on Leona and her mother and make sure that they were set free. Find out where she and Jackson went then follow. Win her back.

* * * *

Somewhere along the English coast

"What do you think, lass?"

"Oh, Jackson. It's beautiful. I love it. Are you sure we can afford it?"

"Lass, you can afford something much bigger if that is what you wish for." His voice told her he would get her whatever she desired.

"No, this is just perfect." She slid her arm around the waist of the tall man next to her as she took in her new home.

It was a small cottage, only six rooms. Built out of stone, it sat on the edge of a cliff overlooking the raging surf. There was a path that led to the water from the house.

A small herb garden had been planted for her and there were rose bushes all around. A forest was not far off in the distance and there was a small stable for her newly acquired horses.

The interior had been done according to her own pleasures, except for Jackson's room. That had been his to redo as he saw fit. It was open and airy, but when the windows were shut the cold damp air was stopped from reaching her.

Her bedroom was done in a pale green. Very open and spacious. Dark mahogany furniture graced her home upstairs and down.

Tucked away where the forest met the edge of the cliffs was her studio. She would be there daily as she painted overlooking the water. It was perfect. The only thing missing was...well, a man to share it with.

Jackson was wonderful, but he wasn't the one she wanted to share it with in that way. The one she wished for, dreamed about, had chocolate-brown eyes, not eyes the color of the ocean. Brown hair, not black. His gaze made her tremble inside and made her want to do things she would never think about with Jackson, who had the honor of being the father figure in her life.

She wanted Trace, just as she always had. Just as she always would.

The arrival of a carriage made her turn. It was a well-sprung ride with an emblem on the side that told her whose it was. Liveried men jumped down as soon as the wheels stopped. Opening the door, they helped out a stunning woman.

The Marchioness of Heartstone. She was exquisite. Her eyes twinkled with good humor as she settled them on Leona and Jackson.

"Good day." She reached for Leona's hand without waiting for introductions. "I know I am a day early, but I couldn't wait to meet you. You must be Jackson. Thanks for bringing her here. Please, call me Ciara." The woman spoke fast, actions from her hands mimicking the speed.

The woman was amazing. She had eyes the color of whiskey and long black hair. Leona looked at her and felt her mouth drop open. She wore pants, buckskins, like Leona did at times. At a nudge from Jackson, she closed her mouth.

Leona stared at this woman who had asked for her. *Her.* To do their familial portrait. A glance down at her own clothes made Leona feel dowdy standing next to the marchioness in pants no less.

Reaching out a slim copper hand only adorned with a single topaz and diamond ring, she squeezed Leona's hand in comfort and understanding.

"My husband is probably right behind me and the kids will be coming tomorrow with the luggage, so we have a little while to get to know each other." She flicked her gaze between Leona and Jackson. "How long have you two known one another?"

"Thirteen years," Jackson said as he slid his arm around Leona in a gesture of affection and support. "I'll go inside and make sure a room is ready for you and your husband. Until later, Lady Heartstone." He gave Leona a quick squeeze and headed off.

Chapter Nine

"He's very attractive." Ciara said, obviously trying to put her at ease.

Leona grinned. "He's the closest thing to a father I've ever had. I don't know what I would do without him."

"Is your husband here?" Ciara asked with a bluntness that shocked Leona.

"I don't have a husband."

With a nod of understanding, Ciara responded, "Just tell me if I'm too pushy. Lucien, that's my husband, says I really need to learn how to curb my tongue." With a grin came, "That's one of the main and many things he complains about in regards to me."

"The other, princess, would be your perchance for running off without me." A deep and authoritative voice broke into their conversation.

At the interruption, both women spun around to witness a man sitting on a horse staring down at them. A handsome man on a horse that looked like it had been running for a while. The man had a stern look on his face but, as he put his stunning blue eyes that were hardened with displeasure upon his wife, they softened to fill with love and more than a little exasperation.

He dismounted and Leona ran her gaze over him with awe. Tall, broad-shouldered, with black hair, blue eyes, a tan, and he was white. He had a good tan, but he was white. Leona's stunned gaze moved between them for a moment before she caught herself.

Her only experience with this type of thing had been with Jackson and her mother, and she'd thought they were crazy for letting others know how they felt about each other. Aside from the master on the plantation using his female slaves how he wished to, though with that there was never any emotion involved between them. Jackson and her mom had never cared what others thought. Apparently neither did the marquess and his wife. Still, it amazed her.

The marquess' eyes narrowed as they fell to his wife and in two strides he had reached her, pulled her into his arms and kissed her. Their kiss was so passionate Leona began to feel the heat, so she turned away out of respect.

"We'll talk later. Don't even begin to think that this is resolved." The deep voice crossed the air, so Leona turned slowly back around to see if it was safe.

Those piercing blue eyes were on her. Assessing. Evaluating. Then he strode over to her, shaking his head.

"I am pleased to meet you, Miss O'Neill. I am sorry about the interruption, but my wife tends to go where she wants, when she wants." He reached out a hand, and as Leona took it, she trembled with the power that this man exuded.

"Not...not a problem. I am very pleased to meet you. I'm sorry." Her face scrunched up with embarrassment. "How am I supposed to address you?" Leona knew her face showed her shame but the marquess did nothing to bring attention to it.

"You will call me Lucien. I can imagine that we will all become very good friends." That statement gained him a radiant smile from his wife. "I will now go and reacquaint myself with Jackson and leave you two ladies to discuss whatever it is you discuss." He gave his wife a quick but thorough kiss before he too headed for Leona's new home.

Leona watched as he strode off. His lazy masculine stride reminded her so much of someone she needed to forget. Trace. She had to forget how he looked, smelled and made her feel.

"Who is Trace?" Ciara was looking at her with a question in her eyes as well as on her lips.

"Pardon?"

"Trace. You just mentioned his name. Is he a friend?"

Unwanted tears filled her eyes. "He's a part of my past. That's all."

The women walked toward one of the benches that overlooked the seas below.

"Tell me how you started to paint."

Leona took a deep breath and began her story. "I was always interested in wildlife. How the animals could come and go as they wished. They were free. I loved to look at them and wanted some way to keep their images around me forever. Since I was a sl...since where we lived we couldn't have that, I began drawing in the dirt."

She rubbed her arms, searching for the words. "One day my mom brought home a piece of paper and a piece of charcoal. I thought I had gone to heaven, I was so excited. I drew her a picture that I had memorized earlier that day. It was of a deer and her two fawns. She kept it close to her chest. When she died I buried it with her."

The women stopped walking and stared out over the cliff.

"Having used my first piece of paper, I wanted desperately to paint. But I wasn't allowed." Bitterness tinged her tone. "I had one friend growing up and he used to get me old pieces of paper and charcoal to draw, but everything always had to be destroyed afterward.

"He taught me how to read and write. I would draw scenes that meant something to me. I used to draw my mom with a smile on her face. I think that was the one I wish I could have given her. She died before I painted one of her with a smile. Growing up, there wasn't much call for her to smile. Not until...well, until she met Jackson. And even after that it took a while."

The whitecaps shimmered in the light as they slammed into the rocky crags below. "After I got good with the paints, Jackson began to hang them in his store on the island. People wanted to buy them, so I kept painting, and they kept buying. I paint because for the longest time it was the only way for me to express myself. I can't hide my feelings in paintings. I'm free to transmit my emotions."

Leona glanced at the woman listening raptly next to her. As she turned her gaze back to the sea below, Leona noticed there were some animals around them that hadn't been there before. They were sleeping in the sun and ignoring her so she just gazed at them, committing them to memory.

"What type of picture were you thinking of?"

"Well, Lucien and I have two children and all of our animals. We would like one of the four humans in our family. I don't think we can have one with the animals for the hallway, something about propriety nonsense, but I would like ones of the animals as well."

Ciara rubbed the head of the large gray wolf next to her. "I think that Lucien would like something serious. I don't know. Tell me more about you."

"There really isn't much to tell. I paint, that's about it. Oh, well, I like to cook, and I do some healing with herbs."

"Really? So do I. What types of herbs do you use?"

The rest of the afternoon was spent getting to know each other and the group of animals that the marchioness had with her.

* * * *

Hawk's Cove

"Well that's it." Trace looked around at his home. Everything was ready. Looking at his butler, a tall black man named Ben, Trace smiled. It was a good day. The local law was due to arrive soon then he could be on his way.

"Ben, I'll leave the place in your capable hands. You and Smythe will be in charge." Smythe was his accountant, a man who had served with Trace in the war and had lost his leg. A well-trusted man who understood what Trace needed to do.

"Yes, sir, Master sir." The distinguished man nodded his white-haired head in deference.

"No, I'm not your master anymore. Call me Trace, or Mr. Morgan if you wish." Trace had freed all his slaves. Those who wished to stay could and would be given wages for their work, while those who wished to leave could.

His divorce from Bethany had finally gone through. She had screamed and denied all the charges against her, but still, now she sat in a women's prison for her crimes. Trace had made sure that even her family couldn't get her out of this one.

He had been so angry when he had finally caught up to her in hiding at her parents' ancestral home, when he had stormed in with the authorities and demanded her arrest and a divorce. Her parents were now living a quiet life after having sold most of their slaves to try to pay to get her out of her sentence.

Trace, being an officer and richer, had pulled strings of his own. With the army behind him he had prevailed and gotten what he wanted — his freedom and his son.

His son, whom he had found living with some slaves who had kept him hidden from his mother and her lover so they wouldn't keep beating him.

Trace had had to do a lot of asking before they would even tell him where his son was. Some begging, when threats had only solidified the slaves into a bigger wall. The slaves had protected him and fed him, an act for which Trace would never forget nor ever be able to repay.

Now, being a single man with a child, Trace had one more piece of unfinished business. Leona.

"Papa, where are we going?" The voice was timid, as if Garrett expected to get beaten for speaking.

Trace looked down and saw his son standing close to Ben, as if for protection, with his lower lip caught between his teeth. A flash of rage flew through him as he thought of the horrors his son had faced while he was gone.

Summoning up a smile, hopefully a gentle one, he glanced into his son's haunted eyes. "We are going on a ship to another island. Do you like ships?"

A small white hand entwined itself into the darker one of the butler. "Don't know, never been on one. Is Ben coming with?"

"No, son. It will be just the two of us." At that his son, Garrett Hawkins Morgan, grew even paler. Flicking a glance at Ben, Trace spoke, "Leave us for a moment, will you please, Ben?"

"Yes, sir." Ben gently pried off the little hand that was in his and walked a respectable distance away.

Trace took his son's trembling hands in his own larger, stronger ones. "Garrett. Listen to me, son. I'm sorry that I was away for so long and for what your mother put you through. I will never hurt you. No matter how angry I get, I will never raise a hand to you. No matter what happens. Okay? I'm your father and I love you very much." Trace stared directly into those brown eyes that were so much like his own as he made his declaration to his son.

Garrett stared back without so much as a blink. Finally he stopped worrying his lower lip and spoke. "I don't like the name Garrett. Momma always called me that before she or Uncle Steve beat me. Can I have a different name?"

Tears flowed into Trace's eyes as he nodded. "Of course. What name do you like?"

His son scrunched up his face in fierce concentration as Ben walked unbidden back over. Garrett looked at Ben and asked, "What was that bird that you kept showing me and told me I was like?"

A gentle smile came to the older man's face. "A falcon, young master. You are like the falcon. Small, yet strong and powerful."

With a deep breath and a squaring of his small shoulders, Garrett glanced back to his father and spoke in a very sure tone. "Falcon. I want to be called Falcon."

"Very well. Falcon it is. And like the falcon, you and I shall take flight to find our own adventures."

"Right. I'm ready now, Papa."

"Flight of the falcon. And flight of the hawk. Very fitting." Ben spoke to them both. "Sir, here come the authorities."

Trace smiled at his son then Ben. This was becoming easier, smiling. He liked it.

The setting of the sun found the two Morgan men boarding a ship to sail out with the tide to another distant island in the Caribbean.

The trip took three weeks with all the other port stops they made. Finally, the day came that they pulled into the port town. Trace was so full of excitement he could barely contain it.

His son, Falcon as he was now known, picked up on his enthusiasm and bounced around. The trip had done wonders for Falcon. His skin had gone from a pasty white to a healthy tan and he had filled out. No longer scared of his papa, he ran with the other boys on the ship all day and slept hard all night. No more nightmares.

As soon as his feet touched the ground, Trace headed for Jackson's shop. The town had grown and prospered. Walking up the street with his son, they both took in the scene.

People of all colors worked side by side. Street vendors shouted their wares and smells intertwined. Finally he saw the sign for 'Jackson's Woodworking Shoppe'. Stopping before the door, Trace felt nervous. He took a deep breath and he felt his son's hand slip into his and give an encouraging squeeze. Together they opened the door and stepped inside.

Chapter Ten

The shop was busy. Most of the paintings were gone from the walls and there was a table with cookies and punch on it.

"Can I go, Papa? Can I have some cookies?"

"Of course. Don't leave the shop without me. Don't eat too much."

With another squeeze of Trace's hand, his son darted off, instantly immersing himself in with the other children. More of the black children, Trace noticed. He seemed to feel safer there.

Trace headed for the counter. A young woman was behind it, waiting on customers. He recognized her as they woman who had been there the day that he had left the island. He waited until there were no others up there before he approached.

She raised bright-green eyes to his and spoke. "Can I help you, sir?"

"Is your father in?" At her inquisitive glance, he continued, "Last time I was here you said that I needed to speak to your father to acquire the information that I required. Is he here?"

Recognition dawned. "You're the one who was looking for Leona." A pout crossed her features, followed by a resigned sigh. "Well, if you're still looking for her then the chances you would want me are pretty much nonexistent."

Trace began to stutter. "I-I... You are very pretty, it's just that—"

"I know. Leona is something special. Don't worry, I won't get too upset." She flashed a brilliant smile. "Wait here and I will get my father."

The girl returned in moments with an older man in tow. "Daddy, this is the man who was looking for Leona." She turned to Trace and said, "I hope you find what you are looking for." With an impish grin she added, "If not, come back here and look me up."

"Crystal. Get back to work, girl." The man's face flushed with embarrassment. "I am sorry about my daughter. She is...well, something else. My name is Wilson, Wilson Kent. My daughter's name is Crystal Kent. Now, what is it you needed to ask me?"

"I'm looking for Leona. You know, the one who did all these paintings. Can you tell me where to find her?"

Wilson stroked his chin while he pondered the question. He cast a glance over the crowd in the store. "Perhaps we should go in the back to discuss this." He opened the swinging door toward the back and waited for Trace to precede him.

"Just let me tell my boy." Trace scanned the crowd for Garrett, who now went by Falcon, and, when he caught his eye, waved him over. "Son, I'm going in back to discuss something with this man. Will you be all right out here?"

"Of course, Papa. I stay inside and don't eat too much." With a wave, he ran off to return to his newfound friends.

Trace took that in stride and went into the back with Wilson. Trace was impatient as he sat in a chair and waited for Wilson to begin. "Well, can you help me?"

"When you were here before, you were on the other side in the war, correct? The side that wanted slaves, am I right? What do you want with Leona? I'm not about to tell you where she is if you want to use her like your kind uses your slaves." The man's voice became bitter and disgusted.

"No, you have it all wrong. I just need to talk to her. She saved my life and —"

"So leave her and Jackson alone. Repay her with that."

"She and Jackson are still together?" His heart shattered into a thousand different pieces.

"And why not? He doesn't believe in slavery." There was no hiding the condemnation in his voice as he spoke the word 'slavery'.

"Look, I don't even own slaves. I don't believe in slavery. I just want to find her." Trace's voice fell tired, full of emptiness. Regardless of how his voice sounded, for the first time he felt proud that he was able to say that he didn't own any slaves.

"Very well, I shall tell you, although if I'm correct about you the answer won't please you. She's in England. She was commissioned, rather handsomely I hear, by a member of the peerage to go and paint their familial portrait. When you get to London, because I know you will be going, ask for Leona O'Neill. And before you ask, yes, that is also Jackson's last name."

Wilson rose and set down his cup. "I don't know what you want her for but know this. If you hurt her in any way, there isn't a person on this island who wouldn't be more than happy to help hunt you down and kill you. Remember my words as you figure out what to do. Good luck in your quest."

Wilson left quietly and Trace remained alone to face his demons. He sat there with his face buried in his hands. He started when a light touch landed on his arm. It was his son.

"What's wrong, Papa?" He was so handsome it broke Trace's heart.

"Nothing. It's just that the one I was looking for isn't here. I have no way of knowing where she is, except to go to London."

"Are we going on the ship again?" Enthusiasm laced his entire body at the prospect of being on a ship again.

"Would you like to go?"

"Oh yes. I love the sea." His eyes sparkled with his affirmation.

"England isn't like the islands, you know. It is rainy and a lot colder. You will have to keep your shoes on your feet."

Falcon colored at the mild admonishment from his father. He was forever losing his shoes. "I am ready. Remember, Papa, Flight of the Falcon."

Nodding himself, Trace stood. "You're right. Let's find and secure ourselves passage to England."

"I can help with that." Wilson's voice came to them both from the door. "There is a ship leaving in the morning. If you want to claim a room on it, I would leave now. There should be some room in the hotel. If not, come back here and I'll be happy to put the two of you up for the night."

As he shook the man's hand, Trace spoke, "Thanks for all your help. I give you my word, I don't want to hurt her. Come on, son, let's go get to the docks."

Trace purchased tickets for him and his son to England then headed for the nicest hotel in the town to retain a room for the night. He and Falcon had a nice dinner in the hotel before they headed for their room to get some sleep.

* * * *

"Come on! Come on! Let's go!" She pulled anxiously on his arm. His arm was strong and yet it still trembled under her weaker grasp.

"Why the rush? What's so important for you to need to go so fast?"

"There's a baby. I want to see the baby. Maybe there are two." Excitement and awe colored her tone.

She was a joy to watch when she was excited. Her eyes glowed with golden fire and she was positively radiant. "I can't seem to tell you no. Lead on, kitten."

Just being in her presence was fulfilling to him, her joy contagious. Her love shone for all to see.

As they moved swiftly but silently toward the new fawns, Trace found himself staring at her more and more. She was watching the deer and fawns as if trying to commit them to memory, every single detail.

As Leona etched the deer into her memory, Trace was etching her to his. This young woman was intoxicating. Some day she would be his. Someday soon.

Suddenly the dream shifted. His brother Steven came into the picture and was beating Leona. David, the eldest brother, was holding Trace back so he couldn't help her. As her blood flowed the more demonic, Steven appeared to become.

"Leona! Leona!" He screamed until he was hoarse, but the beating didn't stop.

"Papa! Papa. Wake up, Papa."

The childlike voice penetrated his nightmare and Trace sat up in his bed, sweat pouring down his face. His son was by his head, fear in his eyes, but he stood tall.

"Who is Leona, Papa? You were calling her name over and over. I couldn't wake you up for a long time and I was getting scared."

As his heartbeat slowly returned to normal, Trace lifted his son up on the bed with him. "Leona is the person I am trying to find."

"Why do you want to find her?"

"She saved my life when I was in the army and I want to thank her."

"Do you think she will like me?"

He smiled down at him. "Of course she will. She is a very nice person."

"People said that about Mama, but she didn't like me."

"Leona is nothing like your mother. I will never let someone hurt you like that again."

"What is she like?"

"You know what your mother is like." Talking about Bethany was just not something he wanted to do.

"No, not Mama. Leona. Tell me about her."

"What do you want to know?"

"Where did you meet her? What is *she* like? Is she pretty?"

"I've known her since I was younger than you. We grew up together at Hawk's Cove. She was my best friend, the one I told all my secrets to."

"What about Uncle Steven? Did he know her as well?"

"Yes, but not in the same way." Never in the same way, no matter what he claimed. "She loved to paint and draw. Those pictures that were in the store, she did those."

"All of those animal ones? Those are just like real animals."

"She came up to my chin. She had black hair and tawny eyes. Her eyes would glow like gold when she was happy. She has a smile that would light up the darkest night—"

"Papa," his son interrupted.

"Yes?"

"Are you feeling all right? Your voice changed and got all deep."

"Fine. I'm fine." Trace was going to have to be careful about that. He shifted to try to get his body into a more comfortable position without revealing his current state to his son.

"I never saw anyone named Leona around the house. Why did she leave Hawk's Cove?"

After lighting a lamp and taking his son's hands in his own, Trace cleared his throat. Now was the time to figure out what his son thought of slavery. "She was a slave, son."

"So were you hidden inside a house like I was?"

"No, we met in secret. After my dad found out about us, she was whipped then she and her mother left the plantation. I never saw her again."

"You stood there and let her get whipped?" The horrified question spilled from his son's lips.

"No, Uncle Steven and Uncle David had me tied up in the closet. I would have traded my life for hers that day. Does that bother you, that I was friends with someone who looked different?"

"Why would it?" His question was direct and honestly confused.

"Son, we owned slaves. Many people feel that they are inferior. What do you think?"

For the first time he had seen, his son's eyes glowed with a fierce fire, bringing out gold flecks. "I know this. The people that have been nice to me were darker. The lighter the person, the meaner they were. I don't get it, Papa. They do all the work and live in nothing."

He scrunched up his face and he clearly thought about his words before continuing. "When I was hidden, I saw Uncle Steven beat them for not saying where I was. He even killed two of them, but they never told where I was. They had very little food and they still gave me some. Over and over they would tell me to hang on until you came home. Mr. Ben would try to slip me extra food. If I was spotted in the house, Mama or Uncle Steven would usually beat me. They wanted me to stay on the back porch, under the steps. The dogs had more to eat than I did."

Trace wanted to kill his brother, but forced himself to stay still.

"I think that they have more…I don't know what the word is, but it is deep within them. More than most of the ones who look like we do that I know. Are you disappointed in me?" Falcon's voice dropped, as if he expected a sound thrashing from his father for that revelation.

"Not at all. In fact, I am very proud of you. Skin color doesn't make the man, or woman, just remember that. Judge a person by what's inside them, not what's on the outside."

"Okay, Papa. Is Leona pretty?"

"I think that she is the most beautiful woman in the whole world." Even though he hadn't seen her as an adult, ever, his voice rang with promise as he spoke those words.

"Me too then."

The easy acceptance and belief brought tears to Trace's eyes as he pulled his son into his arms and they settled back down for the rest of the night, leaving the light on to ward off the bad dreams.

Chapter Eleven

England

"For me? Are you sure? Both of them?" Leona glowed with energy as she spoke to the man who stood before her.

"Aye. For you. Do you like them?" the man with the gray eyes asked. Conar was Ciara's cousin.

"They're beautiful. Thank you. Thank you so much. This is the first time anyone has ever given me a dog, much less two."

"Well, with Jackson traveling so much, we thought it best for you to have some protection."

The dogs were thin, not in a sickly way but in a way normal for their build. They sported coarse wiry coats that were dark blue-gray in color.

"What are they?"

"Deerhounds. I initially opted for Irish Wolfhounds like Ciara has, but when I saw these two, I immediately thought of you. What will you call them?"

"Oh, I don't know. Let me think." Leona ran her hands over the young pups, who both quivered under her touch. The bond between them was instantaneous. The pups vied for her attentions and stayed stuck to her when she sat in a chair. The adolescent dogs always had her in their sight..

"I believe that I will call them Neptune and Jupiter. Oh, thank you, Conar. Thank you so much." Leona rose and placed a kiss on the cheek of the man who had become a part of her small inner circle.

"You are worth it, lass. And as a member of the family we can do nothing less than offer our protection."

It was true. For the past few months Leona and Jackson both had become close to the Marquess of Heartstone and his family. Leona and Ciara were the best of friends and shared many confidences with each other.

"Thank you, Conar. I feel like you are a part of mine as well." She had her family. The only thing missing was the love of her life, and he was gone.

Leona attended operas and dances with the family. She was always escorted by Lucien, Rafe, Conar or sometimes Phillip, who was a friend to both Rafe and Lucien.

The days passed and she did charcoal drawings of the family, both together and separate. With that done, she went back to her cottage and spent her days beginning her portrait. Neptune and Jupiter, never far from her side, grew into large dogs capable of defending their mistress should the need ever arise.

Night was the hardest time. For, when she wasn't busy, her mind was free to wander, and most often it chose the path to Trace.

* * * *

"Hang on, kitten. I am almost there." His deep voice was filled with fear that was easy for her to pick up on.

"I'm fine. I don't need your help. I told you already, I've done this. Since I'm not as tall as you this is the only way for me to get across."

She and her secret friend were crossing a gorge on the island—a crossing that spelled instant death with one slip. The young man crossed carefully even while he watched her weave her way in and out of the many branches. Each time she let go with one hand his breath caught in his throat, he was so worried that she would fall. She could feel his concern for her and how it increased.

Once across, he grabbed her and held on to her. "We will not be doing that again," came the scold. Then he looked down into her eyes and she knew what he saw. Hers were alive with life. That alone melted him. Melted away his fear and anger.

Again, she could feel it inside her. They'd not needed words but had been able to feel what the other did. She couldn't remember a time when she wasn't able to do that.

Leona knew when he saw her at the plantation there was no life in her eyes. She kept them downcast but when he managed to catch them with his own eyes, they were almost lifeless. She knew it broke his heart to see her like that, but the result of him showing her compassion would be even worse if his father or brothers found out.

"What are you so scared of?" she questioned.

"Losing you."

Leona was a lot wiser than she let on. "I am just a slave, Trace. You will be going away to the army soon and will forget all about me."

He jerked her up against his hard body. "No. Don't say that. I will not ever, ever forget you. I am joining the army *because it is getting too hard for me to see you and not touch you, hold you. Not let everyone see how strongly I feel about you."*

He set her down on a large rock and sat by her feet. She watched him absently spinning his ring that his dad had given him, staring at the endless motion. Removing the ring from his finger, he turned and placed it in the palm of her hand.

"I want you to have this."

"I can't. If I am caught with this I will be killed, then who will take care of my mother? I can't take this."

"You will take this." An order. "Put it inside your dress and keep it somewhere safe. I love you, little one. One day I will be able to tell the whole world."

Leona disagreed with his beliefs, but since she had her own childhood fantasy, she agreed to take the ring. They spent the day exploring caves and playing in the surf. Complete freedom and joy filled their day.

On the way back to the plantation, she did as he'd asked and hid it in her dress. They separated a way off from the plantation with a soul-binding kiss.

"I love you, kitten." Trace's husky words flowed over her.

"And I you, Trey." Her own voice was deeper than usual. She slipped away into the woods and headed home. As she entered the shack, she called a home her mother met her with a glare.

"I know what you were doing and where." Disapproval rang strong.

"We were only exploring caves."

"Be careful. You know what would happen if this were to be discovered."

"Yes, Mama, I know."

"All right, I can see that you two have something unique and special so that is all I am saying to you about this."

"I will not forget your warning, Mama."

Leona bolted up. She heard the surf pounding on the rocks below and she shivered as she ran her fingers through the wiry pelts of her dogs.

"A lot of good that was. I may not have forgotten her warning, but I still got caught." She spoke aloud to her companions, whose only responses were to lick her hands. Unable—or not wanting—to return to sleep, Leona rose and dressed before heading downstairs to the library.

Jackson was sitting by the fire drinking a brandy. His hair was streaked with gray, and tonight it stood out to her a bit more. When had he gotten that much? He was still a very handsome man.

"Jackson, when did you get back?"

"Just a little bit ago." He rose and gave her a warm hug then bent to pet the dogs. They stood for the pats then walked over to the chair that Leona had sat in and placed themselves at each side. "They never let down their guard, do they?"

"How did the trip go?" She didn't even begin to answer his question about the dogs, since she knew he didn't require one.

"Very well. You got some requests for familial portraits. I also did some additional investing and got a few more clients. I was wondering, though, if you wanted to have more room?"

Move? From this magical place? "No, I don't wish to leave here. Did *you* want to move?"

"Not move necessarily. We could add on to the house."

"That sounds better. Let's do that. This place helps me paint. I love it here."

"I have noticed that some of your works seem to be with a little something new in them. I couldn't name it before, but now I think that it's happiness."

Jackson rose and walked over to her. He pulled her out of the chair and escorted her to the door. "I don't know what you are doing out of bed, but you should be sleeping. We will have visitors tomorrow. St. Martin will be coming by with his family for another visit."

"Good night. Jackson. I'm glad you're home."

"Me too, lass. Me too. Good night." A chaste kiss on the head and he pushed her out of the door.

Leona and her dogs headed up the stairs to her bedroom. The sound of rain falling made her eyes heavy and she sank into a deep sleep, thankfully a sleep devoid of dreams that had Trace in them.

* * * *

After a three-month voyage, they were finally on their way to London. As their rented carriage bounced over the ground, Trace found himself trembling with excitement. *Soon. Soon*, he told himself, *she will be mine.*

"Papa, how are we going to find her?" His son was all into the adventure of finding this lost woman.

"I guess we'll have to ask someone when we get to London. I'm not really sure. Perhaps we will rent a small house and look for her after. Or we could stay in a hotel. I don't know how long it will take to find her."

His son turned from the small window and looked up at him. "If we get a house, can I have a dog?" He flashed a grin. "I think Leona would like a dog."

There was no stopping the laughter. "We'll see, son. We'll see." The motion of the carriage soon rocked his son to sleep and left him in silence to dwell on his own thoughts. Trace thought back to his time with Elle.

Almost immediately, he too was lost to the world of Morpheus, as he dreamed of a voluptuously curvaceous, perfectly tan, black-haired, tawny-eyed woman who had stolen his heart, his love, his very soul.

* * * *

"Good morning, Leona."

"Good morning, Ciara, Lucien, kids." With a smile, she welcomed them into her parlor. She had a hug for Ciara, kisses for the children and another hug for Lucien.

"I see your dogs are doing well," Ciara remarked as she stopped to pet them on their heads before sitting down on a rich chocolate-colored chaise.

"They're wonderful. Thanks so much for finding them for me."

"Conar was right. With Jackson gone so much, you need to have more protection around you." Lucien looked at her as he spoke. "Are you sure you won't come stay with us at Heartstone? There is more than enough room."

With a genuine smile, Leona shook her head. "No, I love it here. This place holds some kind of magic for me. And I like having a place of my own. But thank you for the offer."

"Well," came the deep reply, "we will just have to keep coming out to check on you."

"And if Lucien doesn't want to come with me, I will come by myself."

"I would never not want to go with you, princess." There was a subtle meaning in those words that even the kids picked up on.

"Papa, please. Don't get all kissy with Mama." That was from Bryn, the eldest child. He was thirteen and positive that girls were icky. Except for his sister, whom he loved with all his heart.

"Just wait, son, someday you will change your opinion of being *kissy* with a girl."

"Humph. Can I go outside with Neptune and Jupiter?" It was obvious he had no desire to be with his parents.

"Ask Leona, as they are her dogs," came his mother's advice.

"You can take them outside. They have been inside with me for most of the day and would probably appreciate being able to run around for a while." With a hand gesture, she released her dogs and they swarmed around Bryn.

"Don't forget to take your sister with you," Lucien broke in.

"I won't, Papa. Come on, Keely, let's go." Grabbing his sister's hand, Bryn headed outside to play as the adults sat down to talk. Jackson came into the room moments later.

"Lord and Lady Heartstone, glad to see you both again."

"Call me Lucien or St. Martin. I consider you both family."

"Very well, Lucien. Might I have a word with you in private?"

"Of course. Ladies, if you will excuse us." The two men left the room.

"How is the painting coming?"

"Well. Very well, in fact. I should be finished within the month."

"I can hardly wait to see it," Ciara said. "Can I ask you something? A personal question."

"Of course, you can ask me anything," Leona responded.

"Were you a slave?"

Panic surfaced in a flash. Would Ciara withdraw her offer of friendship if she knew? Finally, Leona just took the chance and answered. "Yes. Until I was about fourteen."

"Did you escape, or were you set free?"

"We escaped. My mother took me and we left the plantation. Hawk's Cove was its name, and the island."

"Is that why you don't want to live with us? Because owning a piece of property means so much?"

"Part of it." Leona looked at the woman across from her and saw no judgment in her eyes, only compassion.

"Leona, my mom was a slave, so I won't judge you. I only asked because I see you favoring your back every now and then and wondered if you had been whipped. Since you're a healer I was just wondering if it was something that you couldn't have healed properly because you were too young."

Shame, hurt and betrayal flooded Leona's body, flushed her cheeks. Her response was low but steady when it came, no longer tinged with hurt, just a recounting of the event. "When I was fourteen, I received fifteen lashes on my back."

Ciara gasped with outrage. "What was the reason for it?"

Since the scab over her wound had finally been opened up, Leona just needed to get it all off her chest. "I had been found sleeping with the master's son. We were yanked apart and that was the last time I saw him before my mother and I escaped. For the longest time I blamed him. I thought that he had been the reason for my whipping. I believed he had betrayed what I had considered to be our love and friendship. We had grown up together, played together and fought together. One day when I was thirteen, right before I left to go home, he grabbed my arm and kissed me. Our whole relationship changed. That kiss opened up something in me, in both of us. Our feelings became like one. It was like —" She broke off, not knowing how to put it.

Ciara filled in the blanks. "Like your souls had combined to become joined as one for all time."

"Yes. Exactly. How did you know?"

"I have that same feeling. With Lucien. For some reason I can sense his moods and feel his emotions. Makes it kind of scary, doesn't it, to know that someone is that close to you?"

"Absolutely. With Tr...him, it was different. Since he was also teaching me how to read and write. Whenever I got paper and charcoal it was because of him. I owed him so much, but that slate was wiped clean when I was strung up naked in front of the whole plantation and took fifteen lashes across my back."

Her words fell cold and exacting as she were forced between her tightly compressed lips. She shook as she relived the painful memory.

"I grew up fast that day. My childhood fantasies were shattered. After we escaped, and even after I met Jackson, I still had no outlet for my feelings of betrayal. Jackson, with information from my mother, got me the supplies to paint and draw. Art became the way for me to get past my anger and resentment at the pain he had caused me, allowing me to remember the wonderful times that we had. How it felt to be held in his arms. You know, he could make me feel like I was the most beautiful woman in the world. He was three years older than me and I loved him more than anything. I trusted him. Now I just don't know."

Ciara listened raptly to the words that came from Leona. When she was silent, Ciara asked her question. "Do you still love him?"

Tears trembled on her eyelashes before falling gently down her cheeks. "Yes. Oh God help me, yes. I still love him." Leona completely broke down into sobs and Ciara moved to sit next to her and hold her in her arms, providing the comfort that she was so good at giving.

On the other side of the door, both Lucien and Jackson listened to her tale. The men shook with anger at the thought of her being whipped. Lucien remembered how angry he had been when his own son had been struck by one of the duke's men. To hear that this woman, whom Lucien considered to be like a sister, had gone through something much worse made him want to beat someone.

Lucien shared a glance with Jackson, then they walked off a way before he asked, "Did you know about all of that?"

"Not all. I have seen the whip marks on her back, but didn't know the whole story. Every now and then I had to put some cream on her back to loosen up the skin. Her mom told me that it wasn't something that should be brought up. It's a good thing that I didn't know, or I would have beaten him up when I found him in her home."

"He was in her home? On the island?" Lucien was astonished. At the same time, he wished he had been there to help beat the man who had been the cause of her pain.

"Yes, he is a colonel in the army and they were there to battle and try to get more slaves. She found him injured in the field and nursed him back to health. I don't believe that he knew who she was, for he had lost his sight, though only temporarily. When I saw him there he could see shadows. That was when we sailed for England. I am trying to protect her, but now I'm not sure I'm doing the right thing."

Lucien ran a hand over his face as a myriad of thoughts ran through his mind. "He was *for* slavery? Do you think he will come looking for her?"

Jackson appeared resigned. "Yes. Yes, I do. I saw his expressions as he gazed upon her shadow. He always knew where she was and he was more than jealous of me. I don't want to lose her. She's all I have left of her mother."

Lucien nodded in understanding. "I wish I knew what to tell you. I know you want her to be happy, so let's just take it one day at a time. She's family and I'll protect her with everything I have."

The library door opened before Jackson could respond. The two women walked out. Lucien's heart caught in his throat. They were so similar they could be sisters. He stared at his wife and realized that he too had almost lost a loved one once because of other people's prejudices.

The four friends walked outside to find the children. The rest of the day was spent playing games and eating. Lucien and his family stayed for two more days before heading back to their estate. Jackson left as well, to go to London.

* * * *

Left alone again, Leona spent her days painting. She was almost done. She was actually doing four pictures for the St. Clair's. One of the whole family, one of the family with the animals, one of just the kids and one of Lucien and Ciara.

The one of the family was with Lucien standing behind his wife as she sat on a chair. Bryn was standing beside her and Keely was sitting on her lap. Lucien's hand was settled lovingly on her shoulder. The men were dressed handsomely in suits while the women were eye-catching in their dresses.

The one with just the children was with Keely sitting on the chair and her older brother standing protectively behind her. His hand was on the back of the chair.

The portrait with the animals had the family sitting on a chaise, children on the laps of their parents. At each end of the chaise was a wolfhound. In front of the chair by their feet was a gray wolf. In the background was a black bird and curled up under the bird was a smaller catlike creature.

Ciara had told her about a picture she had of her parents, so Leona was painting one in the same pose for her, only this time with Ciara and her husband.

That picture of Lucien and Ciara was the one that Leona was the most proud of. Leona had spent many a day watching Lucien watch his wife to capture just the right look of love for her in his eyes. Ciara's hand rested contentedly on his chest as he looked down into her eyes. The main difference was that in this one the couple was painted on top of another picture. Leona had painted a double picture.

The couple had been painted upon the light backdrop of a lavender rose. After Ciara had told her the story of Lucien and his rose, it had been the only thing she could do. The rose blended in perfectly with the black that Lucien wore and the buckskins that Ciara wore. It was a darker lavender around the edges and paler in the center, where the couple was painted. Leona had made it as a surprise for the people who made her a part of their family and had done so with open arms.

Having painted for most of the day, Leona got up and decided to walk along the beach with Neptune and Jupiter. The dogs ran wildly in and out of the surf, making her laugh at their antics. When they had had sufficient exercise, she headed back to the cottage, where she had a nice quiet dinner before settling into her favorite overstuffed chair by the fire to read a book.

* * * *

London

"This place sure is dirty, Papa."

It sure was. Trace didn't remember London being this bad. Apparently all that time at Hawk's Cove had made him detest the noise and congestion of a large city. "Sure is, Falcon. Stay close to me."

"Okay." He enjoyed the familiar feel of his son's hand slipping into his larger one as they prepared to get out of the carriage.

The carriage lumbered up to the hotel and the footmen got down their luggage. Once inside the hotel,

Trace breathed a little easier. This place was clean. Spotless really. Well lit from the massive chandeliers hanging from the tall, vaulted ceiling. He walked up to the man behind the counter.

"I need a room, please."

"Very well, sir."

As the man was spouting to some other footmen who were waiting to carry the luggage upstairs, Trace wondered how he was going to find Leona in this place.

"Have you heard of Leona O'Neill?" Trace still choked on saying her last name as O'Neill. It just wasn't right. She was supposed to marry him. The man was old enough to be her father, for hell's sake.

The concierge got a condescending and knowing smirk on his face. "Everyone has heard of her. She's made a name for herself painting the peerage. Interesting as she is dark-skinned and all."

"Where can I find her?"

With a shake of his head, he retorted, "Do you really think that you can buy her services? She's requested by many. And if you're thinking that you can marry her to get some of her money, think again. She is under the care of the Marquess of Heartstone." The man leaned in as if he were parting with huge news. "If that weren't enough to scare off most men, then the marchioness would be, what with all her wild animals and all."

He leaned back, overly smug in his knowledge. "If you want my advice, forget about her and find a woman you have a chance with."

Trace boiled with jealousy and anger. Why was she with a *marquess*? "Not that it is any of your business, but Leona and I have known each other since we were children. I was in town, heard she was here and wanted to surprise her with a visit. It is obvious that you don't know where she is, so why didn't you just say so? And for the sake of your health and further longevity, do not, I repeat, do not *ever* take that tone again when you speak about Leona." His words fell like stone on the man behind the counter, shattering through his arrogant persona just as easily as a brick shattering a window.

The man mumbled his apology. As Trace and his son were headed up the wide staircase he called out, "You might leave a note at the townhouse of the marquess. He may be able to put you two in touch."

With nothing more than a wave of acknowledgment, Trace continued up the steps to his room. When the men had left, he looked down into the mistrustful eyes of his son.

"What's the matter, son?"

"You lied to that man, Papa. What's really going on? What is Leona to you?" Eyes that were too wise and old for their bearer bore into him.

"I'm not sure that she will want to see me. I hurt her and betrayed her trust a long time ago." Heartache and pain laced his words and he didn't doubt his son could hear it just as easily as he could.

His son jumped to his defense immediately. "Does she know that you were tied up the night they whipped her?"

"No. I never saw her after that night. It still doesn't matter. I was the strong one. I was supposed to protect her. I didn't know it had been her who rescued me until after I was almost on the ship to come home, so now I owe her for that as well."

"Uh-huh. What is she to you?"

"What do you mean?" Trace wasn't sure he could reveal his feelings to his son. Wasn't sure that he *wanted* to.

"Don't treat me like a baby, Papa. You know what I mean. Do you love her? You get this strange look when you talk about her, and you look so angry and scary when you hear that name, 'Jackson'. Why do you want to find her so bad?"

"I'm sorry. I don't mean to treat you like a baby. I'm just not used to sharing my feelings." Except with Leona. Always with Leona. "Yes. I love her." His words were dragged from his lips. "I love her more than I would ever have believed possible. If she will have me, I will marry her. What do you think about that?" There was a challenge to his son in those words.

Pensiveness and uncertainty flitted across his son's face. "Well, I guess it's a start that you say you love her. I think that you should do what makes you happy, Papa. If you want to marry her then do so. Unless she's married to that Jackson guy."

A low rumble of jealousy erupted inside Trace at that statement. Something so dark and foreboding rose within him. The thought of another man touching her was like poison to him. His lips thinned with fury and his nostrils flared with his anger. Only the look of fear and wonder on his son's face calmed him down.

"Sorry, Papa, I didn't mean to upset you."

He blinked rapidly as he fought to regain control of his raging emotions.. "That's all right. I'm not mad at you." He knew there lingered some of the anger in his words.

"Why do you get so angry, Papa? Are you sure she loves you? I mean, if she did, why would she be married to Ja… That other man?"

125

Rage surfaced again. He was being swirled into a world over which he had no control. He hissed, "She loves me."

"Okay. Okay, Papa. Calm down, you're scaring me."

Tense moments passed as Trace unclenched fists and calmed his heaving chest. He barely held onto an extremely thin thread of control as he spoke softly. His words were more for his own ears than those of his son. "She loves me. She has to. I can't live the rest of my life without her in it. Not anymore. I just can't."

Wisely, his son held his tongue, not commenting on his father's words, which had been spoken from the heart and had not been meant for him to hear.

Together the Morgan men went in search of some dinner. While they ate in the dining room, Trace mentally made plans on how to find Leona. After they had finished eating, he went to the desk and had a note sent to the townhouse of the marquess requesting an audience. He didn't give a reason about what, just signed it 'Colonel Morgan'.

* * * *

Leona stumbled with the force of the rage that surged through her body. Her heart rate accelerated and she had to lean on a chair for fear of collapse. So much rage, so much hate and anger it scared her. And yet. And yet underneath it all was a layer of anguish.

So raw.

So deep.

So *real*.

As she regained control of her body, she sat on the edge of the chair. What had just happened? It must have had to do with Trace, but how? Of course, never had she felt such emotion before. Not unless he was near had she been able to feel him with such strength.

Could he be? Could he be in England? Come to take her back to the plantation?

"I won't go. I'll run away. I'll disappear. I will never be a slave again!" she shouted to the empty room, or so she thought.

"I would *never* let that happen." A steely voice broke through her rants and raves. Surprised, she emitted a very loud shriek as she spun around to gaze upon the large and formidable man named Lucien.

As she placed a shaking hand to her chest, she sputtered. "Lucien. You scared me. How long have you been here?"

"Long enough to hear your comment and witness you almost falling over. You need to take care. If anything happens to you Jackson and my wife will have my head on a platter."

"I'm fine, but what are you doing here?"

"I came to take you to Heartstone, and before you try to argue, do not." Once again Leona was exposed to the single-minded authority and command that this man possessed.

Still, she had to try. "I can take care of myself. I am fine, really."

"No. You are coming with me." His tone booked no room for argument.

"Very well. I'll go pack. Might I ask how long I will be at your home?"

"For the whole holiday. Don't worry, we'll swing by your studio and get your paintings. You need to be with family, and that is us. So go get your coat. Your bags have already been packed, as I spoke to the housekeeper before I came to find you. To your next unavoidable question, yes, your dogs can come and are waiting outside by the carriage. No more reason to stall, let's go."

Leona stared at the man who was like a brother to her and nodded her assent. She gathered her coat and walked down the hall next to him, still after all this time awed by his poise and confidence.

At the door, Lucien placed his hand at her back to guide her down the steps. As she said goodbye to the house staff, who would stay on, she wondered what it would be like to have Trace with her going to see Lucien and Ciara for the holiday season.

Once inside the carriage they headed for her studio. "Thank you."

"For what?" Lucien turned his piercing eyes on her.

"Coming to get me. Allowing me to be a part of your family."

"You are. You are part of *my* family. Don't ever think otherwise."

When the carriage halted by the studio, Leona stopped Lucien with a hand. "Please, let me get them alone. I don't let people in my studio."

Lucien ran his gaze over her face before he consented with a silent nod. "I will be right outside if you need anything."

Leona got what she needed ready in no time at all. The picture of Lucien and Ciara was specially wrapped and she made sure that it wouldn't get damaged. The footmen loaded her paintings onto the carriage then helped her back in.

"We will stop off at an inn on the way to eat and change horses. Since we don't have a chaperone, we will be traveling through the night. Sorry about that."

"That's fine."

A sharp rap on the ceiling and Lucien settled back as the carriage lumbered off. For a way they rode in silence except for the panting of her dogs. Finally Lucien spoke.

"Tell me about Hawk's Cove."

If Leona hadn't been sitting, she would have fallen over. *How did he know?* She felt herself shrinking into a small ball.

Lucien sat forward and grabbed her hands, forcing her to look at him. "I am not passing judgment on you. I know what happened to you. Not because of Ciara, because we were at the door when you told her."

She licked her lips. "It was a big plantation. The main house had four floors, lots of marble and other fancy things. They raised a few things. The largest I remember is tobacco. I don't know much about the house, as the only time I was there was when the master had a party. I was used to serve food and drinks, to make the other men focus on me and their desire to get me in bed so they would not pay attention to the fact that they were losing so much money."

She tried to avoid his intense gaze, so Leona turned her head, which prompted Lucien to tighten his hands on hers until she faced him again. "Keep going," was his only response.

So she did. She told him things that she hadn't told Ciara.

They fell silent as they approached the inn. Lucien got a private room. With a hood covering her face, Leona could pass as his own wife, the marchioness, so no one questioned why he was with a woman.

Dinner was eaten quickly and silently. When it was done, Leona put her hood up and walked without speaking next to Lucien out of the inn and back into the carriage.

Soon she was drowsy, so she leaned back and began to sleep. Her dreams started off gentle enough but then they became violent.

Once again she was stripped naked, hung by her arms until her toes barely touched the ground and whipped. Each time the lash fell her body jerked in response. She cried for her past and all she'd lost.

Finally she woke herself up, to a pair of strong arms that held her tightly, as if she meant something to him. For one of the few times in her life, she felt safe. Whoever held her was a person who she trusted. For a moment she thought it was Jackson.

Leona's entire body blushed as she realized who held her. She scrambled out of Lucien's arms and flew to the other seat. "I am so sorry. I don't know how that happened," she mumbled, unable to look him in the face, not that it mattered in the darkened carriage.

"I moved to you. Don't worry. You had a nightmare and all I did was offer you a shoulder to cry on. I am not going to hurt you, Leona. I was trying to help."

Instantly contrite, Leona glanced across the dark to the man who absorbed most of the room in the carriage. She spoke honestly and from the heart. "I know I am safe with you." That said, she leaned back and shut her eyes, not saying another word but feeling very safe and protected. The carriage was warm despite the cold weather, and it enticed her to fall back asleep.

* * * *

Trace woke silently in the hotel room. His heart pounded and his back stung. He could feel Leona's fear and her shame. Then all of a sudden he felt it fade away and a sense of love and security came through the link. She felt safe, with a man — he could always tell when it was a man with her — who wasn't him.

Jealousy stirred and was fed by his imagination. Leona lying underneath another man. A pair of hands caressing her silken skin, making her moan and squirm. Someone else kissing her full lips and taking the time to explore her luscious body.

Rage was full force as he bolted upright in bed. His chest heaved as he got out of bed and dressed. It was still late, and his son was sleeping soundly in the other bed. So Trace left the room in silence.

As he headed down the stairs, he ignored the looks of the few people he passed. Stepping outside into the night, he began to walk. He had to get away.

Away from her memory. Away from his dreams. Away to find a moment's peace.

Trace strode down the street, not paying attention to where he was going. Therefore, when he came to a club, he just went in.

The noise was what he needed to banish his demons. Settling down at a table, he began to play, not focusing on the men at the table with him.

The night wore on and Trace turned down invitations from some women to go up to their rooms with them. He stayed and played, more than doubling the money he had started with.

As he saw the first beginnings of morning light began to penetrate the smoke-covered city he rose from the table. He took his winnings and, with a nod to each of the men, he left. As he was almost out of the door, he heard her name.

"...Leona. And maybe then I will be able to marry her. Do you know how rich she is? Since she is not a member of peerage maybe I will have a chance."

"Like you would have a chance to marry her. No more of a chance than I do," came another voice.

Trace executed a military turn and walked over in the direction he'd heard the voice. Not married? Could it be true?

Ears open, he listened for that voice again and, when it came, he followed it to the owner.

He interrupted the man with an abrupt question. "Excuse me, were you talking about Leona O'Neill?"

The man looked up at Trace. Any snide remark he had been about to make died when their eyes met.

"Yes. The artist. Why? Are you after her hand as well?"

"I thought she was married."

"No. She is available. Wealthy too."

"Isn't her last name the same as her husband's?"

"Jackson O'Neill isn't her husband. Where have you been? He is her father."

Her father. *Oh my God.* That was why her love for him was so strong and sure. She must have taken his last name for protection. A small spark of hope began to grow inside Trace once again.

"Lots of men are vying for her hand. Most likely, though, she will end up with a broke member of the ton who needs to marry an heiress. But I'm still going to try. What about you?"

Trace had walked off, muttering to himself, "She's not married," over and over as if he couldn't believe it.

Chapter Twelve

It was early morning when the carriage rolled up the drive to stop at the door of Heartstone. There was steam coming from the horses, and as they stopped silent footmen appeared to hold them and open doors. The marquess had returned.

Leona repressed a chill as she preceded Lucien into his home. Winter had definitely arrived in full force. Small flakes of snow were beginning to fall from the gray sky.

The warmth from the house penetrated into her bones, making her realize just how cold she really had been. Neptune and Jupiter were positioned on each side of her and Lucien stood behind her. That was the sight that Ciara saw as she hurried down the wide staircase to greet them, her own animals following beside and behind her.

"Lucien." His name was spoken with such love it made Leona jealous of what they had. "Leona." Her voice still full of warmth. "How good of you to come.

He didn't push too hard to get you here, did he?" She was wearing a pale green day dress, all in all appearing very comfortable as she smiled at Leona and swept past her into the strong waiting arms of her husband.

With the greetings over, Leona went up the stairs with Ciara to the usual room that she inhabited when she stayed with the St. Martins. It was large and comfortable, with a fire already roaring in the hearth, making the blues and silvers of the room shimmer. The two women chatted as they put away Leona's things, having sent the maids away.

"Was he nice or did he insist?"

"He insisted that I come. But," Leona added with a laugh, "his insisting was done in a very nice way."

"Humph. I doubt it. He can be downright pushy at times."

"He only wants to please you."

"I know." A wispy quality entered her voice, and she laughed. "I sound pathetic, don't I?"

Leona responded without thought, "Not at all. You sound like someone who is well loved and appreciated for being exactly who you are."

"Someday, Leona, I believe you will find who your heart is calling too. Who it yearns for."

With a sad smile, Leona responded, "I hope so. Maybe."

"Of course you will."

After she stepped out of the large closet, Leona headed back to her bags. "Can I ask you something? Something personal?"

"Of course. Ask me whatever you want."

"What's it like? You know, being with your husband?"

"For me it wasn't hard. But I also had my parents together for quite a few years. They never made an issue out of skin color. My daddy loved my mama with a passion that, until I met Lucien, I had never seen in anyone else."

Patting the bed next to her, Ciara waited until Leona had settled next to her before continuing.

"Leona, for a love that is true, color doesn't exist. There will always be someone who can find fault with you. We will never be able to please everyone. If you love this man like you say you and he feels the same, who cares what others say?"

"But on the island I grew up on, Eden, it's not allowed. I wasn't even considered a human being, more like an animal." Bitterness flowed through her words. "And not a very well-liked animal. How could...can... would I be able to believe that he would not still see me in the same way?"

"For one, you aren't on the island anymore. Also, love is about trust, Leona. You would have to trust him, trust in his love for you."

"I don't even know why I asked you that question. It's not like I can ever have him. He's married. Or he was."

"You're so much more than you are willing to allow yourself to believe. Look at you. A wealthy, independent woman. You have this amazing ability to paint pictures that touch souls. You are still young. Don't...please don't give up on love."

"I'm just so tired. Tired of longing for something I can't have. Maybe you're right. Perhaps it is time for me to move on."

With a semi-forced smile, Ciara nodded. "Then we shall call in the dressmaker and get you out for all of

London to meet and fall in love with. Before long there will be so many men vying for your attention and hand you will long for the quiet days. Now, show me this painting. We will let the maid finish unpacking." Together the women left the room and walked down the stairs to join the rest of the family in the morning room.

Everyone was there. Lucien, Bryn, Keely and all the animals that hadn't been with the women. As Neptune and Jupiter claimed some floor space by the wolf, all eyes turned to Leona and the packages that were by a table.

Leona shook her head to cover half her face with her hair as she felt a blush steal up her cheeks. She detested being the center of attention.

"Auntie Lea. Do you want some help opening those?" Keely's question snapped her back to earth. Leona had become 'Auntie Lea' since Keely tended to shorten everyone's name. Even Bryn had begun to call her that.

"Of course. Be careful though. Help me take the paper off the first one."

It was the one of the children. As the picture was exposed to everyone's gazes, she heard the awe in their voices. That alone brought a satisfied smile to her face.

Lucien rose and plucked the picture out of her and Keely's hands and looked at it. "Leona, it is amazing. You captured them perfectly. Down to the intellectual glint in Bryn's blue eyes that speaks of his craving for knowledge and the mischievous one that was always present in Keely's eyes that alerts us to her good humor.

"Oh, Leona. It's incredible." Ciara spoke as she rose and stood by her husband to gaze at the picture.

"Auntie Lea. Auntie Lea."

"Yes, Bryn, what is it?"

"What is this little mark down here? What does that mean?"

Bryn pointed to the bottom right corner of the painting, indicating the black outline of a bird.

"Oh, that. It's my signature. It's the outline of a hawk. All of my pictures have it. What do you think of it?"

"I like it."

Lucien and Ciara exchanged silent and knowing glances at that revelation of her signature. She ignored that as she didn't want to discuss what it could mean.

"The next one, the next one," Keely chanted.

So Leona pulled the next one up and let Keely rip off the paper that covered it. The family along with the animals. Again the adults looked on in amazement.

The animals appeared ready to jump off the canvas. After everyone studied that one for a while, Keely was ready for the next one. So she reached for it, only to be stopped by Leona.

"Not that one, darlin'. That one isn't ready yet. We'll open the other one."

"Okay." With her usual enthusiasm for life, Keely took off the plain paper that covered the picture.

The one for the hallway of family portraits. The whole family together. The staff had begun to gather as well to gaze upon the artwork. There was nothing but praise from all who looked upon them.

Lucien took a hold of Leona's hand and pulled her into an embrace as he bent his head down toward her ear. "My thanks, Leona. It was more than I could ever have hoped for."

She nodded her understanding while she inhaled his masculine scent. He was so safe, so warm.

Within seconds his hold on her had changed as he was supporting her. Her body shook virtually uncontrollably.

Leona knew exactly what was going on. Trace's emotions were becoming stronger, and right now he was pissed. In an attempt to rid him of the anger, she made an effort to let him feel her pain, and she knew the instant he did, for like a wave that crashes on the shore and retreats with some of the sand, immediately his rage swept back and carried her pain with it.

"I'm all right. Really, I'm fine." Leona pulled away from Lucien and sat down on a chair. Keely stood beside her and held on to one sweaty hand in her soft one, offering silent comfort.

Ciara took charge, shooing all the staff members out with instructions on where to put the paintings. She sent the housekeeper for some tea and biscuits. The room emptied, leaving the St. Martins alone with her.

"Bryn, will you and Keely see to Neptune and Jupiter so they don't worry about Auntie Lea?"

"Sure, Mama. Come on, Keely, let's go." With one last squeeze Keely, followed her brother out of the room.

"What is going on with you?"

"Nothing, Ciara. I'm fine. Just a dizzy spell, that's all."

In healing mode, Ciara checked her over anyway and, finding nothing that she could see wrong, let it go. Leona trembled inside. *How could our bond be so strong? Especially with the distance between us?*

Lucien took himself over to the fire and leaned against the mantle. After a moment he turned around to watch the two women in the room with him, one he loved so much it hurt. How would it be to lose her again?

As if the object of his thoughts heard him, she glanced up at him and smiled the smile that had knocked him off his feet the first time he had seen it. To this day it could still make him weak in the knees. It told him how much he was loved and would always be loved.

The other woman was an enigma. She had many different faces to show the world. Very rarely did she show the unrestrained, carefree person that he knew she was, but with his kids and her dogs she was unrestrained. Normally she kept her eyes downcast and tried to stay out of the eyes of those around her.

It was time to go to London. Maybe getting her out would help her to feel better. They would spend some time in London then head back to Heartstone for Christmas. Lucien strode silently to the door to issue instructions and to send someone ahead to ready the townhouse.

"What is going on, Leona?" A pregnant pause. "And no lies."

"I just felt something inside me and it just sapped my strength for a moment."

The whiskey-colored eyes that watched her were way too intelligent for Leona to feel comfortable about the way that they were assessing her. However, she held her gaze without flinching. Finally they both looked away, neither winning nor conceding anything.

In silence, Leona tried to figure out what was going on. Closing her eyes, she tried to shut the link down. It was a strain, but she almost succeeded until…

Until a force stronger than she would have believed to be still there forced it back open. There was a low grumble of displeasure at her attempt to shut him out. When she lifted her lids again, Ciara gazed at her with one eyebrow raised in silent question.

"What?"

"That's what I'm about to ask you. You're perspiring. What did you see?"

Perspiring? Not hardly. More like downright sweating. Her face was covered in more than a sheen of moisture. Without another word, Ciara handed her a towel to wipe her face with. Then a gesture pointed her to the tea that had been delivered and already poured. Leona hadn't heard a thing.

"What do you mean?"

"I mean, what did you see? Or feel?"

A sigh escaped Leona's lips. "Do you remember me telling you that we had a link between us?"

"You and Trace? Yes."

How in the heck has she figured out who he was? Now wasn't the time to address that issue. "Well, I was trying to close it down because that was what knocked me for a loop. I don't remember being able to feel him this strongly, and this last time, I could feel him so intensely that it actually hurt. Anyway. I was trying to close our connection down, and just before I had it completely closed, out of nowhere comes this explosion of energy that knocked it right back open. It was as if I could hear him chastising me for trying to close it. So, do you think I'm losing my sanity?"

"No." Complete sincerity was in Ciara's direct gaze. "Not at all. I do wonder, though, if... Do you know if it has to do with how close you are to each other? I mean, would it be stronger if he were closer to you? Do you think?"

"I don't know. Or, rather, I am not sure. I mean, it's not as if I really have had an opportunity to explore what's going on between us. I know that when he was in my home it was stronger, and I thought that was because he was right there with me. But I can't be sure about that at all."

"Can you hear him?"

"No. I get, like, mental images of his feelings. You know anger, fear, pain, jealousy. That kind of thing."

"Did it feel like he wanted to hurt you?"

"No!" She swallowed and tried again without yelling. "I mean, no. As soon as he could feel the pain he was causing me, he retreated. Or it did, whatever *it* is."

"Fascinating! I have heard about people who were able to share feelings and such. My own case with Lucien is minor compared to what you feel."

"You don't think I'm like some sort of unnatural crazy person?"

"Heavens, no. Leona, there is a whole spiritual world out there that we have no idea about. I think that what you and Trace have is not only special, but it tells me that the two of you are destined to be together."

Leona tried to control the rapid increase in her heartbeat. What would it be like to be with Trace again? As a fully grown woman who could appreciate much better what he had to offer her?

"Come, Leona, drink your tea. I assume that Lucien will want to come back in the room soon."

Soon the somber mood left the women and they were laughing at each other's stories of herb-gathering in not-so-pleasant weather. That was how Lucien found them—both happy, laughing and enjoying themselves.

"I was thinking of heading to London in a few days. We know there will be some parties for Leona to attend. And there is, of course, our yearly holiday party. But, there are some things that I need to handle before we can enjoy the holiday, so perhaps I will leave early."

"Lucien, I think that we'll follow you in a week or so. We have some things to plan and discuss."

"The demise of the single male population?"

Ciara arched an elegant eyebrow. "Be careful, Wolf. I would hate to have to join her quest for a man."

"Over my dead body," came the low growl. "As long as I am breathing, princess, there will *never* be a need for you to have another man."

"You are the only man I would ever want. You know it," came the instant response, to soothe her husband's most definitely ruffled feathers.

He glided toward them. When he reached his wife he kissed her so thoroughly that Leona harbored the thought of leaving the room. Finally, they pulled apart and Lucien cupped his wife's face and whispered something to her that made her blush, then he smirked a totally arrogant, completely male smirk and left the room with a nod at Leona.

"I don't think that I have ever seen you blush. Those most have been some powerful words he told you," Leona teased Ciara.

"Be quiet, you," Ciara laughed.

"All right, I won't say anything more about you being"—Leona flicked her eyes side to side as if looking for anyone who might be eavesdropping—"soft."

Narrowing her gaze in threat of retaliation, Ciara lifted her lip in a silent snarl. This just got more mirth out of Leona.

Rising, Leona picked up the last portrait and headed for the door. "I have to go put this up in my room."

"Wait a minute. I got you a studio readied on the third floor. If you want, you can put it there. I promise that no one will look at it and no one will go into the room. I figured that you would probably need a place to just be yourself. Come on. I'll take you up."

They headed up the stairs and entered the room. It was huge. There were big windows on two of the walls, making it wonderfully bright. There were tables that were sitting empty, just clamoring for her to cover them with canvases and paint.

Along one wall under the windows were a chaise lounge and some overstuffed chairs. The fireplace was lit and spreading warmth throughout the whole room. On another wall was a small bed.

A sigh of disbelief escaped her. "Wow. It's amazing. Thank you so much."

Setting down the picture she had on an empty table, she walked into the center of the room, opened her arms as if to welcome the sun and spun in a circle. Her hair fell out from under its pins and floated around her head like a black silk cloud.

She spun until she was dizzy. It was perfect, she could handle this. Stopping, she looked at Ciara's face, which had a motherly look on it, one of joy and pride.

"Can I say thank you for the rest of the day?"

"Just don't spend most of your time up here. You're part of the family and I expect you at meals and to go out with us at times. The bed is for the nights that you stay up here too long, *not* so you can remove yourself from the family."

There was more of the mothering woman. Leona nodded. "Of course. Thank you so much."

With a quick pat to the wrapped picture, she and Ciara left the room and headed back downstairs, where they discovered company. She tugged her hair into a loose clip.

It was Lucien's sister, her husband and their children. They stayed for dinner and the women thoroughly enjoyed one another's company. They all complimented Leona on her portrayal of the families in her portraits. Leona just smiled and shook her head so half of her face was covered with hair.

Before heading to bed, Leona went back up to the studio. She set up one of the easels and put on a fresh sheet of paper. Leona turned up the lamp, pulled up a stool, picked up the charcoal and began to draw. She stayed there for hours before her eyes began to sting.

She leaned back and looked down at her picture. Simply seeing the picture brought tears to her eyes. It was Trace. Only a headshot, it captured the way that she saw him. Sharp features, thick hair, no beard — which is how she preferred him. It was such a good likeness its eyes pierced her soul, and so with a jerk of her hand she covered it up with another sheet. Banked the fire and headed for her room and her bed.

* * * *

She basically climbed up him, his hardened body. She clamored to get closer, if that was possible. They were intertwined and naked on a bed. His strong lean body covered hers as he lowered his mouth. Whispered promises of what he was going to do to her flowed between them. It was a most stimulating feeling to have this man holding her.

His hands tantalized her body. Everywhere he touched flames rose and licked at her skin. Lower and lower they went, moving in small circles, serving only to fan the flames of desire each second.

He hovered above the juncture of her thighs momentarily. His fingers threaded through the hair at her junction, not touching the heat, just teasing. Closer and closer his fingers came.

Leona whimpered as she tried to lift her hips to get his fingers to the center of her heated core. He moved his fingers just out of reach then back again, only barely touching where her body cried out.

Finally his fingers slid through the outer lips and into wetness. Just not quite what she wanted. She wanted that and more. Much, much more.

He nudged her legs apart and settled himself in between her thighs. His throbbing cock teased the entrance of her core. Large hands cupped her hips and lifted her toward him. He positioned himself and —

A loud pounding on her door woke her. Leona's whole body tingled with desire and wanton need. She glanced at the window and realized that it was still dark outside. And nasty, for the wind and rain pounded against the glass. The person still pounded on her door, even more insistent now.

Leona rose and put on her wrapper before she opened the door. It was Lucien. He looked almost panicked, but since he was together, calm, controlled, it appeared more of an unsettling concern. "What is it? Lucien, what's the matter?"

"Ciara needs your help. There's been an accident. She says that you also do some healing. Come now." He grabbed her arm and pulled on it unceremoniously.

"Let me get my bag first." She ran to her closet and picked up her bag and followed Lucien down the stairs.

A fire roared in the receiving room and there were four men laid out on the floor in front of it. Ciara was there, already having gone to work on one of the men. A sigh of relief came out of her mouth as she saw Leona.

Leona hesitated mere seconds to assess the situation, then she headed for another man as she removed her robe to put under his head as a cushion. It took her seconds to bind her hair out of the way then she began to attend the man who lay bleeding in front of the fire.

It took them about four hours to sew up the men to their satisfaction. When they were done both women were covered in blood as well. As she settled back on her heels, Leona looked at the men, who were out of danger now.

Her nightgown was ruined. Not that there was much to it, for it was naught but a flimsy silk item that she had gotten to spoil herself. Now it was covered in bloody patches.

Leona was in front of the fire when she began to rub her neck, unintentionally exposing her back to the other two in the room. Ciara placed her own robe over Leona's shoulders.

Grateful for the extra warmth, Leona nodded her thanks. Completely unaware of what she had just shown her hosts. It had been a long time since she had worked that long on a person, much less worked on four of them, and she was exhausted.

Trace, where are you? She wished more than anything that she had him here to lean on like Ciara was doing with Lucien. Leona rose slowly, nodded to the couple, and headed out of the room to return to her room.

There was a hot bath waiting for her but before she got in, there was another knock on her door. Too tired to open it, she just spoke. "Come in."

Lucien and Ciara entered. "Thanks for your help, Leona. You are a wizard with the needle." Ciara gave her a kiss on the cheek and Lucien placed an identical one on the opposite cheek. They left arm in arm to seek their own bed.

Leona took a quick bath—just long enough to let some of the stiffness leave her body. Then she redressed in a clean outfit and climbed back into bed. Only this time she only had the buffeting winds to lull her to sleep. There was no sign of Trace. She was again alone.

Chapter Thirteen

Over the next week, the dressmaker came and went. Leona and Ciara both were extra careful to make sure that her back stayed covered in the presence of others. When the woman finally left, Leona had more clothes than ever before. Walking dresses, sitting dresses, working — well, painting — dresses, formals, semi-formals and a myriad of others.

She also got a whole new wardrobe of underclothes. There she got some that would be backless, but Leona did not model for them. She had the lady take her measurements from another item of clothing.

This was the day that they were being delivered. Ciara had joined her in the unpacking and repacking to go to London. The women were 'oohhing' and 'ahhing' over each piece, as were the maids who were doing the actual work.

"Don't you think this is a little too revealing?"

"Nonsense, Leona. This is the current fashion."

The dress was stunning. The color was golden-bronze, but it had silver threads running through it to capture the light and shimmer. The fit was tight so those around her could see her figure. The bodice dipped low to reveal her abundant cleavage. The color was so close to her own skin tone it appeared that she was wearing nothing at all.

It was sleeveless and appeared backless but there was a thin covering of gossamer that covered her back and kept her shame hidden. Leona looked stunning in it. But she had just watched as they'd laid it out in the trunk for traveling.

"You will knock him dead with this one."

"Knock who dead, Ciara?"

She had smiled and shrugged. *"Oh, whoever. All of them. Let's get downstairs and go riding before we have to leave."*

Both women, now dressed in buckskins, headed down the stairs and out to the stables. Moments later they rode out, each woman riding astride and bareback off to destinations unknown.

* * * *

He knocked on the door for what seemed to be the umpteenth time. This time was different, since after the dour-faced butler opened the door, he stood back to admit him inside the home.

"He will meet with you in the study, sir." With that, Trace was led down the corridor. They stopped at a door and there was a moment of silence before one pristine white glove knocked once, sharply, on the door.

"Enter." From within came the response, spoken in a deep voice.

The butler opened the door and stood back to allow the man to enter before him. "Colonel Morgan to see you, my lord."

"Thank you, Weeks. That will be all."

"Very well, my lord." The man named Weeks quietly left the room, shutting the door behind him.

At the desk sat a large man. His stern visage glanced across the large mahogany desk as intense blue eyes assessed.

"What can I do for you, Colonel Morgan?" The voice was low, as if he really didn't wish to speak with him at all.

"I was looking for a friend of mine and heard that she had been commissioned by you. Her name is Leona O'Neill."

"Many people say they know her just to meet her and try to marry her for money. How do I know you aren't any different?"

"I have known Leona since we were both children. My son and I are in town and I wanted to stop in and visit for a bit."

"She is not in London at the moment. She will be coming in for the ball that we are giving. You can come then and visit with her if you wish. I will have Weeks extend an invitation to you."

Trace bit back his annoyance. This man wasn't telling him everything. "Perhaps you could just tell me where she is, and I will go see her."

Challenge flared in the eyes of the man behind the desk. "Right now she is at my country estate. You can visit with her once she is *here*."

At his house… Could this be the man she wanted to be with? No, he just wouldn't accept it. Tamping down his anger, although his own eyes grew as sharp as shards of glass, he responded with a flat voice. "Very well. I accept the invitation to the ball."

"Good. Then I…*we* will see you there." The butler appeared as if summoned with an invitation all ready for him.

Trace took the envelope and followed the butler out to the front door. Inside he seethed as he thought of that man touching his woman. *His woman.*

As Trace headed back to the hotel, he watched as couples passed along the walk in the park. Even though it was cold there were plenty of people out. All of a sudden, he saw his son there. With a quick pound on the roof, he got them to stop so he jumped out.

"Falcon. What are you doing here? I thought I told you to stay in the hotel." He was stuck between fear and anger because of what could have happened to his son.

"No, Papa," he corrected, "you said I couldn't go out alone. There were some boys who were coming with their mothers and said that I could come along. They are right over there if you want to meet them." His boy had a sharp mind, for those were the precise words that he had used.

"All right. Let's go meet them."

"Did you find her, Papa?"

"Not yet, she isn't in town. I will have a chance to see her at a ball later on." *No, right now she is being kept at some rich man's country estate.* He was so angry, but he kept it under control.

Ever since he'd understood that his rage could cause Leona pain, he had been keeping better control of himself. He knew that she had tried to close down their link because of his inability to be in command of his own emotions. When she'd allowed him to feel her pain he had immediately tapped down his anger. Anything to keep her from feeling pain. Anything to keep her safe.

Over the next couple of days Falcon spent time outside with the other boys who were at the hotel. They spent their time looking at the members of the peerage as they trotted through the Row.

For himself, Trace spent his time finding something to wear to the St. Martin ball. He went to fittings and tried on numerous suits until he finally found the one that was just perfect. Even so wasn't sure if he should go in uniform or not. It was tailored just for his body, accentuating his broad shoulders and his waist that bore not a trace of fat, and lean muscular legs. It made him look to be the man he was meant to be. Leona's man.

Trace was no longer the sick man who Leona had found near death on the field. Since he had left her, he had once again filled out. He was the solid man that he had been before the war began. A fit man for the military, for he had really only semi-retired.

* * * *

One afternoon, as he and his son were sitting by a lake watching the ducks and tossing them bread every now and then, he noticed a younger boy and girl playing alone on the edge of the water. Suddenly the girl slipped and fell into the water, face first.

As she scrambled to sit, her face bunched up and she let out a lusty wail as her brother tried to calm her down. But to no avail. Her cries grew louder and louder. Trace rose and hurried down to the edge.

"Here now. You'll be all right." He knelt down by the child and wiped her face off with a clean dry linen. "Let's just get you cleaned up a bit."

As Trace tended to the little girl who was watching him with eyes the color of amber whiskey, her brother—at least, he supposed it was her brother—began to speak to his son.

"Who are you?" Falcon asked.

"My name is Bryn. Who are you?" There was an accent to his words that Trace couldn't quite place.

"I'm called Falcon."

"Falcon. What kind of name is that?" No accusation, just curiosity.

"It's one that my father—that's him with the girl there—told me I could have. Not my real name, but I don't like my real name. Is that your sister?"

"I see. Bryn is just a nickname for me as well. Yes, that's my sister. Her name is Keely."

Trace heard that and spoke to the little girl. "Well, Keely, where are your parents?"

"At home. I'm out with the maid. She doesn't keep a very good eye on me, though. Mama will get mad at her for that."

"Why will she do that?"

"'Cause. They are supposed to watch me better." There was a sigh from the girl before she climbed up into Trace's lap and snuggled herself under his chin. "You remind me of my papa. But his hair is black, and he has blue eyes."

"Do you come here a lot?" Bryn asked Falcon.

"Every day. What about you?"

"Only sometimes. I try, but it's not always possible. I prefer to come with my parents, but my father is usually busy."

A rumpled and flustered maid came running up to the children. "Oh my God, there you are. Why did you run off like that?" She leveled a finger at Keely and narrowed her eyes.

Before she could say another word, Bryn insinuated himself between them, as if Trace weren't even there. "Don't you dare threaten my sister. It is your fault, for all you wished to do was meet some man here in the bushes."

Trace was shocked. The boy spoke like he was a very powerful man. Just like someone who Trace himself had seen recently. In fact, the boy's eyes looked familiar as well.

"Don't get smart with me. All I did was turn my back for a second."

"No, we had walked away a long time before that. My father will hear of this."

"We are going home." The woman reached for Keely, who screamed and shrank into Trace even more.

"No! I want him to take me home. I don't like you." There was more than just childlike fear — it was closer to a full-blown panic.

"You don't even know who he is. Now come with me. Keely, this instant." She snapped her fingers as if to drive home her point.

Trace rose effortlessly, keeping Keely pressed to his chest where she was safe and warm with his coat over her. Then he smoothly placed his body between Bryn, who trembled with anger, and the flushed maid.

"She knows who I am. It is no problem for me to escort these children home. For some reason they don't trust you and from what I have seen they have good reason. You, miss, will lead the way. I will walk with Bryn and carry the little lady so she doesn't get any colder." In a tone that booked no room for argument, he stared the woman down and added, "*Now* would be good for us."

Defeated, she spun around and stomped off, leaving the others to follow. Trace adjusted Keely and looked down to the boys, who were waiting for him to follow her first. "Falcon, make sure you stay close to me. I don't know where we are going."

"Okay, Papa."

"Thank you. For standing up for me and my sister."

Trace smiled. "Not a problem. Besides with such a beautiful little lady how could I not help?"

"See, Bryn, he thinks I'm beautiful." She stuck her tongue out at her brother.

Falcon looked up at the girl and saw a mark on the upper part of her arm as she went to put it back under his father's jacket. "Papa."

That one word's tone stopped Trace in his tracks. He swung his gaze to his boy and asked a wordless question. "Look at her arm, Papa."

Trace moved so he could see her arm, There were fresh bruises on it. Anger began to grow. Not saying anything, he looked down at the boy with a question in his eyes.

"Today was the first day she ever did that. It wasn't to me, only Keely."

"You'll be all right, little darling."

"I know. You will keep me safe until I get home to Papa."

So that was how they walked home. Keely was carried and the boys took up positions to either side of Trace as they walked behind the soon-to-be fired maid.

Trace was in shock when they walked up the steps to the home that he had visited in the previous weeks. The same butler opened the door, and when he noticed the children with Trace his face immediately showed concern before he got it controlled.

Before he could say a word though, the marquess came down the steps. "Who is at the door, Weeks? I am expecting —" He broke off as he met Trace's brown eyes. "You. I thought I told you..." Then he noticed his children.

Immediately he held out his arms and both children ran into them. "What happened to you? Where is Lucy?"

"Your daughter got a little wet by the lake," Trace said. He'd seen the woman vanish but wasn't sure where she'd slipped off to.

"What happened, Bryn?"

"Nothing, Father. This man offered to carry Keely home because she was tired and wet."

"Colonel?"

"Perhaps we should speak in private."

"Very well. Weeks, take them and give them something to eat." He looked down at the boy beside Trace and included him in the offer. "You may go as well, if it is all right with your father."

"Papa, can I go with Bryn?"

"Of course."

"This way, let's go." Bryn waved him on.

But Falcon waited. Patiently, he held out his hand and stood there until Keely took it. Then and only then

did he follow Bryn. Trace and Lucien both watched
with a mix of fear and amazement.

Chapter Fourteen

"We'll talk in the study. Can I offer you a drink?"

"Please." After they entered the study, Lucien poured drinks and both men sat in chairs by the fire.

"Thank you for bringing my children home. Where is Lucy?"

"If that is your maid's name, then my guess would be gone. Apparently she only wanted to take them so she could meet some guy by the lake. They were unsupervised when I saw them. She didn't show up until after your daughter had fallen in the water and I had gone down to help her. Your kids were scared of her, and, from the marks on your daughter's arm, I could understand why."

Lucien sat forward in his chair, blue eyes dagger-sharp. "Marks? What marks?" Fire began to burn in his gaze.

"The bruises on her arm. Your boy, Bryn, said this is the first time she had done that. I don't know about that. All I know is your daughter was terrified of this woman."

"She *bruised* my children?" Lucien wasn't really talking to Trace anymore but to himself. Pulling back to the moment, Lucien looked at the man across from him. He offered, "Would you like to come for dinner? Your boy as well? I'm sorry, what is his name?"

"He prefers to be called Falcon. Thank you for the invitation but...yes, I would like to come." What had he been thinking? Leona might be there! "We would both be honored."

"We will be going to the opera later. If you wish you can join us in our box. Your son would be safe here."

"Thank you. I accept, but now I must be going. What time is dinner?"

Rising, Lucien gave him all the information he needed, including the offer of sending a carriage to pick him and Falcon up.

Together the men walked toward the receiving room where the children were and found the boys talking softly. Keely was tucked under Falcon's arm, fast asleep, her little hand wound securely in his, her face pressed to his chest. The boys were close together as they chatted.

"Falcon." When his son looked at him, he continued, "It's time for us to go."

"All right, Papa. It was nice getting to know you, Bryn."

"Maybe you can come see me again sometime." The statement reached both men's ears and they smiled at it.

"They will be back tonight, so you will see them then. They will be here before dinner for drinks and Falcon will be here while his father attends the opera

with us. Right now, you and I have things to discuss."
Lucien beckoned for his son to come to him.

"Good. Then we can finish up our conversation."
Bryn didn't even acknowledge his father's desire to
speak to him.

"Sure." Falcon carefully removed himself from
Keely before laying her on the couch and covering her
with a blanket. It didn't escape anyone's attention how
he brushed his hand across her face before stepping
away from her. "See you tonight, Bryn." He shook the
other boy's hand in a way that bespoke immediate
friendship.

"See you tonight, Falcon."

Trace and his son walked out of the door, escorted
by Lucien. "Let me get my carriage to take you home."
A wave of a hand and a carriage was brought around.
"Until tonight, Colonel Morgan."

"Until tonight, Lord Heartstone." Then he and his
son walked down and climbed into the plush carriage.

As they were heading back to the hotel, Trace's
thoughts were a jumbled mess. A man with children
that old couldn't be with Leona, could he?

"I can't wait to meet Bryn's mama."

"Why do you say that?"

"Bryn says that she has all types of animals. And she
is very beautiful."

"I see. Well, tonight perhaps. Are you sure that you
will be all right staying with Bryn?"

"I will be fine, Papa. He said that when his parents
go to the opera, he says that means game night with the
staff. They play games and have snacks. I can't wait."
He was very enthusiastic about the thought.

Trace let it drop. Arriving at the hotel, they headed
upstairs to get ready for the evening.

* * * *

Leona spent the day with Lucien's sister. The St. Martins had set up another room in their town home that was almost identical to the one at Heartstone for her to use as a studio. She had begun to sketch their likenesses for their portrait. At the moment, she was getting ready for dinner. Conar was coming over to be her escort to the opera after dinner.

She slipped on a fetching dress made of satin. It was a charcoal gray and accentuated the color of her skin. Her hair was pulled up away from her face and left to tumble down her back. Long gray gloves finished the picture.

"Wow. You are beautiful, lass."

She blushed with the comment. "Good evening, Conar. You look pretty dashing yourself." And he did. He was dressed immaculately in a black suit with gray accents. They complemented each other. Very nicely.

Devonna and her husband, Rafe, were dressed to the nines as well. Opening night at the opera was always a huge event. The four friends ate dinner then headed off to the opera.

It was amazing. The beauty of it never ceased to amaze Leona. She'd been a few times with Jackson. The costumes, the music, the atmosphere.

At the intermission couples got up to get drinks and mingle with others. Leona and Conar were no exception. As she walked out of the curtain, she heard her voice being called.

"Leona. Oh good, you're here."

"Hello, Ciara. Isn't it beautiful? I love the opera." They shared a hug.

"You look stunning. Hello, Conar. You're looking pretty handsome as well."

"Careful, lass. I might think you are wanting to get away from your husband."

"Never that, Conar. We missed you tonight at dinner. We had a guest. He came with us. You should meet him."

Ciara's cousin waggled a finger in her direction as he *tsked*. "Sorry, lass, you are not going to be matchmaking for her when I'm with her. Not good for the image."

"Conar, it is just an introduction."

"No way, lass. You are already trying to get her married. I like spending time with her and since she is on my arm tonight, I am going to keep her." He slipped his arm around her and anchored her next to his side.

Leona laughed. "You two are so funny."

"Let's reclaim our seats, lass, before my unscrupulous cousin marries you off right out from under me."

"Unscrupulous? Me?" Ciara muttered something to him that made him blush. Leona had no idea what was said since it hadn't been in a language that she spoke.

"I am not marrying anyone. Not yet anyway. Let's go back to our seat. Ciara, I will see you later this evening once Conar drops me off."

"Enjoy the opera, my dear. You, cousin, behave yourself." Ciara leaned in and hugged Leona once more before waving and walking off.

A shudder went over Leona as she felt a chill run through her body. Conar must have felt it and placed his arm around her waist.

"What's the problem, lass?" He lowered his head so his words were spoken directly into her ear, giving the impression of intimacy to those around.

"I don't know, I just felt my knees get shaky." Her face turned up toward his as she answered.

"Must be my charms finally getting to you, lass."

"Must be. Can we reclaim our seats now? I still feel a little shaky."

"Of course." Without relinquishing his hold on her, he steered her back to the box where their seats were.

* * * *

At the intermission, Trace sat with Lucien, who watched as his wife got up and wandered out of the box. They both knew where she was going. After a bit, the men followed.

It didn't take the men long to find the marchioness. She was speaking to a couple standing by another box entrance. The couple was dressed beautifully.

The man dressed in black with gray accents while the woman was in a shimmering charcoal-gray dress that molded to her body and yet at the same time made those looking upon her wonder about what lingered underneath it.

Trace stared at her and, as the man leaned down to whisper in her ear, he realized who he was looking at. It was Leona. Her exquisite beauty stunned, and he felt his mouth go dry. It wasn't Jackson that she was with. This man who touched her seemed familiar with her as they joked and laughed.

Each giggle thrust a knife deep within his heart. Trace couldn't move. He noticed that Lucien glanced between them with interest.

He looked back at Lucien with what he hoped was a bland expression. It clearly didn't work.

"Why don't you go say hello to her, then? You know, being an old childhood friend of hers and all."

"She appears to be out with another man. I wouldn't want to impose." Couldn't be that close to her and not touch her, or rip that man from limb to limb for daring to lay a hand on *his* woman. He needed time to look over her figure, time to put her beauty in his mind. She was no longer the gangly thirteen-year-old girl who had ignited his passion and stolen his heart — she was a striking woman who took his breath away and made him weak in the knees. In the fifteen years since their dash to freedom she had blossomed from a tiny bud into a magnificent and stunning flower.

"Really. Very well, then we should get back, as the opera will be continuing." Lucien said nothing more on the subject.

* * * *

The rest of the opera passed without Trace seeing any of it. He kept replaying the look of contentment on Leona's face and that man's arm around her. He was silent on the way back to get his son.

"Thank you for joining us tonight, Colonel Morgan."

"Thank you for allowing it, Lady Heartstone."

"My pleasure. Besides, it was the least we could do after what you did for our children today."

The boys were asleep on the couch cushions in front of the fire while Keely lay curled up in a chair. Upon the adults' entrance to the room they all awoke.

"Papa. Is it time to leave already?"

"Yes, Falcon. Get ready to go."

"Did you get to see Auntie Lea tonight?" Keely asked as she left her father's arms and walked over to Trace and put up her arms for a hug.

With the rising of one eyebrow Trace picked up the little miss and wondered how to answer that. Who was Auntie Lea? He did have to admit, he loved how this little girl welcomed him into her life. It was like she'd never met a stranger.

"Keely, that's not polite," her mother admonished.

"But, Mama, they know each other. I know for sure," she added at her mother's look. Turning back to Trace, she touched his face. "I know that Auntie Lea knows you. She has many pictures of you in her studio. She draws you."

Keely had no idea what she had just begun. However, even the boys knew when to leave, and did so after Bryn took Keely from Trace's arms.

As soon as the children were gone, Ciara turned to him. "You. You are the one she calls Trace. You are *that* Trace. The one from her past."

"Yes. I have known her since we were children." She was still drawing him? That must mean something.

Immediately protective, Ciara launched her question. "What do you want from her?" There was warning in her words.

"That is between Leona and me. Not anyone else." He was beginning to feel the need to defend himself.

"I will not allow for any more harm to come to her." That from Lucien.

Finally, the rage overflowed. "What is it about me that makes people think I wish to hurt her?" He was furious by this and anger churned.

Ciara was unmoved as she stared directly into his eyes, a crystal-clear challenge in her gaze. "Perhaps because *she* used to be a slave on your plantation. Perhaps because *she* suffered fifteen lashes at the hands of your father that to this day still bother her on occasion. Or maybe it is the fact that as far as *she* knows you are a married man and have come to take her home and put her back into that degrading, despicable, disgusting—"

"I think we get the point, princess." Lucien looked at him. "Listen to me, Colonel Morgan. She is part of my family and I will protect her at any cost."

His legs were just not willing to hold him any longer. "I don't even own slaves anymore. I have set them all free. Even found the papers on Leona and her mother and set them free as well." He sat down in a chair as he continued, "All I want is a chance with her. I want to get to know her again. I miss her. I want her to know my son. To know me."

The door burst open and in ran Falcon, his face furious as he stood in front of his father's chair. "Don't yell at my papa. He couldn't help her because he was tied up in a closet by Uncle Steven. Papa told me all about it. My papa is an honorable man. He keeps his word."

Stunned by the hostility of the young boy and the words that he'd said, Ciara and Lucien just looked at him.

"Papa loves her, he said so."

Trace put his hand on his son's shoulder and turned his gaze from the couple across from him so they wouldn't read the truth in his eyes. "Don't be mad at them, Falcon. They are only trying to protect her, as I would do. As I should have done. It's about time that someone stood up for her, since I haven't been able to do it properly. Let's go home. Good night, Lord and

Lady Heartstone." He rose on unsteady legs and steered his son out of the room.

"But, Papa, you wanted to protect her, you were just too young. It wasn't your fault," he protested as they headed out.

"Let's go, Falcon."

They walked out to the entrance hall and there, in all her glory, stood Leona. Beside her were two very large grayish dogs, standing as sentries. *Her* sentries.

Her cheeks flushed from the cold, she stood as Weeks took her wrap, handed it back to her and left her there for Trace to gaze upon. The dress cupped her full breasts and lifted them seductively toward him, captivating him. Her waist was still small, and the dress only accentuated that fact.

His hungry gaze roved over her figure. It had been so long, close to sixteen years, actually. He committed all of her to memory. Her face with its high cheekbones, little nose…and those eyes. He'd had many a dream about those beautiful, haunting tawny eyes.

Her hair, long and luxurious. It was thick and full, framing her face with gentle, wayward wisps where it escaped its pins. Full lips that he had missed so much trembled as she gazed upon him.

Her eyes were full of surprise as they lingered over his face before moving all over his body. He could see her shivering, trembling even as he stared at her, an embodiment of perfection.

Trace didn't even notice when Ciara came up and quietly took Falcon by the hand and led him away. The entire building could have been set on fire and he still would not have been able to take his eyes off her.

These years had been wonderful to her. She was a beautiful woman. *His* woman.

That thought made him start, she wasn't his yet.

"Leona." His words came out tortured.

"Colonel Morgan." Despite her trembling in his presence, her eyes grew sharp, wary. "What are you doing here?"

"I came to see you." His hand reached out involuntarily toward her face. The low growl of a dog made him pull it back.

"Why do you want to see me?" Her voice stayed shrewd, as if she had the belief he was setting a trap for her.

"Please, little one." She trembled at that phrase. "You know me. Please."

Her wrap fell to the ground from nerveless fingers and she took a step toward him. The dogs lay down and watched him but made no other movements.

"Why didn't you tell me? Why didn't you tell me your real name? Why say your name was Elle?"

"It seemed safer." Her eyes filled with crystalline tears as she spoke.

"Didn't you trust me? Don't you trust me?" His voice came out barely above a whisper.

"I don't know you anymore."

Even as she said that she took another step closer to him, drawn by an invisible cord, the pull was same on him. The undetectable cord that had tied the two of them together the day they met all those years ago. He forced himself not to move. She had to come to him of her own volition.

"Yes, you do. You know me, you've always known me, kitten."

Her lower lip trembled. "Why are you here? What do you want?"

"You. I want you. I've never wanted anyone but you. You know that, I have never lied to you about that." His words, strong and sure, fell from his mouth without quaver or hesitation, simmered with barely restrained passion.

"You have a wife. A son."

"A son, yes. A wife, no."

"I won't go back, you know. I will die first."

His heart broke. "Kitten, I would never make you go back there. Ever. Can I touch you?" Now his voice contained a slight tremor, betraying the truth that he was scared of rejection from her.

Her answer was to walk right up to him. Her eyes spoke volumes about how she too craved his touch, but there also lingered a look of apprehension in those tawny depths. As if she were unsure about him.

He reached out one hand and caressed her cheek. Leona's eyes fell closed as she leaned into his callused hand. Finally, after all these years, they could look into each other's eyes as they touched. No more dreams, no more memories. Real flesh and blood. Skin on skin. She reopened her golden orbs to stare into the windows of his soul.

A slight smile turned up her lips at the corners. "You can see. You got your sight back."

"Thanks to you." His other hand joined his first and he cupped her face like she was a dewdrop that must not be destroyed as he stepped closer to minimize the already diminutive distance between them.

Trace tipped her face up toward his and his thumbs followed along her full lips. His eyes held hers as he leaned down. "You are even more beautiful than I could have ever imagined."

Their lips brushed. The lightest of touches. Brief, but everything inside him flared to life. To soon, she pulled back. Trace followed — he would not be denied. Would not be refused what he had dreamed about for over fifteen years. Not now. Not after all this time.

Leona's insides melted. How she loved this man. *This* man. Who was a slave owner. A splash of cold water fell upon her, and she retreated for a second time. Also, as before, he followed.

He put his perfect lips — the ones she had dreamed about — back on hers for a second time. This time the kiss wasn't gentle. It was possessive, it demanded, and she gave everything that it expected and more.

She clutched his shirt as she leaned into him, into his comforting strength. As his tongue sought — and gained — entrance to her warm, waiting mouth, she remembered where she was. Just two more seconds, she told herself, unable or unwilling to drag herself away from his intoxicating mouth.

It was more than that when he pulled away, his eyes like melted chocolate that begged to be eaten. There was so much desire in his gaze, it burned her straight through to her core. Until she remembered who he was and what he owned. It was amazing how quickly the thought of being with someone was dashed when you recalled that they owned people who looked like you.

She stepped back, needing to put some distance between them. her heart rate going a mile a minute. At his step forward she held up her hand to stop him. "No. That's close enough."

"It will never be close enough. I want you in my arms, little one."

"I'm fine over here."

Trace paused, tilting his head to the left. "What's wrong?"

"I don't know you anymore."

He narrowed his gaze, disputing her comment with a single, firm shake of his head. "Yes, you do. You know me."

"No. I don't. We have changed over the years, both of us." She took another step backward, away from him.

"Perhaps we could discuss this in private."

She touched her lips, running her fingers over them, reliving his kiss. "No, we have nothing to discuss. It... It was good to see you, Trace. I have to go to bed, I have an engagement...a *meeting* with someone in the morning."

Before she could reach the stairs he was back in her face, his alive with emotions, mostly jealousy. If that wasn't enough, she could feel it within her in their link.

"You can run, little one, but know this. I will not rest until I have you. We belong together, I have not given up on that, and I will *not* give up on you. Your body cries out for mine. You crave my touch, just as I crave yours. We need each other to be complete."

His voice dropped to barely above a whisper, but she not only heard him perfectly, but also felt him. "So I will let you run this time. Just one thing to leave you with before you go to bed. It will be *me* in your dreams tonight, little one. I will be the one who carries you to the plains of passion. No one else, not who you were with tonight, nor whoever you will be with tomorrow." That was a command and there was no doubt in her mind that she would be following that mandate.

His eyes narrowed on her face. "For over fifteen years I wondered what happened to you. Were you all right, did you ever once think of me? I have you again and I will be *damned* if I let you go now. Good night, kitten. We will see each other again, soon. For you are wrong, we have much to discuss."

His arm snaked out like lightning and he hauled her up against him for another bruising kiss, branding her, reclaiming her as his. Leona still leaned flush against him when he pulled away, and as she struggled to stand up on her own, his smirk came back, for he well knew the effect he had on her. "Remember *that* when you are out with your 'friend' tomorrow."

He executed a perfect military spin and walked out of the door, joined by his son, who was silent and clearly unsure of what was going on. Leona watched as he walked away, her fingers having gone back to her lips before she stumbled up the stairs to her room and fell on the bed as her body was just too weak to support her anymore.

He was here. How had he found her? What was going to happen now? She rose and put on her buckskins along with a large old shirt and headed up to the studio.

Once there she lit the fire and curled up on the chaise while she waited for the chill to get banished from the air. Her dogs were with her as usual as she ran through her options.

After a while of sitting motionless, she rose and began to pace. As she walked, she spoke to the dogs, or maybe it was to the empty room. Either way, she had to work through her thoughts piece by piece.

"What should I do? Maybe I should go back to the island. You two would like it there. The mountains would be a good place for you to run free."

Walk. Stop. Turn. Walk.

"Or maybe go back to the coast. He doesn't know where the cottage is. Maybe Jackson could take me to Ireland."

Walk. Stop. Turn. Walk.

"Maybe a whole new country. I heard that Italy was nice, or maybe Egypt."

Walk. Stop. Turn. Stop.

"Why don't you give me some advice? Neptune? Jupiter? Any advice?"

Leona dropped to her knees and opened her arms and the dogs entered willingly. As she hugged them, tears began to fall.

"It has been so long, I just don't know. Part of me wants to just open my arms and take him in them and never let him go. On the other hand, what if it's just a trick and he wants to take me back to Hawk's Cove? I can't go back there. I just can't. I still wake up at night in a cold sweat going over what happened down there.

"Oh, God. What am I going to do? I need to run. I should hide somewhere he can't find me.

"No." A little louder she said it again. "No! Hell no. I will not spend the rest of my life running. I have my own life now. I can do this on my own."

She rose with tears streaming down her face before she crumpled back down on the chaise.

"I don't want to be alone. I want to share my life with someone. I want…I want what Ciara has with Lucien. With someone. Anyone." Neptune and Jupiter both snuffed like they disbelieved what she was saying. She nodded at them and amended her sentence. "I want to share it with him. With Trace. Only with Trace. As always, it's only with Trace."

Leona fell asleep on the lounge completely spent and exhausted. Lucky for her Morpheus had no disturbing dreams in store for her that night. But as Trace had commanded, he *was* the one in her dreams. Luckily they were memories of happier times.

Chapter Fifteen

Sleeping on the lounge was Keely found her in the morning. Leona woke to a small hand shaking her. Opening her eyes, she saw Keely standing there with a sad look on her face.

"What's the matter, sweetie?"

Keely's lower lip stuck out as she scuffed her toe on the floor. "I don't want you to be mad at me."

"Why would I be mad at you?" It was just too early to play mind games with the child.

"Because, Auntie Lea, I did something bad. I thought that was why you left, because of me. Then I thought maybe you were up here so I came and here you are, but now I'm scared again that you'll be mad at me and still leave."

"Keely, just tell me what's wrong." She struggled to sit up, and after that was accomplished, patted the seat next to her. Leona looked over at the narrow bed in the room and mentally scolded herself for not sleeping on that last night.

Climbing up, Keely sat beside her. "Okay." It was the tortured sound of a child about to admit to something horrific. "I looked at your pictures. I came up here and saw your pictures on the tables and looked at them. I know Mama said I wasn't supposed to come in here, but I just had to see them. And Mama really only said that at home in the country. I wanted to know what they were of, if there were any more of me. Then I told Mr. Trace that you had pictures of him. I'm so sorry, Auntie Lea, don't leave because of me." Tears rolled down her golden skin.

"Oh, sweetie. Why do you think I would leave?" *Just because I was thinking that myself last night...* "I'm not going anywhere. I am spending the holidays with you and your family. Thank you for telling me what you did."

"So you aren't mad at me?"

"No, sweetie. Not mad. But you know you weren't supposed to be up here. That cannot happen again. Now, we have a full day ahead of us and I should get up now."

"I was wondering... Will you teach me how to paint?"

Leona was amazed. "You want to paint?"

Kelly beamed at her. "Yes. Then maybe we could be together and paint in here. I like spending time with you, Auntie Lea. Mama says you love it because it makes you happy and it's quiet when you do. I can learn to paint and learn to be quiet as well, promise."

"I kind of like spending time with you too. I am happy to teach you, but later. Right now I have to get ready to go to the park for a ride."

"Who are you going with?"

"The Earl of Danbury."

"Oh. Don't you like Mr. Trace?" She fell into step beside Leona as they walked down the stairs. "I do. He stood up for me and Bryn when Lucy wanted to hurt me again. When I fell down, he picked me up, dried off my face and wrapped me in his jacket. He didn't even know me. He was so nice."

Yes. He was so nice. "Yes, I like Colonel Morgan."

With a child's innocence her next question came. "Then why would you go with the Earl of Danbury?"

"Because I told him I would accompany him on a ride today. That's why."

"Would you go with Mr. Trace if he said for you to?"

'Said for you to.' Just like he would order a slave. In seconds Leona had gone from being happy to shaking with painful memories.

"You mean if he asked me to go?"

Keely nodded. "Yes, that."

"I suppose, if I didn't already have a previous engagement. Why all the questions, sweetie?"

"Just wondering. Can we paint later today?"

"We'll see. I still have to work on the painting for your Auntie Dev and Uncle Rafe."

"Oh. I guess so. Well, until you can help me, I will practice on my own. See you later, Auntie Lea." She ran off down the hall toward her brother's room.

"Bye, sweetie."

* * * *

The Earl of Danbury had just entered the house as Leona began her descent from her room to the main floor of the house.

He was a decent-looking man. Okay, better than decent. Tall and fit, he sported light brown hair and had startling green eyes. He had a pleasant enough voice that made her insides feel a little funny. All in all, she enjoyed the time she spent in his company, for he was witty and made her laugh. Also, he didn't look down upon her for her painting.

"Good morning, Miss O'Neill."

"Good morning, Lord Danbury." She felt a little flustered as she gazed upon the man who waited for her at the bottom of the stairs. Waited for *her*. It was most definitely a heady feeling.

As she approached, he bent and pressed a quick kiss on her gloved hand. "My dear, as always, you are a vision."

With a blush, Leona ducked her head. She wore a dark blue dress with gold accents.

"You really should get used to hearing compliments like that. You deserve them." She shook her head and he stopped. "Very well, I will stop. For now. Shall we go?"

"Yes. I would like that."

"Well, even though it is snowing, I know how you value your walks, so would you like to walk?"

"Really, you wouldn't mind?"

"Keep smiling at me like that and I would *never* mind. We can also take your dogs. Each of us walks one. How does that sound?"

"Wonderful!" *Thoughtful.* As Weeks held her coat for her, another maid brought out her leashes for Neptune and Jupiter.

When all was ready, they stepped out into a morning of gently falling snow. The weather was crisp, just how Leona liked it.

Side by side she and her escort walked down the street, with the dogs out front, stepping easily. They chatted about little things as they headed for the park. Their chaperones followed an acceptable distance behind.

One moment Leona felt a stab of anger on her link with Trace, but it only lasted a moment before it was gone, so she didn't focus on it at all. Well, not too much anyway.

Trace and his son were walking up from the other way as he saw his woman—he refused to think of her in any other terms—leave the house with another man and those same two very large dogs. Fury surfaced before he tapped it down.

He may have figured out what *he* wanted, but he did understand her hesitancy. After all, she did have a horrible childhood, he knew that. What he didn't understand was why she didn't trust him.

Who was he kidding? He knew that answer as well. He'd never gotten a chance to tell her where he had been that fateful night. He was counting on the fact that her feelings hadn't changed for fifteen years. Maybe she didn't find him attractive anymore.

No, that couldn't be it. She had definitely responded to his kiss last night. And the kisses they'd shared at her home, before he had regained his sight. Also, Keely had said that she had lots of pictures of him up in her studio. They needed to talk. Alone. Just the two of them.

"Why don't you just call on her, Papa?"

"What did you say, son?"

"Why don't you just call on her like all the other men?"

Children made things seem so easy. No muss, no fuss. Just plain and simple solutions.

"You're right. I should. I'll leave a note for her when I drop you off."

"About time," his son muttered, so low that Trace almost didn't hear it.

Almost.

Falcon was right. It was time to begin wooing his woman. Time to make her realize that he wasn't after her for anything less than forever. His love was true and would remain so for the rest of their days. It wasn't often that someone met their soul mates at the age they had been, but they had, he just had to remind her that what they had surpassed anything from their past. They could face it, move on and be together.

After Trace dropped off his son and left a note for Leona, he headed off back to his hotel room. He had work to do.

* * * *

Leona was escorted by the very dashing Earl of Danbury to Viscount Harrington's house after their walk. For the rest of the day she spent time working on more sketches of the family and compiled her work into a pile to take back to her studio.

It was dark when she returned to the St. Martins' townhouse. The snow fell much heavier and Rafe had insisted that a carriage take her home. She hadn't argued since it was cold, snowy and late. Not to mention she had the dogs and her artwork to haul as well.

As her coat was being taken from her, Weeks was there to hand her the platter with a note for her. It was addressed with simple lettering and had only her first name on it.

She opened the note as she walked up the stairs to go change for dinner.

Leona –
I was wondering if I might once again have
The pleasure of enjoying your company.
Perhaps a walk or something where we could
Spend some time together. Alone.
I have things that I need to tell you.
Things that I can't say in a note.
I am no good at flowery words. But I will
Learn if that is what you like. Remember,
There is nothing I wouldn't do for you
Kitten.
I will await your reply with bated breath.
You hold my heart, now and forever.
~Trey
PS: I want you to meet my son

Damn him. He'd had to call her kitten. She had to see him. If for no other reason than to face demons from her own past. She owed it to herself and to their previous relationship to give him her undivided attention.

But where to meet him? The days were getting colder, so maybe here would be the best place. She would have to clear it with Lucien and Ciara first, as she didn't want to have any notions of impropriety to fall on their family.

Could she? Should she? *Would* she?

She had to. Trace was right. Every single traitorous fiber in her being craved his touch. He knew it, she knew it, so why pretend otherwise? No matter what had happened in the past, the only thing she was absolutely positive about was she was still in love with him.

For years she may have had her doubts, but they had all vanished the second she'd recognized his body on the ground. They shared something special and unique.

* * * *

At dinner, she asked the opinions of the marquess and his wife. Since it was just the three of them and since Ciara still disliked eating formally in that specific room, they were at the breakfast table with the dinner before them to serve themselves.

"Colonel Morgan left me a note asking if he could call on me." Leona just blurted it out.

Her friends put down their utensils and turned to look directly at her. When that was all she said, Ciara prompted, "And?"

"I was thinking I might accept."

"Just spending some time in the receiving room talking? It is getting much colder now, so a walk may be out of the question." Ciara's sharp mind missed nothing.

"He said he had something he wished to discuss with me. So, I thought..."

"About damn time," Lucien mumbled more to himself than to the women at the table, although they heard his comment. A comment that earned him a reproachful glare from his wife and caused a blush to run up Leona's skin.

Finally Leona gave up all pretense of eating, dropping her spoon with a loud clank. The noise echoed in the silence. "I know you both know about him. I need to be able to spend some time with him alone. But I also don't want to besmirch your name or home."

Lucien put down his cup and exchanged another glance with his wife. His words were concise and clear when they came.

"If you need to talk to him then invite him here and do so. You have the gardens in the back if you want to be outside, or there are plenty of rooms inside if it is cold. You are like family, and after your *last* meeting with him, I think it is safe to say there is still something between the both of you. That kind of behavior would be much better done under this roof than out in the park."

Leona noticed that although she stayed silent, Ciara was nodding in agreement to what her husband was saying.

"Also, this way there will be no talk of impropriety, since I will be here as will Ciara. Have him bring Falcon along also."

Falcon? Who was Falcon? Was that his son's name?

"Very well. I will send a response this evening."

"For tomorrow?" He raised an eyebrow at her.

"Yes, Lucien. For tomorrow." She loved how pushy and yet protective he was of her.

"Good."

And still, Ciara remained silent.

After dinner was over and the three adults were in the library, Leona penned a short response to Trace. She rose silently and handed it to a waiting footman to deliver.

The rest of the evening was spent with Leona sketching and Ciara and Lucien snuggled together on a couch, all of them warm and protected against the winter weather that swirled out beyond the windows.

* * * *

Around ten-thirty, Trace heard a knock on his hotel door. He opened it to look down into the face of a footman who held a letter with a crest he recognized as belonging to the Marquess of Heartstone.

"Good evening, sir. This note is for you and I am to wait for a response, if there is to be one."

Trace backed up from the door and gestured for the man to enter his room. "It will just take me a second to write one." There would be one all right.

The footman nodded and stood by the fireplace to warm up as Trace read the note.

Across the front was penned 'Colonel Trace Morgan'. The script was blended together perfectly, showing the expert penmanship of the writer.

Could it truly be Leona's writing? He had only seen her write as a child and teenager. A tiny sliver of dread reared its ugly head. What if she didn't want to see him?

Tamping it down, he opened the envelope to pull out the folded ecru-colored paper. There was the faint smell of orchids, taking Trace back to the last time he had seen Leona in his father's house and actually spoken with her.

They were having a ball that evening. At sixteen there were other things that he would have preferred to be doing but since he had no choice, he would be attending the ball. He strode into the ballroom, to see what it looked like, and there she was.

Leona was alone in the huge room, which was good, since it was becoming increasingly difficult for him to not expose how he felt about her in the presence of others. His control slipped just looking at her, it was so hard to keep in check — her eyes, hair, body, every part of her called to him like the sirens calling sailors. Those men had no will or control of their own actions.

She stood on the far side of the room, wearing nothing more than her tattered one-piece dress. If that was what you could call it.

Leona had the faded gray article cinched at the middle with a piece of twine that accented her thin waist and her breasts — without doubt. She had matured. Her hair was braided down her back and tied off with another piece of twine.

Even in her ragged clothes she was beautiful to him. Leona moved with a grace that made her seem untouchable, unattainable. Like the horrors that were around her stopped short of touching her. Trace's knees were wobbly as he shut the door behind him, sealing them in together. Closing it with complete care. And silence.

Leona was humming to herself as she cut and arranged the flowers on the table in front of her into vases. She worked very quickly. All the flowers were orchids.

With a quick second glance to make sure they were really alone, Trace moved toward her. He stalked her silently until he was directly behind her. Placing his arms on either side of her, he whispered softly into her ear.

"Hello, kitten. Miss me?"

"Please go away. Don't get me into trouble." He knew she'd known he was there as she didn't even jump a tiny bit.

"Answer me and I will."

"Go away." There was a noise in the hall.

"Answer my question."

"All right. Yes. I've missed you. You already know that," she hissed in fear.

"I knew that before." He brushed a kiss across her neck, savoring in the way it made her shudder. "Do you like orchids?" *She smelled like them. She smelled good enough to eat.*

"*Please step away from me.*"

"*Do you?*"

"*Yes, I love them. They are so beautiful, now, please. Someone is coming.*"

The handle was turning on the door, slowly. Trace didn't care, his headiness making him reckless. "*Meet me later.*"

"*I'll be here at the party.*"

"*After then. I need to hold you. I don't want to share you with anyone. I want it to just be us so I can touch you. Agree to meet me.*"

The door pushed open. Leona remained focused intensely on the flowers. Trace sprang away from her and pretended interest in the decorations. He had pulled himself together and had the look of boredom and indifference on his face. Damn it, it wasn't easy.

It was Ben. The tall, jet-black slave who was in charge of all the others that worked inside the plantation house. His brown gaze swept the room, seeing all then some as he stepped completely inside the room and shut the door behind him.

"*Good afternoon, Master Trace. Are you almost done, Leona?*"

Without turning from her work, she replied, "*Yes, Mister Ben. Not much longer.*"

"*Very good. Don't forget to get your clean clothes from your mama. She has what you are to wear tonight.*"

"*Yes, sir.*"

Trace hated this. Hated how she was treated. How they all were treated, but most especially his Leona. Ignoring the other man in the room, Trace picked up an orchid and walked back over to Leona.

He waited until she brought her eyes to meet his own, then he repeated his question in a low tone. "After the party? Usual place?"

Her eyes dropped back to her work. "I can't."

"Look at me," he commanded.

She lifted her ocher-colored gaze to his and waited in silence.

"Meet me." Forceful this time.

"All right." Her words were barely louder than a whisper, as her head was lowered toward the floor.

His eyes held hers as he ran the orchid down her cheek and under her chin, bringing her head up to meet his stare. Surely, she knew how much he loved her. Without further consideration to the third person in the room, he replaced the orchid with his fingers so her chin was caught. Anchored between his long, lean fingers.

Trace stepped into her and lowered his face to hers. He placed a kiss so tender it would make a single snowflake give the impression of being harsh and foreboding upon her lips. Straightening, Trace set down the flower and walked out of the room without looking back to Leona or addressing the shocked look on Ben's face that the man worked quickly to smooth away.

With a hard swallow Trace opened the note. In the same elegant script were the words —

Trey:
Breakfast is at eight.
Bring your son.
Until tomorrow,
~Leona

She'd called him Trey. Probably hadn't meant to or realized it, but she had. Her simplicity made him smile. *Ever to the point.*

Trace grabbed a piece of paper and a pen to write his response, before handing it to the waiting footman.

After the man had left to deliver his message, Trace sat heavily in a chair and just thought about her. Every last detail of her beauty was burned into his brain, and he enjoyed his perusal of each and every one he recalled. He began to count down the hours until he would actually see her again in the flesh, not just a memory.

* * * *

Leona waited for the footman to bring his response. Not that she would ever willingly admit it out loud, but she was ready to climb the walls with nervousness.

When the man finally arrived and delivered said message, she opened the note without even acknowledging the expressions on the two witnesses to her actions. Leona slid her finger into the envelope and pulled out the paper. Anxious. Tense. She opened it.

In his scrawl were two words —

Until tomorrow.

"Well, what did he say? Is he coming?" someone asked her. She wasn't sure who, since she reeled with the prospect of being alone with him again.

"Yes." Her voice was all breathy, like she had just climbed to the top of a mountain. "For breakfast tomorrow." That said, Leona got up, walked out through the door and headed to her room.

* * * *

Trace woke early. He was restless. Scared, as if he were going into battle his very first time. He sent for hot water. Trace shaved and dressed himself in a nice set of clothes. He roused his son.

"Falcon. Wake up. We need to get ready to go for our breakfast appointment."

His son stirred and cracked open one eye. "Okay, Papa."

Trace sent for another batch of hot water to be brought up for his son. As he watched Falcon get ready, his mind raced through Leona's potential reactions to his son.

"What's wrong, Papa?"

"Nothing, just thinking." Would she be harsh to him?

"What if she doesn't like me?" Worry had obviously begun to surface within Falcon.

"Why wouldn't she like you?"

"She didn't even look at me the other night. It was like I didn't exist."

"I'm sure she will love you, like I do. I imagine that seeing me was quite a shock to her. That's why she didn't speak to you."

"If you say so." It was easy to tell that Falcon didn't believe that for a second.

With an attempt to put him at ease, Trace asked, "Don't Bryn and Keely like her?"

"Yes. They call her Auntie Lea. But what if I make her think about the plantation?"

Trace grabbed his son's shaking shoulders and steadied him. "She would never blame you for something that happened to her in the past. Never! She is going to love you. Come on, we should be going. They'll be sending a carriage around."

Smoothing down a wayward piece of hair, Falcon took a deep breath and shrugged. "All right. I'm ready."

Trace noticed his slight tremor but made no mention of it, just placed his arm around his son and walked out of the door with him.

Partway down the hall, Falcon stopped. "I have to go back."

"Why?"

"I forgot something. Can I have the key?" Trace handed the key over wordlessly and watched his son dash back to the room, unlock the door and reappear moments later. He locked the door behind him and ran back to his father's side.

Trace noticed a small smile of hope on Falcon's face as they began to walk down the hall. There were a couple times Trace noticed that his son's hand had gone to his pocket, as if to make sure whatever he had in there stayed in there.

Outside, the morning was downright cold. New snow fell from thick slate-colored clouds. He noticed all the servants were the only ones out this early. A well-sprung carriage with the seal of the Marquess of Heartstone awaited them.

It was warm in the carriage with the heat that radiated from the bricks in there. They were on the move just as soon as the door was closed. Heading toward his destiny.

Although he climbed out when the coach stopped, Trace hesitated before proceeding up the freshly shoveled steps with his son. With knowledge beyond his years, his son slipped his hand into his father's before giving it an encouraging squeeze.

They entered into the warmth of the home and were directed to the breakfast room after giving up their coats. They were expected, and told to go right ahead. As he walked through the doorway, Trace found Leona immediately.

There were plenty of silent footmen setting down platters of steaming-hot food that smelled heavenly along the sideboard.

Leona stood at one end with a plate in her hand. She'd leaned over to hear what Keely told her before she would put the food on the plate. It was apparent that she was fixing a plate for the child.

A pale lavender dress made of sprigged muslin and matching shoes was all Leona wore. Her hair was pulled back into a single thick braid that fell down the center of her back. As usual, there were a few wisps that had gotten free of their confinement to settle gently around her face.

"Falcon, you made it." Bryn spoke loudly as he shoved away from the table to meet his friend. "Come, get something to eat, we can continue our discussion."

Leona's hand trembled as she turned to face Trace. Again. He clearly noticed, but stood silently as she pivoted to cope with his presence.

"Good morning, Colonel Morgan." The words were a little raspy, but not too bad considering.

"Good morning ki…Leona." Eyes met, challenged and spoke volumes to each other with a mere glance. Trace blinked, looked at her again, and she noticed that his gaze changed. The expression in his chocolate-brown eyes seemed to beg for something — perhaps it was understanding, maybe compassion—before he added, "My son."

That was it. This was her introduction to his son. Even Bryn and Keely watched as the scene unfolded in their presence.

Leona flicked her gaze down to scrutinize the young man who stood in front of his father. In his eyes, which looked like a softer version of his father's, she recognized what she saw. It was fear.

Fear of not being wanted, not being accepted.

After she set Keely's partially filled plate on the sideboard, Leona walked toward them both, her steps sure.

She stopped in front of the young man to look him directly in the eye. "Hello. You must be Falcon. Bryn has told me a lot about you. How are you doing today?"

"I'm fine, thank you. What should I call you?"

"Well, most call me Leona, Miss O'Neill or Auntie Lea. You can call me whatever you want."

"Can I just call you Lea?"

"Of course you can." The boy visibly relaxed before smiling at her, another reminder of how Trace had looked at that age. Casting one more smile at her, Falcon headed off to get some food with Bryn. Leona was left alone with Trace.

"Good morning kitten," came his purring statement.

"Don't. Don't call me that." Iron laced her tone.

Trace seemed to realize he tread on dangerous ground and so without even a blink he backed off that approach. "What's good?" At her glare, he said, "I was talking about breakfast." He walked past her and headed for the sideboard, only to stop dead in his tracks.

Trace had stopped so suddenly that when Leona spun around she almost walked right into his broad back. She edged out from behind him before she too halted in her tracks at the sight unfolding by the sideboard.

Trace's son had picked up Keely's plate and was filling it for her as she walked along side and pointed out what she wanted. The two adults exchanged glances as the rest of the servants left the room. There was something familiar about the way those two children were acting.

A moment of strained silence floated between them. "All of it. All of it is good." At his single raised eyebrow, Leona amended, "The breakfast. All of it is good."

They filled their plates and were well into the meal when Lucien and Ciara arrived to partake of the meal. There was no need for anyone to ask where they had been.

"Good morning, Colonel Morgan."

Trace's eyes migrated to Leona and softened before circling back to settle on his hosts. "Yes, it is a good morning, Lady Heartstone. Good morning to you both."

It wasn't long until everyone had food and the room was filled with easy chatter, mostly led by the kids. Leona ate silently, not really contributing to the conversations buzzing around her.

Her attention was completely taken up by the nut-brown-haired man who sat almost directly across from her. He still looked so damn good. He looked better than good. Every movement was beautifully choreographed, making them appear flawless. He was a predator in his own right—graceful, fluid, dangerous and extremely confident.

She ached to touch him.

To run her hands under his crisp, pristine white shirt. Place her hands on his muscular chest, which was broad and spoke of his power. Intertwine her fingers with the light smattering of brown hair that covered his chest, enjoying how it felt against her hands.

To place kisses all along his rugged jaw. Up his cheeks, across his forehead. To delve her fingers through his head of thick silky hair.

But most of all, she longed to gaze upon him naked as she had done so long ago. To have him look upon her like she was the most important thing to him in the world. To see desire flare in his eyes, not as a lad, but as a man.

He looked across the table at her. As if he could read her mind, his eyes darkened. The emotion swirling in those chocolate depths was very clear to her. He desired her. Now. Still. After all this time.

Unable to keep her own gaze unheated, Leona looked away. She tried to focus on the exchanges around her but every time she glanced in Trace's direction he was staring at her. Straight through to her soul, where he read what she wanted in big block letters.

After breakfast the children ran to go play outside for a while. Lucien and Ciara were going with. They left Leona and her guest at the door to one of the receiving rooms. There was tea and biscuits already set out. With a nudge, both were in the room and alone.

"Missed you, kitten."

Leona struggled to maintain her control, so she walked over to the window and looked out into the backyard. "What was it that you needed to talk to me about?"

"Can we sit down?"

"Go right ahead." She stayed facing the window.

"Will you sit down with me?"

The hesitation was long enough to geld him. Leona walked back and sat down in a large chair before she pinned him with two tawny daggers.

"I need to tell you—" He broke off. After all this time, he couldn't find the right words. "I have gone over what to say so much it should come to me, but it won't."

"Start at the beginning."

"I'm just so confused." He made a fist with his hand over and over so he wouldn't jump up and touch her. Had to get through the talking first.

"Can I ask you some questions?" Leona sat primly beside him but her gaze, as always, was direct.

Relief? Most likely. "Please. Ask whatever you want."

"Where were you?" There was no need for her to elaborate on that question, for he knew exactly what she meant.

"Steven and David had tied me up and locked me in one of the closets. They came back after and told me bits and pieces of it before they beat me into unconsciousness."

Her eyes stayed on him. There was a war raging inside her and he saw it. He didn't blame her. Hell, it was nothing more than an excuse, talking about how he'd been tied up and beaten by his own brothers when he was well aware of the hell she'd gone through.

"I know now it doesn't mean much, but I am so sorry for that. I promised that I would protect you. I failed. I *failed* you."

She watched him without flinching, but neither did she move away. He took that as a good sign.

"I was laid up for about two weeks, then I found out you and your mom had escaped. I prayed that you two would find safety somewhere and that you would not believe what Steven told you about me being with my next girl. That you were just a passing fancy. That was not true. There was never anyone else for me."

Continued silence from Leona, and it made him uneasy. Did she believe him? Had she already made up her mind about him? His son?

"A few months later I went into the army. Since I had nothing to live for, I was dangerous and reckless. Apparently good qualities for what they were looking for. Once they got rid of my recklessness, I moved up through the ranks quickly. One of my trips home I met Bethany, from up the road. We were married and Falcon came later. I still don't know if he is my son or Steven's, not that it matters, for I love him all the same."

He wanted to believe she softened at that. "Then the need for more slaves began." Leona's eyes grew sharp and shuttered. "I took a regiment to your island – still don't know why, other than we were ordered there – and apparently walked into a trap set up by Steven. Then I woke up in your house. Did you always know it was me?"

Leona nodded. "From the second I turned you over on that frozen ground."

"After all I did – or didn't do – for you, why did you save me?"

"I had to."

"Why?" He needed the reason.

"Because."

"Tell me." A command now, and he didn't think it would be disobeyed.

"Because I had to."

"Tell me." He implored not only with his words but also his eyes.

"Because I was still in love with you. Because at one time you were my friend. Because I couldn't sit there and let you die without trying to save you."

'Was. Was in love with.' What the hell is with the past tense? "And now? How do you feel? About me? About us?"

"There is no us. Don't you get it? You were the master." She spat the word with disgust. "I was the slave. What we had…it was not real. It was just a disillusioned childhood fantasy for me, and I'm not sure what it was for you."

"No! Damn it, I won't accept that. You can't sit there and tell me that it was nothing. There was something between us, there still is. I can feel it and I know you can. We are connected, Leona. We always have been."

"You have a son, Trey, by another woman. You *own* slaves."

"No, I don't. I do not own *any* slaves. There are workers on my plantation, but they're paid. Very well."

There was no denying her shock at his statement. "What do you see when you look at me?"

He had zero hesitation when he answered. "I see the most beautiful woman in the world. I see the adolescent girl who stole my heart who went and grew into a stunning woman who takes my breath away every time I look at her. Yes, at one time you were a slave, but make no mistake, I do not see a slave when I look at you. I see the other half of my soul. I love you, Leona. I always have."

"What about the color of my skin?"

"What about it? It looks wonderful on you."

"I'm different."

He shook his head. "You need to get over this. I love you *for you*. Stop throwing obstacles in our path. I am declaring myself to you. I *will* be competing with the other suitors to win your hand. I hope I am not wrong about where your heart already lies. I'll find a way for you to trust me again."

When she said nothing, Trace shuttered his eyes to conceal his pain. He realized that he had a long battle ahead of him.

"Tell me about your son."

Perhaps a safer topic for the moment. "Well, his name is Garrett, but he prefers to be called Falcon. When I got back from your island, I found that he had been living in the slave quarters. Steven and Bethany beat him often. He was scared and timid, but we're working through it."

"I *am* sorry for what he went through. No one deserves that. Especially a child."

Trace stood up and walked over to where Leona sat. Pulled on her hand to get her to her feet. Then he walked them both over to the chair closest to the roaring fire. He sat himself down in front of the chair, placing Leona between his legs so her back was flush with his chest.

"Tell me about it."

Chapter Sixteen

Leona shuddered and tried to move away, but he held fast. She inhaled deeply before she began. Again, there was no need to clarify the request, for she knew exactly of what he spoke.

"After I was ripped away from you, I was taken to the pit. You remember that, right? The pit?" Her body trembled against his but she stayed there and soaked up his strength. "After dinner they brought me out. Stripped me naked and hung me by my wrists until my toes barely touched the ground. Then they whipped me in front of everyone."

Trace's hands caressed both of her wrists, the motion gentle and soothing. Calming. "After that?"

"After that Mama was allowed to take me home and she nursed me. I believed that you had betrayed me. Steven stopped by just to tell me that you were with your newest slave girl. That hurt worse than any beating I could have received, for I fancied myself in love with you and believed that you felt the same about me. I dreamed that one day we would be together. Married. Not having to hide our feelings. That was just a dream. As soon as I could move Mama ran with me. To the island, Saba. Once on the island, Mama met Jackson. They were in love and not afraid to show it."

She licked her lips, glad he couldn't see her face. "He encouraged my painting habit and sold my first painting for me. He has been investing my money ever since. Anyway, then I saw you again and came here to England."

"I'm so sorry. I promised to protect you and I failed," he murmured. Then his words became even fainter. "I would have given my life for you. I would still to this day."

Leona snuggled up against his chest, the heat from the fire warming her front and the heat radiating from the man behind her keeping her warm from the back. How perfect was this? For the first time in years she felt perfectly content. She turned a little to the side and placed her face against his rock-hard chest.

He smelled like sandalwood and spice. She fell asleep as he sat there stroking her hair, lost in thought.

* * * *

After a while, she roused from her sleep. She was still warm and content on the floor in front of the fire, wrapped up securely in Trace's arms.

"Sorry, I didn't mean to doze off. That was really rude of me."

"Don't worry about it. I like holding you in my arms while you sleep. Can I ask you a question?"

"Um-hum."

"Does it matter to you that I have a son?"

"No. Should it?"

"Well, he was concerned that he would remind you of the plantation. And to be perfectly honest, so was I."

She sat and tucked some hair behind her ear. "Trace, *you* remind me of the plantation. But I would never take anything out on a child."

"I know. But I had to ask."

"I think he looks a lot like you did at his age." She smiled at him.

"Do you? I don't see it but between the two of us, you were the one who looked at me more," he teased.

They shared a moment of silence.

Trace cleared his throat. "Where do we go from here?"

"What do you mean?" Leona was still leery, but she knew that he would ever be the only man for her.

"I mean, where do we go from here? I love you, Leona. I want to fall asleep every night with you held in my arms and wake in the morning to you as well. I want to learn your body all over again, and show you just how beautiful I think you are. I want to spend days making love to you. Most of all, I want you to look at me like you used to, as though I had just handed you the moon and the stars. I want to see you grow large with our child. I want to spend the rest of my life with you." His hands curved around her abdomen as if he already anticipated a child growing safely in there.

"What about Falcon?"

"What about him?"

"How do you think this situation would make him feel? Not to mention how giving him a sibling might make him feel."

"He'll be fine."

"This is too fast. I need time to think. To sort out my feelings."

"What's to sort out? You love me, right?"

"I...I...I just need some time."

"All right, kitten. Some time. I'll not stop coming around. I will be here every day to make sure you don't forget me."

As if that were possible.

Traced closed his eyes for a moment before he continued, "I'm not much for flowery words, or soft sentimental feelings. I never have been, and you know it. If that's what it will take to get you to only want me then that is what I will do. I only want to make you happy. Please tell me you understand. Tell me."

Back to his commands.

Trace tightened his arms around her. "Do you remember anything good about Hawk's Cove?"

"Yes. The time I spent with you. The adventures that we had, the times we spent together as we explored Eden. All of that is a happy memory for me. *Every* second that we spent together was wonderful. You taught me what it was like to love, to be loved. What it was like to be a woman. It doesn't matter, Trace. None of that will change that what I need now is time. Can you understand that?"

He stiffened slightly. "Yes, I understand. Will you at least give me a chance to make you see things as I do? That we belong together, always. I'm not in this for one night. I want to be with you until we're both old and gray."

"So I get time, but you'll be there to try to influence my decision? Is that right?"

"Every step of the way, I *will* be there. I'll not lose you to some dandy from this island. I will not lose you to anyone."

He'd begun to caress her, fanning the flames that burned within her. Within moments, her body arched against his. Soft mews were born deep within her throat.

This time they were not teens bumbling around in inexperience. They were adults and knew just what they wanted. Every hair on Leona's body stood on end — it was electrifying, being held in his arms.

Leona struggled to regain her control. She slid out from his arms and stood. "Come with me. I have something I want to show you."

Trace rose with his usual fluid grace. Leona had to swallow a few times before she calmed herself enough to precede him out of the room and up the stairs.

Trace followed her willingly. He stared his fill as he walked behind her and watched her body move under her dress. Her hips swayed gently with each step she took. He still couldn't get over how gorgeous she had become.

They went to the third floor and he realized what room they had entered once they got there. It was her studio. There were portraits and sketches in an organized mess all over the room.

A warm fire blazed within the hearth and it made the room very comfortable. She led him silently over to a table and stood there with apprehension on her face as she waited for him to look over the papers that lay scattered there.

Keely hadn't been lying. Every single paper that covered the large table was of him. Different poses, head views, profiles and full-body sketches. And every single one of them had him happy with a sparkle in his eyes — the same sparkle that was in the picture she had given him when she'd returned his rings.

His mouth dropped as he stared at the sight before him. Her ability astounded him. She was absolutely amazing. And her artwork wasn't that bad either.

Her mute admission about her feelings rocked him to the core. What she couldn't say to him downstairs had just been yelled loud and clear.

She still loved him.

With a deceptively casual movement, he turned to her. Leona's eyes were downcast, and her hair had fallen over part of her face, keeping her in the shadows. His body was tense and ready to pounce but he kept his actions calm.

"Look at me." His tone was husky and seductive.

Her head came up slowly. A faint flush had settled on her cheeks but her eyes were what hit him hard. They glittered like jewels with unshed tears.

"Oh, kitten." His voice was like velvet, and it reached and embraced her, he had no doubt it encased her in its softness. He could feel it too.

She made to step back and he acted. Just like a bird that swooped down on its unsuspecting prey, she was in his clutches.

It took mere seconds for his lips to find hers. That was all. Leona ran her hands up his body to lock around his neck. Everything she felt was in that kiss.

His tongue gained swift entrance to her mouth, where it proceeded to tangle with hers. His body was on fire. From her reaction, so was hers.

He backed her up to the bed that was along the wall and stopped. "Are you sure?" The question was guttural, admitting he had a hard time asking it.

"Yes. Please, Trey."

It was his nickname that did it, did him in. He had her dress off in mere seconds, to pool on the floor. Her undergarments followed without delay and soon she was naked in front of him. He stopped and took in the sight before him.

She was magnificent. Her body was firm and tight. Her breasts were full and begged to be touched. Her legs were slim and long.

Trace stepped up to her and took the pins out of her hair so it cascaded down around her. She looked like a darker, more beautiful version of Venus as she came out of the water. As soon as her hair fell, he smelled the normal scent that he did around her, only this time he could place it. *Orchids.*

"You still smell like orchids. You always did." His words were murmured as he stepped back to her.

"My turn." Leona ran her eyes over him.

She slowly removed his shirt from his pants, then she began to unbutton it. Little by little his chest was revealed to her.

It was still broad, still firm. Still covered in that dusting of brown hair. He had a few scars, though, which she kissed as they became exposed.

With his shirt on the floor, she moved on to his pants. Leona unfastened them and pulled them down over his lean hips. His arousal pushed against his undergarment. Moments later he too was naked.

Trace pulled her back into his arms. It had been so long and all he wanted to do was ravish her, and yet at the same time he wanted to go slowly.

He placed kisses all over her face as he lowered them onto the little bed. His hands ran down her body to massage and tease her until she writhed with desire.

One large hand covered her as a finger dipped between the glistening curls to seek access to her heated core. Her thighs spread wider to accommodate him.

She lifted her hips to meet his finger. She was wet. More than ready for him.

"Please, Trey. Now."

"Not yet." He moved his mouth to her breasts and sucked them. First one, then the other, until they had hardened and were tender.

"Trace," she moaned.

"Yes, kitten? What is it? What do you want?" His words were coarse with the strain of maintaining control of the situation.

"You. I want you, Trey."

Trace settled himself between her legs, guided his hard length to her velvet heat and with one stroke encased himself fully within her.

She was so tight, almost as tight as that first time, when he'd taken her maidenhood. She hissed.

He stopped and looked down into her eyes. "How long has it been?"

"A little over fifteen years."

He blinked away tears as he realized that he really had been the only man for her. Trace moved slowly until she got used to him inside her.

As soon as she started to whimper and push up to meet him, he lost the hold he had on his control. The slow lover was gone and in his place was a man who needed to find his release.

Trace slid in and out of her with increased speed. He went deeper and deeper. Long strokes, short strokes, faster and faster he went.

He placed his hands on her hips and pounded into her. Leona met each and every thrust with an undulation of her own. Moans and grunts.

Trace's body was covered with sweat and still he moved his hips back and forth like a piston. Leona's cries got louder, so Trace leaned down and placed his mouth over hers and swallowed her cries of passion.

Leona crested first, her body shuddering around his. The feel of her molten heat gripped around him sent Trace over the edge. He was so lost in what he was doing he didn't pull out of her, not that it would have mattered, for Leona had her legs wrapped around him like an iron-clad vise. They were anchored together. Fused as one.

With one last plunge, Trace spilled his seed deep within her womb and collapsed on her. They were totally spent. Both of them fought to catch their breath as their limbs stayed intertwined.

"Are you all right?" he asked into her neck.

"Fine."

"Am I too heavy?" Trace moved to get off her, but she tightened her hold.

"No, stay. I like the feel of you on me."

Too tired to argue, he remained like that for a bit then rolled off and hauled her up against his side. Like they had never been apart, she fit her head right on his shoulder and cast a leg over his waist.

"Sleep now, kitten. I will…"

"I know. You will keep watch and keep me safe." Leona was fast asleep in no time as Trace covered them with blankets, laced his fingers so she was anchored against him and fell prey to the world of the sandman within moments.

* * * *

For the first time in ages, Trace slept a peaceful sleep. He awoke before Leona and just lay there in silence and held her. The smell of orchids tantalized his senses and stirred his lust once more

He edged out from under her and laid some more wood on the fire to build up the blaze. Then he walked back over to the bed and gazed down upon her form as she slept. She had curled up into a smaller ball since he had left the bed. Her hair fell around her like a silk cloud, framing her in gentle waves.

Leona moaned in her sleep and turned over onto her stomach. Trace reached down to pull the blankets up over her shoulders, and as he pulled them away from her body, he saw *them*.

The scars on her back. The marks criss-crossed her skin, marring the perfection of her back. Trace folded down the blankets and completely exposed her back. He sank down on the floor beside her and stared in horror. *The pain this must have caused her.*

Trace reached out and hesitantly touched the lines. They were smooth, but he could feel some pain in them. "Little one, what did I do to you? I didn't realize, I just didn't realize. I am *so* sorry. No wonder you don't want to trust me."

He rose over her and covered her up before he slid in beside her. Leona instinctively moved toward his body and curled up against him, like she belonged there. Which she did, she just didn't—or wouldn't— realize it yet.

* * * *

It was her dream again. It had to be. She was on fire and there was someone sucking on her breasts, alternating between them. Then they moved down her body and licked and nipped everywhere.

When her legs were spread and a pair of wide shoulders settled themselves between them, she knew it had to be a dream. Maybe this time she wouldn't wake up before coming.

There was a tongue that probed deeply within her secret place as it looked for its reward. Her legs tightened around his neck and held him there. *If only it was Trace.*

"Trace. Where are you?"

"Right here, little one. Who do you think is between your legs?" A hint of anger tinged his question.

Leona rose up and looked down at the man who was settled between her widespread legs. "I thought it was a dream. You're really here? It's not just a dream?"

"No, kitten. I am most definitely not a dream. Does this feel like a dream?" He flicked his tongue back over her nub and smiled as her hips rotated to press him more firmly against her.

She whimpered. "No. It's not a dream. You're real. I...I... Oh God, Trey. It feels so good, don't stop. Please don't stop."

"No chance of that, kitten."

Trace slipped two fingers inside her and moved them back and forth. Leona contorted as he continued his relentless attack on her body. Over and over she came until her body shook with exhaustion.

"Trey, please."

"What?"

"More, I want more."

He didn't make her ask again. He rose up over her and in one swift move he slid his entire length inside her. They fit together like a hand slid into a warm glove. A perfect fit.

They were one again. Trace went slow.

For the second time that day Trace came deep within her and she found himself wondering if she would end up pregnant. And if she did, how she would handle everything.

"You know this doesn't change anything." She spoke to his neck, where her face was buried.

"What do you mean? Of course it does. You could be pregnant."

"I mean I still need some time to think. This is happening so fast."

"Very well, I will give you until the ball that they are throwing to be alone or with your other 'appointments'. I will stay away from you for the next two weeks. After that, though" — he put his face millimeters from hers — "all bets are off. I will come after you with everything I have." There was a dangerous edge to his tone, informing her that he meant exactly what he said. That warmed her much more than it scared her.

"Two weeks isn't much time for me to figure things out."

"The other guys can't make you happy. I know what you want. I know what you love. Do they know your favorite flower, your favorite color and animal? I know that you like to sleep curled up in a ball if you are alone, I know that you hum to yourself when you concentrate on something like cooking. I know your dreams, kitten, and I will not let you go. Not without one hell of a fight."

"I have to sort things out."

"I know, kitten, but to be fair you have to give me the same chance that you give everyone else."

She was silent for too long and he frowned, reaching out to her.

"What's wrong, kitten? What are you thinking?" He caressed her cheek.

"Just thinking."

"Perhaps we should get up now. I don't know how long we have been up here."

"You're right. Keely will probably come looking for me soon."

Leona looked at the man on the bed in her studio. He looked upon her like she was the only thing in the room. His eyes grew darker and she knew what thoughts raced through his mind.

"No. You need to get up."

"I am up." He shot her an arrogant male smirk again.

"I meant out of bed. Get dressed."

He rose languidly. It was clear he wasn't ashamed of his current aroused state, he made sure she could see it. Leona's eyes never left his body for a moment.

My God. He was perfect. Her body leaped in response and began to tingle and twinge. Nipples hardened and begged for him to touch and stroke them.

Trace obviously knew his effect on her and reveled in it. Slowly, ever so slowly, he put his clothes on. He held her gaze and made sure that she didn't take her eyes off him for a single second.

Fully dressed, he helped her make the bed. "Can I see some of your other work?"

Leona took his hand and led him to the other table, where there were multitudes of sketches. He recognized some of them but not all.

"You are amazing. These are wonderful."

"That is just the beginning. I do many sketches then sort through them to find the ones I think capture them people the best, depending on what type of picture they want—serious, relaxed or even fun. Then I start over here." She headed to the easel next and flipped back the sheet that covered it. "This is one that I just started of Rafe."

"Who the hell is Rafe and why are you drawing a man alone?"

"He is Lucien's brother-in-law. I did him first since he will be behind the chair where his wife, Devonna, will sit." *He is still jealous, even after what we just did together.* She smiled to herself.

"Oh."

"Then once I get what I consider to be a decent idea of what they will look like, I start on this canvas and begin my painting. I only get to the canvas when I am sure that I will get it right."

"What is this?" He pointed to the corner of a finished picture her dogs that was going to be for her own house.

"My signature."

"Is it the symbol of a hawk?"

"Yes."

"So you did think of me." When he put it that way, it was in no way a question.

"Every single day."

Trace cupped her face and lowered his lips to hers. "Thank you. That means the world to me." He placed a fast kiss on her lips and moved back. "Tell me more."

He was interested in her work. It was amazing for her to be able to share this with him. He had been, after all, the one who had gotten her the items for her first start in this career.

"I mix oils and try to get the right colors for people. Or for whatever I am —"

"Mama! I found them, they are in her studio." The childish yell pierced the hall and the room.

In ran Keely, and she was followed by her parents. All they found was Leona as she stood next to an easel and talked to Trace. All clothes were on and there was no hint of disarray anywhere. Her dogs lay on the bed content to just watch their mistress.

"Everything going all right with you two?" Ciara asked, as her sharp eyes swept the room.

"Fine. Leona was just explaining how she did her painting."

"Well, we are about to have some lunch. You two have been up here long enough. Come eat with the family," Lucien spoke.

"Very well. Leona, thank you for sharing this with me." He gazed at her. His eyes sent a different message — *Thanks for sharing yourself with me.*

Chapter Seventeen

The adults headed down the stairs after Keely and the dogs to the dining room, where Bryn and Falcon were already seated.

Trace and Leona took a walk after lunch outside in the gardens. He was a perfect gentleman for most of the time.

"I have missed you, kitten."

She leaned her head on his arm as they walked. "I missed you too."

"So why are you making me wait?"

"It's just not that simple."

"Sure it is."

"No. It's not."

"You make everything so difficult. It doesn't have to be." He looked around, then he pulled her under a large arbor covered with ivy.

In mere seconds her back was against the arbor, his hand was under her dress and his fingers had worked her into a frenzy.

"Auntie Lea? Where are you, Auntie Lea?" Keely's voice reached them.

"Trace," she panted, even as she arched against his hand. "Stop this. Keely is coming."

"Not before you." He nipped at her neck and kissed her deeply.

"Auntie Lea? Where are you?"

Leona pulled away from his mouth. "Trace, stop. Please, she will be here any second."

"Tell me you love me." A command.

"Trace, stop."

"Tell me or I won't stop. How are you going to explain my hand up your dress to a six-year-old?"

His fingers moved faster and faster. Her mind became blank. What was it she was supposed to be protesting? Moans began in her throat. Louder and louder they got until Trace lowered his head down by her ear and whispered, "Shhh. Don't give away your position. She's getting closer."

"Please." It came out so faint maybe it never got said at all.

"Please what, kitten? Stop?" His fingers slowed minutely.

"No, don't stop. Please, Trey, let me get there."

"Now you *don't* want me to stop? Make up your mind. Keely is almost here. I can hear her footsteps."

"You win. I love you. Now, please."

"As you wish, little one." With an expert flick of his wrist and fingers, Trace sent her over the edge to find her rainbow of pleasure.

Leona was still on the high plains of pleasure when Keely careened around the corner and into sight. At least Trace had taken his hand out of her dress and just stood there as the child stopped by them.

"There you are. Why didn't you answer me? Didn't you hear me? What's wrong with you, Auntie Lea? Your face is all red."

"Must be the cold air. I'm fine, darling. Sorry I didn't answer. I must not have heard you."

Trace smirked. "Yeah, that must be it. Did you come to walk with us, little one?"

"Yes. I don't want to be inside, and the boys won't let me play with them." She pouted.

"Well, that's not very nice of them, now, is it?"

"No it isn't, Auntie Lea. They can be so mean."

"I agree." Leona threw an eyebrow up toward the sky, which Trace took to mean that she included him in that assessment of males.

Trace wasn't a fool and kept his mouth shut. As they walked, Keely ran ahead at times and was a true joy to watch. The few times that she left them, Trace took the opportunity to kiss Leona thoroughly and get her all hot and bothered.

"Would you quit that?" she snapped after he had slipped his hand down the bodice of her dress to tease her breasts.

"I just want to you to remember what you will be missing when you are out with those other men. I want you to remember that I am the only one who can stir you up like this."

With a quick glance to make sure Keely was still off ahead, he pulled one breast out and sucked it. When his mouth came off it, the cold air hit it and made her gasp again.

"Are you wet for me, kitten? Do you want me yet?"

Leona was barely back in her dress when Keely came back again. Her breaths came rapidly and he knew she fought for control.

As they walked, Trace took every opportunity to brush his erection up against her so she knew how he felt and what he wanted to do to her. Each feel, each intimate press against her, weakened her resolve a little more. He could see it and sense it, as it took her longer and longer to push him away each time.

Much more of this and he bet she would be reduced to a little puddle on the ground.

"Keely, is there any holly around here?"

"We have some, Trace. I know where it is, come on."

They followed her deeper into the gardens and reached a place that was full of holly. "Do you think we could cut some and take it inside?"

"Uh-huh. I know where there's a basket. Don't go anywhere, I will be right back."

"Okay, we'll be right here." Trace observed Leona as she watched her savior run off to find a basket.

The second she was out of sight, Trace had her up against a tree. He yanked her dress up, exposing her legs to the chill in the air, but from her moan of need, she didn't care. She was on fire, as was he.

He fumbled with the catch on his pants, and as soon as he freed himself he slid into her silken folds. "I can't get enough of you, kitten."

"Oh God, Trey. Faster, please. Faster."

He obliged and looked down at her.

Her eyes were closed, back arched as she wrapped her legs around his waist to try to get closer. Fingers dug into his shoulders as whimpers escaped her throat. She bit her lips to keep silent but sounds still slipped out.

Trace felt her start to convulse around him and saw her eyes open. She was bliss to watch as she came. Her eyes darkened to gold and he noticed the sheen of tears in them.

"Oh God, Trey. I...I..."

"Come with me, kitten, come with me," he purred. With one last powerful stroke, he felt her come around him then he joined her, pouring his seed deep within her.

Once again, time was on their side, for just after they'd pulled themselves together, Keely came back with a large basket. They gathered holly and decided to head back to the house for some chocolate.

Keely chatted the whole way home. "I like it here, but I like the other home better. Will you come and see me there, Trace? I like you and so you should come see me. Maybe the three of us can go on another walk together. It was fun."

"Sure was." Trace knew he sounded a little husky. He walked beside Leona and whispered, "You have some tree bark in your hair."

Leona panicked. "Get it out."

"I'd like to put more there." But he obliged her anyway. So when the three of them mounted the steps back to the house they were all straightened, pressed and ready to face the others.

Trace and his son also stayed for dinner. The adults played whist in the receiving room as the children talked and planned for the holiday.

Leona and Trace were not left alone after that, so he had no more opportunity to try to sway her toward his way of thinking. As they said good night, he had no doubt his eyes told her what his mouth couldn't say in the presence of the others.

"Good night, Leona. Thank you for a lovely day. I enjoyed getting to know you after all these years. Pleasant dreams."

"Good night, Trace. I also had a wonderful time today." She looked down at the boy, who stood beside his father. "Good night, Falcon. Maybe someday we'll be able to spend some time together and get to know each other."

"I would like that, Lea." He beckoned for her to come down to him. When she did, he whispered into her ear, "This is for you. It is from Ben." He slipped what he had in his pocket into her outstretched hand. "Good night, Lea. Good night, Bryn. See you later."

Trace wondered what she had been given, but she slid it into her own pocket. They took their leave out into the snow and climbed in the carriage before it took them back to their hotel.

* * * *

"What did you get, Auntie Lea?" Keely asked.

"I am not sure." Leona was distracted. Ben. She remembered him fondly.

"Come, children, time for bed. We'll be up later to say good night," Ciara spoke.

"I wanna know what she got," Keely whined.

Her mother didn't have to say a word, just arched one eyebrow, and her daughter scuffed her toe and quietly followed her brother up the stairs.

After the children had left, Leona walked back into the room they had just vacated and sat in a chair by the fire. She reached into her pocket and pulled out the wrapped gift. It was covered in a shiny paper tied with a big bow.

It was heavy, and she had absolutely no idea what it could possibly be. She opened it. When the paper was off, she realized what it was.

There had been a slave on the plantation named Monk, who had worked with glass. He'd had amazing talent, and it showed with what she had in her hand.

It was an orb, made of glass that ranged from clear to blue and purple depending on how the light hit it. Inside the glass was a hawk in full regal flight. Clutched in his talon was a long-stemmed orchid. She trembled as she unfolded the note.

Leona:
Don't forget about your own
Happiness. Your mama would want
You to be happy.
He truly does love you and he always
Had, since the day you left. He
Swore to me then that he would find
You. Trust in him, he needs you
More than he will admit.
~Ben
ps: come visit me for I miss you.

Tears clouded her vision and before long they were streaming down her face. When she got herself under control, she realized that she was the only one in the room. Ciara and Lucien had left her alone to unwrap her present.

Leona fell asleep with the orb beside her on the table. When she woke in the morning, it was still there and still just as breathtaking.

* * * *

Trace stayed true to his word. For the next fourteen days he did not show his face once to Leona. She saw Falcon every now and then, but never his father.

He still made his presence known, however. Every day a huge bouquet of orchids came for her. There never was any card, but there was no need. She knew who they were from. No matter how many flowers she received from others, it was the orchids that made her smile.

She missed him so much she ached inside. He was right—when she went out with the other men it was like being with a brother. There was nothing there. But the second she thought she may have seen Trace, or heard his voice, her heart rate sped up and her palms became damp

"Miss O'Neill?"

Leona blinked a few times before she realized that the Earl of Danbury spoke to her. "I'm sorry. What did you say?"

"I asked if I might have the honor of a dance with you at the annual Heartstone Ball."

"Of course. I will save one for you. But now I really must get back, I have a lot of work to do."

"Of course, my dear. Let's get you back. Don't forget about my dance."

"I'll see you tonight."

"Until tonight, my dear." He bowed over her hand and took his leave.

Leona turned around and came face to face with Falcon. "Good afternoon, Falcon."

"Good afternoon. Can I have a word with you?"

My goodness he is serious. "Yes, of course. Will the library do?"

"That would be fine." He led the way down the hall and waited for her to precede him into the room. Falcon shut the door behind them.

Chapter Eighteen

"What can I do for you?"

"Why are you doing this to my papa?" His words were sharp, accusatory.

"I'm sorry. I don't understand. What exactly am I doing to your papa?"

"He loves you. He said that you love him. Why are you going out with other men if that is true?"

"It's not that simple, Falcon. Your father and I talked about this and he knows that I need some time to get my thoughts worked out."

"You are hurting him. Just like Mama did." Angry tears sprang into his eyes.

"Oh no. I am not trying to hurt him, I swear to you, Falcon. What your father and I shared once is very complicated and..."

He gave a furious shake of his head. "It's not complicated. You were a slave and he was the master's son. What difference does that make? He loved you. You aren't a slave now. He doesn't think of you in that way. He still loves you. He came for you after he came and saved me from my mama's sick and twisted ways. Do you know what he told me when I asked him about you? Do you? Do you!" His voice had risen to a high pitch.

God, she wanted to pull him close and hug him to her. "No. What did he say?"

"He said that you were the most beautiful woman in the world to him. Always had been and always would be. I never saw him once, not once, have the same look in his eyes when he looked at Mama that he gets when he talked about you." Tears ran down his face.

Leona reached out for the boy. He struggled against her, but she didn't give up and pulled him into her arms to snuggle him against her breast. Slowly she rocked him back and forth until his cries had subsided.

"Falcon, I don't want to hurt your father."

"But you are."

"I just need some time to work things out in my head."

"Is it because of me? Do you not like me?" His question was muffled, as he kept his face tucked against her.

Tears of her own burned her eyes. "No, honey. Never because of you. It's me. I am so confused right now. For the longest time I was angry at him and now... This is all new to me. I just need some time."

"I don't think he has the time. He misses you. I know he does, even though he tries to keep it from me. His face looks tortured." He pulled back and gazed into her face.

Leona wiped his tears with her thumbs and smiled softly at him. "Falcon, your father is a very special man and you are right, I do love him. I always have."

Without asking, he climbed up into her lap and laid his head on her shoulder. He murmured softly, so softly she almost didn't hear, "I think I will like having you for a mama. You smell good, like flowers."

Leona wrapped her arms around him and held him tight. Out of the corner of her eye, she saw Lucien standing silently. He met her gaze and nodded in her direction, and she knew that he had heard their exchange.

* * * *

Later that day, Leona was in her room getting ready for the ball. She and Ciara stood in front of her multitude of dresses as she tried to decide which one to wear.

"So, you never did tell me how your visit with the colonel went?"

"Fine." Her cheeks heated.

"That's it? Nothing more than fine?"

Leona looked at Ciara and saw devilish humor floating in her eyes. "That's all I am going to tell you."

"How was it?"

"How was what?"

Ciara just arched an eyebrow and grinned as another blush raced across Leona's face. "You know what I mean."

A knock on her door interrupted their banter, and Lucien stuck his head in.

"Husband, I think you spend too much time in this room. Is there something you needed from Leona?"

"Jealous, wife?" He grinned and winked at Leona.

"Humph. Not on your life, because I know that you don't stand a chance with her. Too moody. Go away, we're having girl talk."

"I just wanted to let you know that it's almost time."

Pure exasperation filled her features. "I hate this part of being a marchioness. I don't like it at all."

"I know, sweetheart. We will leave tomorrow and go back to Heartstone for the rest of the holiday." He came in for a quick kiss, and, with an evil glint of his own, he pointed at the golden-bronze dress. "Leona, I think you should wear that one. He won't know what hit him."

Leona flushed. Lucien laughed and walked out of the room.

"He's right, you know. You should wear that one. Besides, that way we will match, I'll wear the one that I have like that. Lucien doesn't know about it yet. What do you say?" Ciara had a dress in the same style but in copper to match her own skin tone.

"All right."

"Good, now tell me everything about Trace. And I do mean *everything*."

The ladies spoke and laughed together for the rest of the time while they got ready.

* * * *

The party had been going for a while when the major domo announced to the room, "Colonel Trace Morgan." Leona felt her heart skip a few beats. He was here. She stood along the side of the room, since she'd just finished a dance with the Earl of Danbury.

She watched as he walked into the ballroom. Instead of a uniform, he wore a suit that was tailored just for him. It accented his wide shoulders, lean hips and strong legs. He moved with the same elegance that she had noticed in Lucien. He was dressed in black with a midnight-blue waistcoat. Her favorite color.

His hair had been cut to taper perfectly to his collar. The lights shone on his hair, bringing out his highlights. He was freshly shaven. She had no doubt that he would smell like sandalwood and cinnamon. Such a shame she couldn't go dance with him now, but she had another already promised.

As she stepped into Viscount Hadley's arms, she cast a final look toward Trace, wanting to be with him.

* * * *

Trace's eyes scanned the room as he looked for the object of his desire. He couldn't find her but knew she was there. He saw Lady Heartstone and laughed to himself as he also saw the scowl that seemed to be permanently fixed to her husband's face.

Another dance began. He stood by Ciara and Lucien as couples took to the floor. All at once he saw her.

She danced with a pale-haired man and she looked... *What the hell is she wearing?* It looked like nothing. The same style of dress that Ciara wore, but it was so close to her skin tone that she appeared almost naked.

It fit tightly, showing her body to everyone, and everyone looked. All the men stared and Trace felt his blood begin to boil with jealousy.

He heard a loud grumble, and at the expression on Lucien's face he knew that he himself had emitted the sound. "How could you let her wear that?"

"I think she looks fetching in it. Don't you?" Ciara asked.

"Yes, my lady, I do. As do you." That earned him a growl from Lucien.

It still didn't stop him from wishing he could cover her up and take her away from prying eyes and ravish her until they were both too exhausted to do anything else except sleep the sleep of the dead.

When the dance ended, he walked up to her. "Good evening," he purred as he strode through the men who surrounded her.

Her eyes darkened as they fell upon him. "Good evening, Colonel Morgan."

"Perhaps you have a dance yet open on your card that I might have?"

"I have one left. A waltz."

"I'll take it." He left no room for argument from the others around her. Trace leaned over and signed her card and walked off without another word.

If she only knew how hard it was for him to leave her there. His entire body trembled with desire and the need to smash in the faces of those fools who slobbered all over her. She was his and it was time for them to realize that.

Trace had secured the last waltz of the night with her. And he wasn't about to give this opportunity up for anything. It killed him to think that they had never danced together before.

* * * *

When the time arrived for the dance, Trace came to collect her from Lucien's side. "Miss O'Neill, I believe that this is my dance."

"Of course, Colonel Morgan. If you will excuse me, Lord Heartstone."

Lucien just inclined his head in that regal way of his and swept his own wife out onto the floor.

During the dance, Trace spoke to her in a much more intimate way. "That dress is scandalous."

"You don't like it?" she teased.

"I don't like that others are seeing you in it. What were you thinking?" Trace spread his hand along waist, swearing he could feel her heat.

"There is no need to get nasty about it."

"I want to rip it off you and take you here on the floor. How does that sound?" He forced the words from between clenched teeth.

"I don't think that Lucien would like that very much." Leona smiled at him.

"Who cares? From the look he leveled at his wife, he would be the first to follow my lead. What were you two trying to do to us? Kill us?"

"I didn't think you would notice." She gave a small shrug.

"Kitten, I notice everything about you. Don't *ever* forget that."

"Thank you for the flowers." A slight pause as she licked her lips. "All of them."

"Did you like them?"

"You know I did."

"Did you miss me?"

"Yes. I missed you."

Trace loved how quick her response fell. "You're getting better at this, kitten. I didn't have to ask more than once."

It was heaven, being in his arms as they spun around the room. He was a fantastic dancer. Leona barely felt like she had to work. It was as if he lifted her and carried her through the dance.

When it was over he took her back to Ciara and left with a bow over her hand.

Trace wanted to stay beside her, but he wasn't going to force it. He would see her later. There were to be fireworks later and while in reality it wasn't that long, to him it was forever, everyone was bundled up for the show.

Leona stood off to the side alone and watched as couples wandered off into the shadows to steal a kiss or two as they observed the spectacular show. Moments after the show started, she felt a presence at her elbow.

A warmth flowed over her and she knew right away who it was. Trace. "I thought you had left for the night."

"I would never leave without hearing your answer." He spun her into his steel embrace. "Or without my good-night kiss."

Leona reached up and placed her lips on his and kissed him. She slid her tongue in between his lips and stroked his tongue. Trace responded immediately, and he quickly got control of the situation.

Trace pulled back and placed her back against his chest and set his chin on her head. His hands worked their way around her waist and her hands covered his. They stayed like that for the whole fireworks display

As the display wound down, he stepped back. "I must take my leave now. I will have your answer, please."

"Yes. Yes, Trace. It is you. It always has been you and always will be."

A smile that was part happiness and mostly arrogant male smirk crossed his rugged features. "Good answer, kitten. I have to go. Until tomorrow."

Once again he moved like the wind, and she found herself surrounded by bands of steel as his lips laid waste to hers. She responded with everything she had and soon they both panted as they separated.

"Good night, little one." Then he disappeared into the darkness.

"Good night, Trey." Leona watched as the bushes swallowed him up like a ghost.

Later, as she was undressed by her maid, she felt giddy. "Thank you, Sara. I can finish undressing if you want to start the packing. I'm leaving tomorrow. Just do a little, for it is so late and I am sure you want to get some sleep as well."

"Yes, ma'am." Her quiet maid got to work.

Chapter Nineteen

The next morning Leona and Ciara were reading in the library when Weeks came in and announced, "My lady, there is someone here. Miss O'Neill, you have a visitor."

"Send them in if you please, Weeks." Ciara spoke.

"Very well, my lady." He departed silently.

"How is my little lady?" A deep voice speared the air.

Leona jumped up with a squeal. "Jackson. You're back." She threw herself into his arms and hugged him with all she had as he wrapped his arms around her in return.

"I've missed ye, lass."

She leaned back to look up at him. "And I you. And I you."

"So how was the ball? Sorry I missed it."

"Wonderful." Leona couldn't stop the smile from turning up her lips.

"Hello again, Jackson." Ciara spoke as she poured him a cup of tea.

"Good morning, my lady." He gave her a small bow before putting his attention back on Leona.

"How was your trip?" she asked her friend.

"Everything was good. Don't worry about a thing. Tell me what you've been up to."

"Well, shopping and dancing. The opera and lots of things like that. As well as painting."

"Anyone special I should know about?" Jackson leaned back in his chair.

"Just me." Trace's voice cut across the room.

Jackson rose with a growl. "You again. What are you doing here?"

"I came to speak with St. Martin, but since you're here, I will ask you instead. I would like your daughter's hand in marriage."

Ciara sat down on the chaise, avidly glancing between the two men.

Jackson sputtered, "In marriage? Why would I do that?"

"Because we're in love. And there is a chance that she might be pregnant."

When he'd said all bets are off, he'd meant it! Leona flushed and kept her eyes on the floor.

"Lass? Would he be speakin' the truth?"

Leona struggled to get the words out of her mouth. It was just so dry. "I...I...love him."

Before she could say anything else, Weeks appeared back in the doorway with Lucien behind him, who took in the scene with interest.

"Yes, Weeks?"

"Excuse me, but there is a woman out here who claims to be Colonel Morgan's wife."

Leona blanched. *No, it couldn't be. Not now.* She glanced at Trace and saw nothing but disbelief on his face. As one Lucien, Ciara and Jackson formed a protective barrier around her.

In through the door burst a small, brown-haired woman. She was wild-eyed and panicked-looking. "You! Trace, you did this to me. Where is my son? Where is he?" She went after him with raised hands, swinging at him. Trace blocked her attacks, but his eyes stayed on Leona.

"Tell me!" she screeched. "Why won't you look at me? Who are you looking at?" Her head followed his line of sight and saw everyone else in the room. She summoned a smile and patted down her dress before she walked over to them. With a small curtsy, she nodded to both Lucien and Jackson.

"I am sorry for my behavior, gentlemen, but I have been so worried about my son." Her tone was smooth, too smooth. Like a woman who knew just what to say to get exactly what she wanted. One who used her looks to cover up her ugliness.

Leona noticed that she deliberately ignored the women. She continued, "Is the lady of the house home? I would like to talk to her. Perhaps one of these…these…servants…could go get her." As if they were less than her.

Blue eyes narrowed. Bethany was about to learn what it was like to insult a marquess.

"You have just insulted my wife. She is standing in front of you." His strong hand settled on the shoulder of his whiskey-eyed wife as his voice lowered to a hiss that had enough danger in it even a deaf man would be able to pick up on it.

Bethany flicked her eyes over both women and sputtered. "You don't mean one of *these* is your wife, do you? Oh, I get it. This is a joke! Trace told you that we own slaves."

"Weeks, remove this woman from my home." Both Lucien and Jackson had a grasp on the women in front of them, mostly Ciara, who was more than ready to do battle.

"With pleasure, sir." He grabbed the woman and pulled her out through the door.

"Trace, Trace, don't let them take me. Trace!"

The door slammed shut on her wails.

The room was silent for a moment as everyone looked at Trace. "I am so sorry. She was supposed to be in prison for conspiring to kill me. Leona?" He held his hand out to her.

Leona stayed next to Jackson. Trace shook his head in defeat, lowered his hand and slowly turned around to face the door. "I'm sorry."

Before he could walk off, she spoke, it was hushed and he almost didn't hear it, but she spoke and he did hear it.

"Trace?"

He spun around and his eyes, almost frantically, searched for some sign in hers. "Yes, kitten?"

"Are you really divorced?"

"Since I made it back to Hawk's Cove. I don't want her, I never did."

His eyes melted away the rest of her resistance, like butter placed in a hot frying pan, as they said — *It was only you. It was always only you that I wanted.*

Leona walked on shaky legs into his arms and just let him hold her. She stood protected by the strength of his embrace. She pressed her head against the wall of his solid chest and she listened to his heartbeat and felt her own fall into the same pattern, so they beat as one.

"Are ye sure about this, lass?"

Without removing herself from Trace's hold, she maneuvered her head so she could look at the man who had been a father to her. "Yes. I am sure."

Trace dropped his arms slowly, as if reluctant to let her go, and stepped closer to Jackson. "You never did answer my question. May I have your daughter's hand in marriage?"

Jackson stepped up flush against Trace. They matched stare for stare, neither backing down. Water versus earth, two amazing forces. Blue-green versus brown. "What makes ye think that ye be the right man fer her?"

Trace never missed a beat. Never blinked. "I am the *only* man for her. Just as she is the *only* woman for me."

He reached behind him and pulled Leona back into his arms and placed his hand under her chin, bringing her eyes up to meet his as he kept speaking. He took his eyes off Jackson only to look into her eyes.

"I have loved her since we were children and I swear that I will love her beyond my dying day. I want to be with her until I no longer have life left in my body, and when that day comes, I will wait for her to join me in Heaven so we can be together once again. We are two halves of the same whole. I need her to be complete."

Trace brushed a tear from Leona's face before he pulled her back tight into his arms.

They stood together for a while before someone cleared their throat. Lucien. "Well, since my family has just apparently grown by two more, I...*we* extend the offer to you and your son to spend the holidays with us out at Heartstone Manor."

Trace lifted his head and stared back at Lucien. "We would be honored to join you. I think that it would be the first Christmas in a long time that would mean anything to the both of us." As he spoke, his arms tightened around Leona to silently include her in his reason for a wonderful holiday.

"Well, we are leaving today. We can send the wife and kids and luggage off ahead and you can ride with Jackson and me. How does that sound?"

"Fine. It won't take me long to get our things." Trace glanced at Jackson, who still had distrust in his startling eyes.

"Send off the wife and kids? Excuse me, husband, do I not get any say in the matter?" Indignation rose fast in Ciara.

"No." His lips found hers swiftly and fiercely before he swatted her on the bottom. "Get ready to go. I want to get there at a decent time."

Ciara grabbed Leona's hand and pulled her away from Trace. She dragged her out of the room behind her, leaving only a "We'll see who gets any say in the matter" to her husband.

* * * *

Trace rubbed the back of his neck as the night fell. They had taken rooms at a local inn on their way. The marchioness wasn't feeling the best and Lucien hadn't wished to continue traveling. He understood, truly he did, however, here he wasn't allowed to be with Leona and he hated with a passion being away from her.

He wasn't sure how his ex-wife had found him, or how she had managed to get out of prison. The only reason he cared now was because she posed a threat to his happiness, his son's safety and, without a doubt, Leona's.

A low rumble rose within him. He would kill the woman himself before he allowed her to cause any more pain to their son or Leona. He paced the room he'd been given.

He went to the door and opened it to see a serving girl approaching. No, correction, she wasn't a girl, she was more of a barmaid age and, from the looks of her, she was hoping to find a bed to warm at night. *If her intent is my direction, she is going to be disappointed.*

She bit her lower lip and cast a seductive glance up to him. He gave her a nod, solely because when he'd been in uniform he had been instructed to be respectful. It surely wasn't anything his old man had taught him.

"Anything I can get you for the night, sir? Anything you want, we can accommodate."

"No, ma'am. Thank you."

Trace made his way downstairs after making sure his room was locked. What he didn't need was to go back later and find her in there waiting.

Claiming a lone spot in the back, he looked up when the proprietor walked up.

"Everything okay with your room, sir?"

"Yes, it is fine. I just came down for a drink."

"Right away." He paused. "Whiskey?"

"Please."

He gave him a nervous smile. "Of course."

Trace got it, he did. He'd come in with a marquess. If Lucien were not happy with anything, this entire establishment could be ruined. Not that he saw the man doing anything like that, but still, coming from a commoner's position, he got it.

He nursed his drink, and looked up when a shadow blocked the light for a moment. Lucien stood there.

"Do you mind?"

"Of course not. Everything okay with your wife?"

Ciara had instructed him to call her by her first name, but he didn't feel comfortable doing that to the woman's husband. A bit too personal.

"Leona is in there with her, getting her to feel a bit better."

Worry pinched the corner of his eyes. It also explained why the man was down here instead of in the room with his wife. He was concerned.

"Thank you," Trace said after a few moments of silence.

"For?"

"Everything. Inviting us to share the holidays with you. I know our boys enjoy spending time together."

"I thought you were thanking me for not having you killed when your ex-wife showed up."

There was no humor in the man's expression. At all. Trace leaned forward, elbows on the table.

"I have been trying to figure out why she came, how she got out of jail and what her desired ultimate resolution with this is."

"And?" Lucien leaned forward as well, his blue eyes sharp and calculating.

"Blank. When I left Hawk's Cove and went to her parents', where she hid, I was with the army to arrest her, I was told she was not going to get out, that she would die in the jail. So if she is out, it makes me wonder if my brother has also found a way to escape."

"And your brother would be a threat to Leona and your son?"

"Yes. My brother is a level of evil you cannot begin to imagine."

Lucien's smile was more of a baring of teeth. "Perhaps." He finished the rest of his drink. "What is your plan?"

"I think I have to go home. I need to discover what's going on and figure out what steps I have to take to stop this." He shook his head. "My former wife is crazy and there is no limit to what she will go to in order to achieve whatever twisted reality she is living in for the moment."

"And while you're gone? Are you telling me you want to expose your son to that place once more?" Lucien turned his cup.

"No, I have wish to do that. However I have to make sure he is taken care of, and that is my only option. I cannot expect Leona to take on that responsibility for me."

"No, I suspect you cannot."

Trace finished his whiskey and set down the glass. He leaned back in his chair, wishing all the answers would just fall into his lap.

"Are you taking her with you?"

His body tensed at the thought of Leona being exposed to what was going on back there. He saw the understanding in Lucien's gaze before the man responded.

"Will you stop her from going?" Lucien asked another question.

"With everything inside me. There was very little that went well for her during our younger years, and the last thing I wish to do is dredge up more memories. I know the place is changing but, I cannot stop her pain. But I can protect her now."

"You care for her."

He skimmed his top teeth with his tongue. "I have loved her since the day I first laid eyes on her. That will never stop, nor will it ever change."

Lucien nodded and rose from the table. "Your son is more than welcome to stay with us while you take care of what you need to. I go to check on my wife, so I will bid thee good night."

"Good night, my lord."

Lucien gave a brief nod and walked away. Trace didn't linger downstairs and exhaustion ate at him, mind and body, as he climbed back to his room. Slipping inside, he closed the door behind him and rested against it, a large sigh escaping.

He needed to talk to Leona.

* * * *

That chance didn't arrive for another day. Not until after they made it back to Heartstone Manor did he manage to find her alone.

"Hello, kitten."

She turned from where she worked on a portrait and gave him a smile that, same as it had when they were younger, contained the power to take him to his knees.

"Trace. What are you doing in here?'

"Wanted to talk to you."

Her expression shuttered immediately. With a single blink, he was staring at a blank slate as she placed her pencil down on the easel's tray.

"About?"

He moved closer. Not as near as he wanted to be, but the door was open and this wasn't about sinking between her thighs, but explaining to her that he was leaving.

"I have to head back to Hawk's Cove."

Trace waited. She didn't speak, just watched him in return.

"Say something?"

"What am I supposed to say? Congratulations? Beg you not to go? Inquire as to why you feel the need to go now that your ex-wife has shown up?"

He breathed a bit easier the moment he heard the jealousy in her tone. This he could handle, but the lack of anything had scared him, because he couldn't address what wasn't there.

"Kitten, there is no one for me but you in the world. Can you believe me when I say that?"

That she didn't agree with him in that instant set off concerns of his own.

"Are you staying through the holiday or are you leaving now?"

He skirted the easel and stood by her, trailing a finger down her arm and the soft material covering it.

"Staying. I have not been with you or Falcon during a holiday and I am not about to miss this one. But I will be leaving after. Lucien said Falcon could stay here with them." Unease peppered his skin and gut. "She was not supposed to get out. I have to know if my brother did as well."

"Of course you do."

"I do not want to leave you."

"We all have things we must do." With that, she went back to her drawing and picked up her pencil once more.

That hadn't gone at all how he'd intended. Bending at the waist, he brushed his lips against her cheek.

"I love you, kitten." Then he left her there before he forgot his manners. At the door, he gazed back once more, but she wasn't paying him the least bit of attention, nor were her dogs. They were sleeping and she, sketching.

Chapter Twenty

After Christmas

Leona squealed with laughter as she ducked a snowball thrown by Bryn. Holding up her hands, she cried off. She wrapped her stole around her a bit tighter and burrowed into the warmth it offered.

The day was cold and windy, but the kids had wanted nothing more than to come outside and play. She'd gone with them, aware she'd been holing herself up in her studio working on her drawings. Some time outside would be good for her.

And she'd believed that until they'd started pelting her with snowballs. Now the icy slush ran down the inside of her clothing.

"Where are you going, Auntie Lea?"

"Inside, Keely. I need some dry clothing and some hot chocolate."

As she'd hoped, all the kids stopped and ran to her. "Do we get some too?"

She nodded and wiped some snow off Bryn's face. "Of course, but we have to get inside, change and make it."

"Can I help make it?"

Leona picked up Keely and held her close. "Yes, you can. We should head inside."

She smiled at the maids and footmen who were also out in this and didn't mention all the grateful looks they gave. The wind had whipped up and the temperature had gotten ugly and cold fast.

Inside was warm. Fires were burning, and she sent the kids along to change then did the same herself. Meeting them once more in the kitchen, she waved at the cook and told her they were going to make some hot cocoa.

"I can make it for you, miss."

"No. Thank you, though. I promised Keely we would do this together. I promise I will clean up after us."

As she heated the milk, she glanced over her shoulder in time to see Ciara walk in, a glow about her.

"Good afternoon, my lady."

"I heard there was chocolate being made in here." She kissed her children and Leona's heart tripped when she didn't leave out Falcon. "What can I do to help?"

"Cinnamon?"

"We have some of that. Are you thinking a bit grated off into the chocolate?"

Leona nodded. "I am. That is how my mother used to make it." For Trace and his family, but that wasn't where she wanted to go with her thoughts right now.

Keely stood on a chair beside her, stirring the milk, while Ciara and the boys added some cinnamon. The room smelled just like Leona's childhood and tears pricked her eyes as she remembered her mother.

Making enough for the staff, as they had to be cold as well, they eventually took their drinks to the sitting room. The children gathered by the fire and played some make-believe game. The adult men were not there, and when Ciara sat beside her on the settee, Leona knew a talk was about to happen.

"Are you upset he is leaving?"

"In a way, yes. I don't understand why. He said he was done with all of that, but the moment she showed up, he has to go." Her insecurity and an ugly feeling of betrayal rose like the tide.

"And the fact he thinks you and his son are in danger?"

"I do not know what his ex-wife could do to me that I haven't already experienced in my life. She cannot inflict more pain on me. She has already taken him from me once." Leona shrugged. "I thought I was ready to be with him but now, I am not so sure."

Ciara lifted her cup to her lips and sipped. "I understand. What about his son?"

"Yes, do what is necessary to protect him, but again, what we both went through is different. I don't wish ill on Falcon, I love the boy, but my heart is still unsure."

Lucien and Trace walked in.

"Hello, princess," Lucien muttered, kissing his wife.

Leona dropped her gaze to the porcelain cup in her hand. Trace stopped behind her and touched the back of her neck.

"Hello, kitten." His voice wasn't loud enough to carry to the children, but she didn't doubt that Lucien and Ciara had heard him.

It wasn't fair. All he had to do was speak to her and she felt all the walls that she'd erected to try and keep herself safe falling.

"Trace," she said with a small smile.

He returned it, then claimed a seat near her but far enough away that there was a respectable distance between them. Unlike the marquess and his wife. Lucien sat right beside his wife and had Ciara curled into him, his arm around her, holding her. Showing everyone that this was his woman and he was oh-so protective of her.

Jealousy burned Leona's throat and she swallowed hard while she averted her gaze. Focusing on the children, she immediately viewed them there, playing, in portrait form. It would have been rude of her to escape, so she committed the scene to memory, promising herself she would sketch it out later that night.

Before the night was over, the room teemed with family. Lucien and Ciara's family. Jackson was there as well, but as time ticked by, Leona moved closer and closer to the edge, feeling as though she were an imposter. This wasn't her world. She wasn't a member of the peerage and never would be.

She cried off as the men poured another round of drinks.

Up in the studio they'd provided for her, she moved the lamp closer to where she needed it and sat on the lounge, sketching the scene she had been honored to see. Her dogs were with her and the wind howled outside but she was warm and safe.

Time passed as she sketched, and when her body screamed at her to move, she moaned as she stretched, setting the pad to the cushion beside her.

She found Trace leaned in the doorway.

"What are you doing here? And how long have you been there?" She hadn't heard him arrive.

"I came to tell you good night, but you were so deep in concentration and I did not wish to disturb you. Instead, I opted to watch you."

"Good night."

His laugh was warm and familiar.

"It is never going to be that quick between us, kitten. I plan on saying good night for a long time." He shifted his stance. "Are you heading to bed now?"

"No. Why?"

"Come downstairs with me. I missed talking to you tonight."

"Can we not talk here?"

His eyes flashed in the flickering light. "I do not have that kind of control around you, kitten. This is why I am still standing over here, because were I to go there…" He took a deep breath. "There would be a sudden lack of clothing."

Heat flushed through her. She stood, closing the notebook by her side. The dogs rose as one and trailed her to the door. Trace stood back and let her by without a single touch. Together they returned to the first floor. Instead of to the sitting room, he guided her to the library. The fire still burned well there and warmth pushed throughout the room.

"Can I get you two anything?" a maid questioned.

"No, thank you," Leona replied, then looked to Trace. "At least, not for me."

"We will be fine, thank you." Trace smiled.

The maid curtsied and left.

Leona saw why he said that. On the floor by the fire were a thick blanket and a tea service with cookies on it as well. Trace led her there and helped her down. Curling her legs under her, she smiled at him.

"I have not had a picnic in a long time."

"Last one I had was with you." His expression sobered and he shook his head. "I'm sorry, I have no wish to bring up bad memories."

"Trace, our past is not going to vanish just because we do not speak about it. I know how our situation was. You were the master's son and I was the slave girl. That did not change how *I* felt when we were together. We were just two people and I was in love with you." She clasped her hands together. "Even my mother could not understand. She thought that you were threatening me and I could not possibly want to go be with you. And I do understand, from her view. She didn't have a choice with your father. But I did with you."

He picked up her hand and kissed the back of it.

"Part of me thinks she believed all we did was have sex, but I tried to tell her how you brought me paper and I would spend the entire afternoon drawing while you lay beside me."

He pressed another kiss to her hand. "I love watching you draw. Tonight reminded me of that." He released her and gave her some tea and cookies. "The way you studied the paper, the sparkle and pure love in your eyes as you put pencil or charcoal to the sheet for the first time, as if being allowed to see something no one else could at the moment. You were complete joy, and I wanted so much to keep that look on your face all the time."

He brushed some hair that had escaped the clip at the nape of her neck back from her face.

"It is freeing. Taking a blank canvas or sheet of paper and envisioning where you're putting your first stroke." She sipped her tea and shook her head. "The one I remember the most from then was the twin fawns." Leona squeezed her eyes shut. "I wanted so much to share that one with Mama."

Trace stretched out, his head toward the fire. "You know she is so proud of you and watches all you do."

"I like to think so."

"And do you think she approves of us being together again?"

Leona stared down at him. His gaze was straightforward, the brown hue warm and inviting.

"I believe Mama wants me happy."

"Even if that happiness comes at the expense of being with a man like me?"

"We were each born into a life, Trace. Each of us had a path laid out for us and both of us diverted from those paths and made our own. Others may look at you and see the plantation owner who had slaves, but I see more. So much more."

She moved the tea service and adjusted how she sat, beckoning him to rest his head in her lap, much as he had used to do when they were younger.

"I see the boy who taught me to read. The one who would follow me on all my crazy adventures. The one who kissed my injuries and held me until I stopped crying." She stroked his hair away from his face. "You grew into an amazing young man and I fell in love with you. Even when you were around your family, you were different than they were. Now here you are, a man with a son who you would protect no matter what. How can I *not* be happy with you?"

"Because I was *not* there to protect *you*."

"And we both know that you would not have been able to stop what I endured."

"I love you, Leona. You will always be in my heart."

* * * *

Four months later

Trace stood at the rail and watched the small port town come into view on Eden. The weather here was much warmer than it had been in England when he'd departed. A bevy of mixed emotions rolled inside him.

He didn't want to be here. He wanted to be with his son and Leona, getting ready to marry her. But he couldn't leave a potential danger to either of them out there. Lucien had said they would be on the lookout for Bethany if she tried to come back.

The journey had been long and hard. They'd lost a bunch of men overboard during some of the storms they'd encountered. Retreating to his cabin, he packed up the last of items he'd brought with him, and waited for them to dock.

He hadn't let anyone at Hawk's Cove know he was coming back, not wanting to give Steven or whomever he was working for advance notice. Hiring a hack by the dock, he waited while the man loaded his trunk. Then he gave his destination of where he was to be taken.

The ride wasn't all that long, but he would have been happier riding a horse instead of being cooped up once more. As the carriage slowed, he instinctively straightened his shoulders and sat up. The general's large house's pillars gleamed in the warm tropical sun.

Trace hopped out and smiled at the men who came to remove his belongings. "Is the general home?"

"Yessir."

"Could you let him know that Colonel Morgan is here to see him?"

"Right away, sir. Miss Ella will get you something to drink inside where it is a bit cooler, if you would like to follow her."

Trace nodded and trailed the young woman inside.

"I would be lying if I did just hear a rumor you had returned."

The general's booming voice had him looking up to the second floor.

Trace smiled at seeing his old commanding officer. "Good to see you again, sir." He hadn't changed, still looked fit, like he could vault on the back of a horse and lead his men to victory in battle.

"And you, son. What brings you back here? I thought you were after your woman."

"She's waiting for me back in England."

"And your boy? How is he?" The general looked around. "Did you bring him with you?"

"Much better now, thank you. No, he did not make this journey with me. I left him in good care with some friends of mine while I returned."

"I need him well. I want him to join the army. If he's half the man his father was, I need him."

Trace gave a shake of his head. "I think my son is a bit young to be leading men at the moment."

The general smiled. "Just do not let him go join the navy or anything like that." He sobered. "What brings you back?"

"My ex-wife showed up in England."

The man's bushy brows slammed together, giving him a unibrow look. "How the hell did she get out?"

Trace lifted his shoulders and flattened his lips. "That is why I came back. I need to make sure that

Steven didn't escape." He used to call this island home but, he realized that his home was Leona and would be where she was.

"There will be hell to pay if that has happened on my watch." The general's expression was full of danger. The general had been willing to fight by his men's side.

"You will stay here for the night and we will head off in the morning. Right now, we can drink and catch up."

Trace wanted to go now, but one didn't simply refute the general and his decision. He got settled in his room and went back down to have conversation with one of the men in his life he could say he actually liked and respected.

* * * *

By the time he retreated to his room again, his exhaustion was complete. Trace crawled into bed and closed his eyes as the warm breeze flowed over him. The island had always been a great temperature and it was a definite improvement over the cold he'd left behind in England.

One thing England had that this place doesn't is Leona. God, he missed her. Grinding the heel of his palm along his thickening cock, he moaned and shifted on the mattress. Eyes closed tight, he pulled from his memory the way she looked lying beneath him, skin flushed and lips swollen and parted as her breathing fell fast and short. The smoky way she watched him as he thrust in and out of her heat.

Trace gave in to the need and pushed his hand down the front of his bedclothes. His erection was hard and demanding release. He wrapped his hand around it and stroked slowly, wishing it were his woman's touch as opposed to his own. It wasn't to be, and he had to accept that. She was nowhere near him, and until he'd resolved this mess and gotten back to her over in England, it was only going to be his familiar hand on his cock.

Stroking fast, he alternated his grip as he moved. Soft. Hard. In between. Pinching the head of his dick, he moaned, denying himself his release. On and on he tormented himself, desperate to hold on to the imagery of Leona's expression as he brought her to orgasm. How she shuddered around him and bucked, keening as she fell to pieces, trusting he would be there to catch her.

That did it and he came hard, losing his breath. After lying there for a few moments, he cleaned up and crawled back into bed, determined to get some sleep. It was the first night in a long time that he wasn't on a ship, traveling.

* * * *

The following morning, after they'd been served breakfast, the men climbed on their waiting horses. The ride was silent, much how riding with the general as a solider had been.

The two-hour trip gave Trace time to think about how he was going to handle things if Steven had escaped. He would have to hunt him down, because the man was too damn dangerous to be left to his own devices.

Side by side he and the general entered the jail. The rancid stench of the jail was powerful and he struggled to recall how he had ever been used to smells like this when he'd served. It wasn't easy. Dirty smelled like shit.

"General Harrington and Colonel Morgan. We need to speak to one of the prisoners."

"Of course, sir," the young soldier there said, standing at attention. "Who may I take you to?"

"Steven Morgan."

Trace held his breath, waiting for the man to inform them he wasn't in there any longer.

"Yes, sir, right away. If you two will follow me."

He could breathe a bit easier. Still not confident until he actually laid eyes on his brother, he and the general fell into step behind the man and walked through the darkness to a line of solid-door cells.

"He is all the way at the back, sirs. On the left. If you wish to talk to him out of here, I will have to bring him up to a different room."

"There is fine," Trace said, not wanting to be in this place longer than he had to.

"Very good, sirs. The small access door will allow you to see in the room and speak to him." He saluted and turned to walk away.

"Want me to wait here?" General Harrington questioned after they were left alone.

"If you don't mind, sir."

"Not at all. Take your time. I will be here."

Nodding his thanks, Trace walked down the passageway to the indicated cell and with a deep breath, reached out and opened the small door that allowed him to see in the cell. It was like a door inside a door. When it was opened, you could see in but the person there couldn't get to you.

A few tiny windows at the top of the cell allowed for a soft filtering of light to penetrate, but it wasn't a lot. His brother lay on the cot, looking toward the hard, cold stone wall.

"Steven."

The thin shoulders shook as Steven coughed. "Well now, this does not bode well for my state of mind. Why, you ask? Because I am suddenly hearing my brother's voice in my head. And which brother would that be, you may inquire? Happy to tell you. The one who let me get locked up in the first place. My baby brother, who I did all I could to protect when we were growing up."

Trace barely held back his snort of disbelief. Steven was insane if he was under the impression he'd been helping and protecting Trace as they'd grown up.

"Stand up."

The blanket moved, allowing the man to rise and make his way to the door. Hatred overflowed from Steven's blue eyes as he glared at Trace, even the low lighting couldn't stop that.

"So it is you. What? Come to gloat? Decide now I should be killed?"

"You should have already been killed. You plotted against a superior officer."

Steven spat at him. "Fuck you. Nothing about you was or is superior to me."

Trace wiped away the wetness without allowing any flicker of expression change. "*Everything* about me is," he said, tone low and assured.

"I protected you," Steven seethed, jabbing a finger toward him. A dirty digit with jagged and disgusting nails.

"You tormented me and made my life hell."

"I was showing you how life was. You were the stupid fool who thought you fell in love with a slave. We were just showing you how that doesn't happen. We are *superior* to them. We want to fuck them, we do. We want to beat them, we do. Animals don't have a choice."

Raw fury pumped through Trace's veins as the words fell from his brother's lips.

"You have never been so wrong. We were, are, for having thought that way."

"She was just a fuck. A good one, but just a fuck. How is it you can let a slave come between your brother and you? That you would take her side over mine?"

Trace longed to reach through the space in the door and choke his brother until air no longer flowed, but he didn't.

"She is *not* a slave. She is the woman I love and if this barrier were not between us, I would show you how fucking much I will always take her side over yours — or David's, before he got himself killed."

"Not this angry about your white wife. What does that say about you?"

"That I do not give a fuck about a cheater and someone who would try to kill me." Steven inched closer. "Tell me something, do you ever wonder if he is your son?"

"The brat Bethany popped out? Hell no. I will admit to fucking her, hell, even enjoying it because bitch is a sex fiend — loved me fucking her ass and having more than one dick in her at once — and plotting against you with her, but that brat? No way, he's not mine." Steven's face morphed into evilness personified. "You have no clue, do you?" The laughter wasn't kind.

"No clue about what?"

"Your supposed brat." He inched closer. "If I gave a damn about you, I might think of telling you, but as I do not... Keep wondering. If he's not my seed, and he's not yours, who else's could he be?"

"Why?" Trace asked the question he'd sworn to himself he wasn't going to ask. "Why Steven?"

The reason he'd told himself over and over on the boat ride, and even this morning, was that Steven's actions back then hadn't mattered, nor had they when he'd plotted to have Trace killed and taken his name. Yet, somehow, the youngest brother who had always wanted to be accepted by his older siblings pushed the question free. It made its way by the man Trace had become. The soldier. The father.

"Is that why you came all this way? To wonder why I hate you so much? Or is the why asking why we did what we did? Not that there is a difference really."

"Be a decent brother for once in your life, Steven, and tell me what I want to know." His throat hurt from forcing himself to maintain a calm tone.

"Is that all you want?"

"That is all you have that I want."

The man leered at him. "Fine, just know that when this is over and your little slave bitch comes back to the island, I am going to fuck her right in front of you before I kill her."

"You will never have the chance to touch her." He clenched his fists and narrowed his eyes, wishing again that there wasn't this door between them and that he could return the favor of all the beatings he'd gotten as a boy from this one who had been supposed to protect him.

"The sad part is you actually believe that. See you when you wake."

That was his only warning before something heavy hit him in the temple, sending him crumpling to the floor, his brother's evil cackle echoing in his ears.

Chapter Twenty-One

Leona wrapped her arm around her waist as she stood outside and allowed the crisp wind to flow around her. The days had been nicer and more spring like, but today had teetered closer to wintery weather. It didn't matter. She enjoyed being out in the fresh air.

Her dogs ran and played without seeming to understand the turmoil swirling within her. Bottom line — she missed Trace. She also missed his son, who still currently stayed with the St. Martins at Heartstone.

She and Jackson had returned to her cottage. The additions had been completed and her work had picked up once more, so it wasn't like she didn't have things to do and to occupy her mind. None of that mattered when night came and she lay in bed thinking about the man she wanted more than her next breath.

Worried for him, and worried about Bethany who was running around somewhere, she tried not to think much about it. Failed in exceptional fashion, but she tried.

"Lass, come back inside."

With a smile for Jackson, she whistled for her dogs and did as he'd bade. Closing the door behind her, she shrugged out of her wrap as she watched him pace in front of the fireplace.

"Everything okay, Jackson?"

"You have been sequestering yourself away ever since that man jumped on a ship and left. I'll nae have it anymore."

She got he was angry because his accent leaked through. Shaking her head, she said, "I have been working. I have a lot of requested commissions I have to finish."

"Sequestering."

"Working."

"You turned down three invitations from Lady Heartstone to come for a visit."

Because going there would mean seeing Falcon. Which would only intensify her thoughts of his father.

"I do not get work done if I am spending my days traveling in a carriage, Jackson."

"Stop lying to us both, lass. We both know the reason, and it's not healthy. I knew he was not good for you."

"Is that what this is about? Because you do not approve of him?"

"Of course it is," he roared. "That man and his family treated you worse than animals."

"There is *no* reason to remind me how I was treated there. But that was his father. Trace has never been anything but good to me."

"That man, lass, is going to be nothing but more pain for you. Your mother knew this and hoped you would come to understand this as a fact of life. But no, all I see is her crying because you are still holding onto some childhood fantasy that this man is the one for you."

"Why are you saying this?"

He raked a hand through his salt and pepper hair. "Because it's killing me to hear you cry yourself to sleep every goddamn night. Hoping and praying that he will come back to you."

Tears sprang to Leona's eyes and she swallowed hard, not wanting them to fall.

"If you feel this way, perhaps you should move out. This way you won't have to hear me and you can be disappointed in me with the memory of my mother."

"I only want to look out for you."

"You want me to marry a man who is scared of you and that will not go against you. I do not need your protection. How about this. You stay here and I will go and visit Lady Heartstone. I think we could do with some time apart. I will leave right away."

Spinning around, she walked away, the tears sliding free and dampening her cheeks.

"Leona, lass. Talk to me."

She didn't stop. There was nothing more for her to say.

Despite the fight, Jackson still had the carriage ready for her and the dogs. The tiger hopped down and secured her trunk before helping her in. The dogs jumped up and lay down. Without saying anything to Jackson, she leaned back against the seat and waited for them to depart.

* * * *

The entire trip she alternated between dozing and going over what Jackson had said. The words didn't sting any less each time she revisited them.

When Heartstone came into view, she watched the sprawling home grow larger the closer they came. This wasn't her life, she didn't belong in a place like this.

After being helped down, she walked in and smiled as Keely came running toward her.

"Auntie Lea! You came to visit me."

Leona sank to her knees and hugged the girl, feeling a sense of home when those arms tightened around her. *Maybe I do belong here.*

"I missed you," she said, pulling back and touching Keely on the nose. "How have you been?"

"I am growing, the boys are mean, and I do not want to be the baby anymore."

"That is a lot going on for you." She pushed to her feet, heart softening as Keely wrapped their hands together.

"I know, it's a lot for a little girl."

She tried not to laugh. Bryn and Falcon appeared on the steps behind the footmen that had come to carry her bags up.

"Gentlemen," she said with a nod.

Both boys gave her a bow and Keely let go of her hand to run up toward them. "I told her how you were mean to me."

They shared a look and shrugged before waving in her direction and scampering down the stairs, leaving Keely behind.

The marchioness entered the front room. "Leona."

The smile came so easily this time. She curtsied. "Lady Heartstone."

Ciara walked up to her and hugged her. "I think you enjoy reminding me of my title."

"I am giving you the respect you deserve." Leona hugged her once more before stepping back. "How are you?"

"Grateful you finally decided to accept my invitation. I was almost to the point of coming out there to drag you back." Her whiskey eyes narrowed. "What's wrong? What happened?"

Leona's chin wobbled as she shook her head. "I will okay. Just a row with Jackson."

Ciara slid her arm through Leona's. "Men. I am guessing this had to do with Trace?"

She squeezed her eyes together once more. "Yes." With a sniff, she lifted her chin. "I will be fine."

"We'll talk later. Right now, I want you to meet someone. A friend of Lucien's." She directed them toward the receiving room. "He just got here about an hour ago."

Allowing herself to be led, Leona composed her features right before they moved into the room. Seated in two chairs, drinks in hand, sat Lucien and his friend.

When the women walked in, both men rose as one. Lucien smiled as he looked at his wife, then turned his smile, less powerful, to Leona. The other man was as tall as Lucien, his sandy brown hair cut in the latest style. He had no facial hair and his eyes were gray, arresting.

"Leona," Lucien said, "this is Phillip Vallence, Earl of Edais."

The man came to her and bent over her hand, brushing his lips along the back. "My lady."

She blushed and ducked her head. *Definite flirt.* "I am not a lady, just Leona."

"It is an honor to meet you."

He smiled and winked before stepping back under the extremely watchful eye of one Lucien St. Martin, the Marquess of Heartstone.

Ciara took her arm once more. "We are going to the sitting room to talk. We will see you gentlemen at the midday meal."

They went to walk out when Leona heard, "Princess."

She turned back when Ciara did. Lucien said nothing but his wife as he strode toward her, tipped up her chin with two fingers and kissed her. He slid an arm around her back, bringing them flush to each other.

Leona glanced away and found Phillip's amused gaze on her.

"They always make me feel as if I am intruding." He shrugged easily.

"You are," Lucien said, releasing his wife. "Remind me again why I keep you around?"

"We are such good friends," Phillip replied without any heat.

Lucien grunted. "We may have to revisit this."

"Come along, Leona. They get this way, and it can be hours before they stop." Together they went to the sitting room. Not much later, there was hot cocoa and sandwiches before them for a snack.

"Who is he?"

"The earl? One of Lucien's oldest friends. He, Phillip and Rafe grew up together, causing trouble and breaking hearts. There was a time when they were at odds, but Phillip has changed." She waggled her finger in Leona's direction. "He is not one who will be doing a lot of flirting with you though. Even if you were not with Trace, Lucien would not allow that match." Ciara took a drink. "Not because of what you are thinking. It has nothing to do with your lack of title or skin color, but purely because he looks upon you as a sister and would not let a man of such loose morals in your life like that."

"Surely people can change."

"And he has, but not enough to be okay for his sister."

It was oddly comforting to hear herself being referred to as sister to a man with Lucien's status.

"Tell me what happened," Ciara ordered.

"Jackson continues to remind me that Trace is not the right man for me and that my mother would be disappointed in the knowledge I am happy with him."

"What do you believe?"

"That she would be happy I am happy."

"I think you are right. Jackson sees you as his daughter and therefore no man is going to be good enough for you, not in his eyes. My grandfather did not wish my parents to be together but he loves me unconditionally and I know this. Lucien's father is coming around."

"All Jackson sees when he looks at Trace is a man who owns slaves, and in his eyes that is all he will be good for."

"What do you see?"

Leona trailed her finger along the accent pillow, following the jacquard pattern. "The man I love, the one I have always loved."

"Do you not think, after all your pain and heartache, you are worthy of being happy?"

"I suppose so."

"Then do not let anyone stop you." Ciara squeezed her hand. "If being with Trace for you is like being with my Lucien for me, hold on to him with both hands and do not let go. Take flight with him and live your adventures together."

"I am so lucky to have you as a friend."

Ciara tugged her close and kissed her forehead, perfectly motherly. "It will all work out, you will see."

If only she had half the confidence the marchioness did.

* * * *

Trace heard the *plip* of water and struggled to make sense of what had happened. One moment he had been questioning his brother in a jail cell and the next he had been clipped in the head.

Struggling to a seated position, he squinted through lowered lids, wishing his head would stop pounding. He didn't recognize where he was.

"General?" Was the general here too?

His question had been pitched low because he wasn't about to announce to the world he had woken. But his inquiry was not responded to. He tried twice more before he stopped and rested against the cold stone wall behind him.

He wasn't tied, so there was the opportunity to escape. After making sure he hadn't sustained any injuries, other than the hit to the head, he slowly pushed to his feet, utilizing the wall as support, for he was still weak on his limbs.

He checked his pockets and found they had been picked clean. Current status — unknown location, no money, and no way of proving he was who he said he was.

Panic rose for his son and Leona before he squashed it. Falcon was well protected under the watchful gaze of the Marquess of Heartstone and his family. Leona had them as well as Jackson to keep her safe.

It wasn't the same as knowing he was there to do the job, but it did set him at ease a bit.

He checked the perimeter of the small space he was being held in. No handle on this side for him to try to open the door. Feeling through the darkness, he drew an image in his mind.

This was a jail cell. Smaller than the one he had been talking to Steven at, which meant he had been moved to a new location. Unless that place had an underground cell, which was possible. They hadn't when he had been there last. That, however, did not mean one hadn't been added since that time.

Who did this to me and for what reason?

Moving around a bit more to get his blood flowing, Trace latched onto an image of Leona and held it tight, unwilling to let her go. The door opened he heard the squeak of hinges, yet he still couldn't see anything because everything remained dark. A net was tossed over him and he was dragged kicking and struggling out of the small room.

Not too much later he was strung up, and as he dangled from a hook two men strode in carrying lanterns, allowing him to see their faces. Men he didn't know. They were soldiers though, that much he knew. They carried themselves in a certain way.

One was large and one smaller with wiry musculature.

"Colonel Morgan," his larger captor said, setting his light down. "I have to tell you, it saddens me to do this to you."

"Do what?"

"Punish you."

"For?" He could barely touch the floor, so all his weight was pulling on his shoulders.

"Picking the wrong side."

He growled low in his throat. "Where is my pitiful excuse for a brother?"

"Steven? In a jail cell last I knew. This has nothing to do with him, although later he may be used as a scapegoat when they find your dead body with that of your slave whore."

He memorized their features for later, when he found them again to kill them. "Who hired you then? And why are you doing this?"

"Hired?" The smaller one spoke up. "We volunteered for this duty. There's no pay involved."

The larger one began unbuttoning his shirt, exposing a powerful torso. "This is honestly not going to bring me lots of pleasure, you understand, Colonel, but it will bring some. You have to learn the order of things again, as it is apparent that you have forgotten."

He didn't even fight. Whatever punishment they wanted to dole out, he had no problem accepting. He deserved it and more, by his estimation.

"What exactly am I supposed to learn?"

After the thinner man set down his light, he removed a whip from the bag that had been attached to his belt. Memories slammed into Trace as he stared at the three-foot leather whip with the tapered end.

Father's favorite whip. His old man had preferred this one over the rest at his disposal.

"We fought to keep our way of life. To keep our lines unsullied. You not only disrespect that, but you take what does not belong to you."

"Shut up and get on with it." He closed his eyes once more, knowing this was going to hurt.

* * * *

Twenty minutes later, he continued to hang, spin and bleed. The man wielding the whip was worn out and had taken a break. All Trace could envision was his Leona enduring this at barely fifteen.

"I do not think he'll break."

"He will," the larger one said, his voice deeper than the other's. "We have a long time to get him to do so."

"I will never break."

He opened his eye and glared at them through the one eye that hadn't been swollen shut. It hadn't only been a whipping. They had taken great pleasure in beating him, using him as a bag to work out their frustrations on.

"Sure you will."

The smaller one handed over a clean rag to the larger one, who wiped the blood off his meaty fists. The whip had drug through the dirt to be mingled with his own flesh each time they'd connected.

"What do you want from me?"

"We want you to return the slave you stole. And the boy."

"They are safe in England and it doesn't matter what you do to me, they will never be back."

Their smiles turned his gut over. He could hang here and take anything they doled out, but if Leona or his son were in their clutches, he would not be able to handle it.

"They will be here soon."

"Not a chance."

"Of course they will. We sent them a letter shortly after you landed saying how you needed them both back here right away to save your life."

He spat out the blood pooling in his mouth. "They'll never believe that. Nor will they come."

"You think this because they would not trust such words from just anyone. But we did have one person, well, two, whose words, we were informed, would be believed."

That unease that had been fluttering in his belly grew in a second, nearly overtaking him.

"Who?"

"Well now, son, that would be me." General Harrington turned the corner of the doorway, leaning against the wooden frame. "And that Ben slave. He signed it as well, before I slit his throat."

Betrayal unlike anything that had swarmed him when he'd learned of his brother's treachery consumed him.

"I trusted you," he gasped.

"As you should. I was your commanding officer. It was my job to instruct you and teach you right from wrong. You have to believe I have your best interests in mind now. You will see, I am right."

"Never," Trace bit off. "Why do you need them back here?"

"Because you need to learn the punishment for someone who goes against me." The general took a deep breath and lit a smoke. "Also, I want my son."

Trace's heart stopped for a moment before he blinked and tried to convince himself he'd been hearing things.

"Falcon is *my* son."

The man laughed and blew a thin line of smoke toward the ceiling. "No. He is mine. I've been fucking your wife pretty much since you married her. All the times I sent you away, purely so I could have access to that pussy. And she gave it to me so willingly. She truly is a whore." He walked closer. "I don't give a damn about that bitch of his mother, but my son, I want him back. He needs to be here so he can be raised and taught the proper order of things."

Drawing hard on the rolled tobacco, until the end glowed, General Harrington then put it to Trace's skin. Trace hissed in pain but never lowered his gaze from the man doing this to him.

"He is my son," he uttered with conviction. "When I found him he was living in filth because his mother and her current boyfriend, my *brother*, had been treating him like a dog."

"Adversity makes for a stronger man."

"You will not get your hands on him."

"Of course I will. She'll get your note and she will come with him, to save you. She will come alone because I know all the people around her and if they show their faces, I will slit your throat in front of her and my son. Once we have her again, she will stay here for the simple fact that she is under the misguided conception that you'll be turned free."

A cold haze settled over Trace and he nodded. "I may be hanging from some ropes right now, General, but if you do not kill me now, I will escape and I will kill you. Without hesitation or remorse."

Another few burns on his chest.

"We will see how your tune changes when your slave is within my grasp. Sleep well, Colonel. Leave him there for the night, he should survive. If he does not, then he's not the man I believe him to be."

Within moments Trace was alone in the dark, still dangling from the hook. The tears snuck past his defenses. Again, for the second time in his life, he was not able to protect those who meant the most in the world to him.

He willed Leona to stay away, but knew if the note made it to her, she would come. And this time, he would lose them both.

No! Not this time. I will not let her be hurt again because of me.

Chapter Twenty-Two

"Do you think he's forgotten about me? About us?"

Leona reached for the boy beside her as she thought of the best way to word her answer. On the tip of her tongue to immediately deny Trace had forgotten him, but she did understand where he was coming from. The reason behind all of his fear.

For a moment, Falcon resisted her tugging him into her lap. Then he went willingly. She looped her arms around him, lacing her fingers, not forcing him to have eye contact. Just holding him. After a few moments he settled against her, relaxing.

"Your father would never forget about you. His work may take him away, but I promise you, you're always on his mind."

"He has been gone so long. I think maybe he found somebody else. A boy who will make him proud."

Leona pressed the side of Falcon's head into her chest. Eyes blurring with unshed tears, she wished Trace had returned.

"I have known your father a long time and I have never seen him more proud than when he watches you. You are everything to him, and even if there were some kind of trouble, he would move mountains to get back to you."

Falcon tipped his head up to stare at her, eyes full of worry and so much older than they should have been. "And you."

All she did was smile and hug him tight once more. This was not the time or the place to get into her own misgivings and concern about what was going on. Spring had passed in the summer and they were creeping toward autumn with no word from the man who'd left right after the new year.

What she couldn't tell, and didn't, was about all the nightmares she had. The way she would wake covered in sweat body, aching with pain. None of it made any sense, aside from the fact that she knew she and Trace were linked. However, given the distance, she wasn't sure they had anything to do with him. They were quite possibly just her own memories coming back to haunt her.

"Do you think I will ever have a title, like Bryn?"

Grateful to be on a separate topic, she smiled slightly. "I am no expert on how the titles work with the members of peerage. What I do know is that if anyone could acquire a title, it would be you."

Falcon turned in her arms and hugged her. He kissed her cheek and hugged her once more.

"I love you, Leona." Then he ran off without a single look back.

Folding her hands upon her lap, she stared after him until she could no longer see him. "I love you too."

Today was a rare day for her. She had no work on her schedule and was planning to go to the opera later with the marquess and his wife. She was looking forward to it, not having been in quite a while.

After a leisurely dinner and saying good night to the children, they were on their way to the opera. Leona watched intently, wishing from time to time that she not only had the talent but the courage to be up on stage before people performing like this.

The ride back was done in silence, as everybody seemed to be lost in their own thoughts. The moment they were inside, everything changed.

A member of the cops waited for them in the receiving room. After speaking in hushed tone to his butler, Lucien led the way to where the law enforcement officer waited. The man stood immediately and offered a low bow.

"Forgive the intrusion, my lord. I fear this news is of great importance and could not wait until morning."

"Speak your piece."

Leona wasn't sure what to make of what was going on, however the tension in the room continued to climb. Remaining toward the back of the room, she debated leaving to allow Lucien and his wife privacy, as she doubted the news had anything to do with her, or was anything she needed to be involved with.

"Few of my men were out on patrol and we ran into Ms. Bethany. You had requested us to keep an eye out for her?"

Leona struggled not to collapse to her knees. The fact that Bethany had resurfaced scared Leona more than she cared to admit.

"And?" Lucien's tone dropped.

Ciara moved closer to Leona, who noticed that the mother of two didn't touch her, but was definitely in a protective position.

"When we caught her, she was coming out of a less than reputable business with a man who, once we questioned him, said he had just gotten off a boat that had docked earlier in the day."

Bile pushed up in Leona's throat and she swallowed, not wanting to miss whatever this man had to impart.

"Is she in custody now?" The man nodded. "I want her kept there, for threatening my wife and I want her held and tried. What about this man who had been with her?"

The officer swallowed and stepped forward. Pulling a folded parchment from his pocket, he handed it over. "We found this on him."

Lucien accepted the parchment from him and stared at it. He turned and looked at her. "This is addressed to you, Leona."

Her feet were rooted to the floor. She didn't want to approach him and take it, aware deep down that there was bad news. Ciara glanced to her as well. She forced her feet to move.

"Thank you." The whisper had to fight to make it past dry lips.

"Yes, ma'am," the officer said. Then he turned his gaze back to Lucien. "We have them both if you care to question them. I will see myself out. Thank you for your time, my lord."

The man was seen out and Lucien and Ciara stared at her.

"Do you want me to read it?" Lucien posed the question.

She didn't want *anyone* to read it. Whatever the horrible news it contained, she didn't want it to come to light and be true. Even still, she handed the parchment over, knowing she couldn't handle reading it.

She held her breath while Lucien took a knife and split the seal on the letter. He unfolded the letter and skimmed it, his expression not giving anything away to her. Perhaps Ciara knew how to read him, but Leona didn't. To be honest, she wasn't sure if she would be able to handle finding out.

Lucien flicked his gaze to her then back to the letter.

"Do you know a General Harrington?"

It took a few moments for his deep voice to penetrate her cloud of worry. She stared at him, thinking once more how lucky Ciara was to be with a man like him.

"Leona?"

She dampened her lips and nodded. "I do. That was Trace's commanding officer and the man who helped him put away his brother, and his ex-wife." She shifted closer to him. "Is that from him?"

"It is." Lucien's dark brows converged and he shook his head. "I do not like it. There's also the name Ben on the paper. Do you know him?"

"I do. He was a slave at Hawk's Cove when I was. Trace said he is still there but works for a fair wage."

Leona held out her hand and he passed the document over. She could see his reluctance in doing so.

He remained beside her as she read the words on the parchment.

To Miss Leona,
I know you do not know me but I have heard of you through the stories Colonel Morgan would tell of you. I am

his commanding officer, General Harrington. I am writing this letter on his behalf.

He is in trouble and needs you to come as expeditiously as possible. Also, we need Mr. Garrett to accompany you. At the moment, Trace is unable to write this, and as I know you do not have any reason to believe a word I say, I have asked Ben to vouch for my words.

General Harrington

Her heart seized and tears gathered, pushing hard in an attempt to get free of their confinement. Blinking in rapid succession, Leona lifted the letter once more in her trembling hand.

My Leona, I hope you know how much you mean to me. Please take this man's word. Mister Trace is in trouble and needs both you and his son by his side. There are two tickets included in there for you and young Garrett to return. I had hoped to see you again but am saddened this is the situation that will get you here to Hawk's Cove once again.

Respectfully Ben

* * * *

She woke lying on one of the chaises in the room, Ciara beside her, dabbing her forehead with a damp cloth.

"It is a trap," the marchioness said without hesitation as she continued to touch Leona's clammy skin.

"Yes."

"You will not go." Lucien stood behind his wife, arms crossed and a thunderous scowl on his face.

"I must." She sat up in slow increments, allowing and appreciating that Ciara assisted her. "I do not want

Falcon to go, but if we do not, they will kill him for sure."

"We will come with you."

"No," she blurted out. "You have far too much to lose. And I would guess that your descriptions have been passed along. They will be looking for anyone traveling with the two of us."

"I'll go," Ciara insisted. "You will *not* do this alone."

Interjecting before Lucien could dispute his wife, Leona shook her head and gripped her friend's hand.

"No. You are a wife and a mother. Two children and a third on the way, you cannot risk this." She tightened her hold. "Plus, we know if you went, your husband would come, and that puts us right back to this situation."

"I do not want you going alone."

"I have an idea," Lucien said, backing to the door. "I need to send for someone. Then, *wife*, you and I will discuss why you did not see fit to tell your loving husband you are carrying his child once more." His eyes burned a path across the room before he stepped through.

Leona stared down at the letter beside her. How Trace must feel, betrayed by the ones he had trusted. Again. Her heart went out to him, and she wished she were close enough to hold him tight.

She sat there in silence for a while.

"Are you sure this is what you should be doing?" Ciara watched her with a concerned gaze.

"I cannot leave him there. I *will* not."

"Why do they want you back?"

"My guess is to be a slave once more." It churned her stomach to imagine going back to that life. But for

Trace, she was willing to risk her freedom. "But I do not know. Perhaps they just wish to kill me."

"And his son?"

She worried her lower lip. "I know he was not sure if Falcon was his." She spoke in a low tone, as if they could be overheard. "Perhaps the true father wants him back. I do not want to take him, but I do not think he will let me go without him."

"I do not think he will. He is so much like his father in that way, protective of the woman he loves. His mother. *You*."

Leona hugged her. "Thank you, for everything."

"Do not think we won't come after you, because we will. You have a lead on us, but trust me, we *will* follow, and you will not be stuck there."

Lucien stepped back into the room and Phillip followed, his normally teasing expression serious. "Phillip will accompany you. They will not know about him, and he can fight."

"I am ready. I will secure passage on the ship. We will not speak, Leona, but I will be there, watching over you." The Earl of Edais put his gray eyes on her.

"I cannot ask you to put your life in danger," Leona insisted.

He gave her a flirting smile. "And you did no such thing. This is me doing right. You mean something to this family and, while we just met, that means you are also important to me. I will leave now and see you on the ship." He sketched a bow and left.

Lucien pulled Leona to her feet and hugged her. "My wife was right. I will follow. You will not be returned to that life."

"If it means freeing Trace and letting him and his son —"

"No," he interrupted. "That man would not want you trading your freedom for his. He is going to be furious enough that you went. We will not let you three stay."

Leona held on to the conviction in his tone and the knowledge that she did have family. They loved her and would protect her, as best they could.

* * * *

Time had blurred into nothingness as Trace was rotated through a regimen of whippings, beatings, being burned and always with the taunting. They didn't let him die, however, and he wanted nothing more than to find a way out.

They had taken his right eye and now he had a patch.

Unfortunately, the general knew what he did in terms of being resourceful and made sure there was no way he could escape. Guards were forbidden to speak to him, and there were never less than four present any time the door was open, regardless of the condition of his body.

Occasionally someone would come in and clean up his injuries, perhaps to keep them from becoming infected and ruining their fun if he died. He was no longer sure of anything.

But he refused to tell them more about Leona or his son, holding onto the belief the two he loved more than anything in this life were safe in England, away from the clutches of this island's evil.

Then the beatings stopped. He was allowed to recover, and fear grew within him as to why. No point in him asking, as they didn't speak to him. Trace pushed himself as best he could to remain in decent condition. He ate what they gave him, small though it may be and he worked to keep up is strength. He didn't want to be unable to fight if he had to, or was given the opportunity.

One day the door opened. Trace ignored the ever-present four guards and stared impassively at the fifth man there. General Harrington.

His lips were turned up in glee.

"My son has returned."

Trace longed to deny it, but nothing passed his lips. He refused to argue this with him. Falcon was his! All he did was wait to see what the general said next.

"No questions? Do not worry, you'll get to see your whore once more before I get her. Seems she's unaware of her place. No one came with her. Perhaps living over there has made her assume she can do what she wants without consequences. She believed that Ben and I were concerned for your well-being, and has brought my son back to me." He crossed his arms. "I mean, Ben was concerned, but as that old bastard is dead, it does not matter."

He gestured with one hand and the four men stepped in to get Trace up.

One on each side of him, they headed for the door.

"Nothing to say to me?" General Harrington asked, as he trailed him.

"Do you remember what I told you when this first started?"

The man hadn't lied. Trace could feel Leona within him, her warmth and strength the calming presence in his life. As strong as it was, he knew the love of his life was close. Too close to danger.

"That I should have killed you?"

Trace nodded.

"I will kill you, but not until I have your whore before you and my son, so you know as he does, there is a place for everyone in this world. And her kind is *not* equal to ours."

"You are going to die a horrible death at my hands." Trace dismissed the general and stared out of the cell that had been his home for the past few months.

"Always so arrogant, Trace Morgan. One of the things I had admired about you. Right now, you seem desperate."

Trace didn't respond, and as the men took him somewhere else, he heard the general yelling after him, "You could have had it all with me."

His bath consisted of being shoved into a tub and getting cleaned up a bit, not a lot. One man trimmed his beard and hair while another held a gun on him the entire time. Trace didn't fight it. He sat there in the warm sun and gathered his energy for the fight he knew without a doubt would be coming. For the moment he could be the perfect subdued prisoner, giving them no reason to do anything more to him.

Later that morning he was loaded into a carriage, with guards around him, and they set off. By the direction, he knew the end destination was Hawk's Cove.

Trace was chained in his bed once there and no one entered the room. He assumed the general had threated his workers. The bed was heavenly to be in and he just lay there for a moment.

"Who is the Earl of Edais?" General Harrington demanded, bursting into the room.

"Who?" He shook his head and pushed himself back so he was a bit more upright in bed, the clinking of the chain holding him a reminder of his current situation.

"You do not know him?"

"I never met an Earl of Edais while I was in England. I met and befriended a marquess. And a viscount. But no earls." He adjusted himself again. "Why?"

"There's one downstairs asking to talk to you."

"And you think I what, sent a letter asking him to come while you held me prisoner? Because I knew the exact date you would be bringing me back here." He didn't even try to hide his sarcasm.

The general snapped his fingers and one of his men stepped through the door with a young girl in hand. "I am going to let you go talk to him. You give anything away and this one here will be a gift for my men. She is young and tender and my men have not had a woman in a long time."

"She is but a child," he growled.

"Then I suggest you be a good lord of the house and do as I say."

"You have my word. Just leave her alone."

"Johnny here will keep her with him until the earl leaves." Another man came over and unlocked the cuff keeping Trace to the bed. "A *long* time without a woman, remember that."

Like he would forget. He straightened his clothes and headed down the stairs, using the railing to help support him.

His visitor stood there, back to him as he looked at a painting that hung in the entryway.

"My lord? You asked to see me?"

The man turned, a slight smile on his face but nothing more than that. Trace knew right away he was being sized up, and found lacking.

"I did, if you are the owner of this plantation."

"I am. Trace Morgan."

"Phillip Vallence, Earl of Edais."

They shook hands when Trace was on the ground floor.

"And how may I be of service to you, my lord?"

"Do you mind if we talk outside? It is so nice here and, after leaving England, I would love to have the sun on my face."

"Of course not. I will have some refreshment brought out," Trace said, looking at one of the staff. "We will sit out front." Personally, he could go for some more sun.

General Harrington came out with the man who carried the whiskey, introduced himself and sat down beside Trace.

"I am interested in buying this place. I have heard people say you no longer frequent it and wanted to inquire if it was for sale?"

"Odd, is it not, to be making the inquires yourself instead of having one of your men do it?" General Harrington asked.

"I am an earl, General. Not a fool. I keep a close eye on *all* my assets. I do have men who make purchases on my behalf, however, as I had not seen this place yet, I traveled here to make sure it was something I would like. I have to say when I landed I was impressed with the island, and being here, from what I saw riding in, I know I do want this land." His tone held a slight reprimand that Trace had heard Lucien use from time to time when he wanted to make it clear he believed his station to be above another's.

Sipping some whiskey, he relished the burn as slid down his throat. "I had not given much thought to selling," he admitted, and that was the truth.

"I would appreciate it if you did." Phillip stood after finishing his drink. "I will be in town for a while. Please contact me there, after you have had some time to think about it. I thank you for taking the time to speak with me."

A carriage came up and Trace wanted to scream at this man to take the woman he *knew* would be stepping out away with him.

Trace stood and shook his hand. "It was my pleasure, my lord."

Sure enough, behind them, a footman held the carriage door and out jumped Falcon. He was followed by Leona. His son waited and took her hand.

The earl turned and went to the man holding his horse. He barely slowed, just tipped his hat at Leona. Then he swung up and rode off.

Neither she nor Falcon showed any recognition of the man who had just left. Trace knew General Harrington had been waiting for that.

"Papa," Falcon cried out, dashing up the steps and grabbing him tight. "Are you okay? What happened to your eye? The letter Leona got said you weren't doing well."

A bevy of mixed emotions poured through Trace. He held his son again, but the boy was in so much danger.

"I'm getting better. Thank you for coming." He cut his gaze to General Harrington, who had fixated on Leona. "Both of you."

He could see her emotions all over her face. And what wasn't showing, he could feel through their link. She was torn about being back at Hawk's Cove and seeing him here once more.

She lifted the hem of her skirt and walked up the steps to where he and Falcon stood. With a curtsey, she put her brown eyes on him. What did she think of him only having a single eye now? Did she think him less because of the loss?

"Good to see you again, Mr. Morgan." Then she looked to the man beside him. "Are you General Harrington?"

"I am."

"Thank you, sir, for letting me know he wasn't well. I am glad to see he is doing better."

"You don't even care about your place, do you?" the general growled.

"Papa?"

"That man is not your dad, boy. I am." General Harrington yanked Falcon from Trace. "You will stay here with me and I will teach you how things are supposed to be. Where people's places are this world."

"I do need to tell you, General," Leona said, "the Duke of Stokley and the Marquess of Heartstone and their families are on the way. I was with them when the note came and they too wish to make sure that their friend Mr. Morgan is safe and recovering well."

Trace knew where this was going and wanted to stop it.

"Your point?"

"If you want me to pretend that you were not the mastermind behind this, and that you are a better man than you are, you cannot leave a mark on Mr. Morgan, or the boy. They can go with the duke and marquess when they leave."

"Why would I let my son go?"

"I'm *not* leaving here without you, Leona," Trace thundered. The pain tearing through him was so much worse than any of the beatings he had taken.

He knew exactly what she was doing. She had known precisely what she would be walking into. A trap. To keep her back in the one place she hated. And, still, she'd come. To save him.

Chapter Twenty-Three

Leona refused to look away from the general. "You do not need this child. He is happy over in England. Agree to let them both go and I will tell the duke and marquess any lie you want. I'll say I am staying, willingly."

"What if I threaten everyone else? You do not hold any bargaining power over me," the general spat.

"I don't care about the rest. I am willing to trade my life and my freedom for those two. And you are wrong. I know you recognize the Duke of Stokley's name. It was all over your face."

"You will pay for this insolence."

"I know."

She beckoned to Falcon, who yanked free from the general and ran back to her. Sinking to her knees, Leona hugged him then drew back, cupping his face.

"You are perfect. Never forget that. No matter what anyone else tells you, Trace is your father. He loves you and will give his life for you if needed. I need you to hug Jupiter and Neptune for me when you get back."

He shook his head. "You have to come too."

"No, I will not be going back with you and your father. I was raised here and it was time I came home." She used her thumbs to move the tears from his eyes. "You own a place in my heart, Falcon. Thank you for being part of my life." Her heart was being ripped in two. "Be good for your father." She kissed his cheek and stood.

With a deep breath, she looked between the general and Trace then back to the man she'd despised from the moment she'd received the letter. He nodded. Lifting her chin, she walked to Trace.

He looked gaunt, and she knew his time had not been an easy one. He had a patch over his right eye. The change had been shocking, and gave him a much more dangerous air.

"I am *not* leaving you, Leona."

"I love you, Trace Morgan. Now and always. It is my turn to do the saving."

The corners of his mouth pinched. "No, you saved me on the field. It's my turn."

She wanted to touch him but didn't think the general would allow that. "You have always saved me. Never forget that. Take your son and go to England. Live the best lives you can."

He must not have given a damn about the general, for he grabbed her upper arms and yanked her close.

"Do you think I give a fuck about any of that if it means you are left here?" The question was tortured.

Her body flew to life at his touch. "I think you're a father who will do what is best for his son."

"You are what's best. For him *and* for me."

"Him growing up with the general in his life is not what is best. *We* know this. I am sorry it couldn't have been different for us, Trace. Go, be free. Sell this place and take flight."

She saw the flicker of understanding in his eye. Giving in to her need, she touched his face and brushed her fingers along the strap for his patch. "I like the look. Very dashing."

"I am not leaving without you."

She stepped back. "Goodbye, Trace."

The general gestured and two men appeared to take a struggling Trace back inside. Falcon stepped in front of her when two other men moved toward her.

"No harm comes to my son. Not yet. Take him to a room and chain this one up in the back." The general glared at her as he made the command.

Leona didn't resist when she was dragged through the house, past faces she'd not seen in years to a small windowless room in the back off the kitchen, where the house slave had slept. The room was a lot like she recalled and as the man tossed her to the floor, she bit back a cry of pain.

The heavy door slammed shut before a lock was engaged. She scrambled to the corner pallet, wrapped her arms around her legs and sobbed. Holding images of Trace and her open home in her mind, she tried to figure out how in the hell she was going to go through living like this once more. This time would be worse, of that she had no doubt.

* * * *

For two days she barely saw anyone. All the men did was let her out for a few moments, then it was back in there.

After she had gotten cleaned up on the second day, the general was there when she was pushed back in the room. He was a large man, and she could see where he had made a good leader.

"We have someone coming to talk about buying this place. I want you there to serve. It was Trace's stipulation. I guess he thinks I am beating you like you deserve. What he doesn't understand is I want you unblemished when I take you to my bed. Then I will beat you to within an inch of your life. Right now, you will serve. You will not speak unless spoken to. You *will* remember your place."

"Yes, sir."

He gripped her chin. "It's been so long since I've had one who was as pretty as you. I cannot wait to make you choke on my cock." He released her and gestured to the wall, where a dress hung. "Change."

Knowing there was no point in asking him to leave, Leona just went to the maid's outfit. Undoing the buttons on her dress, she shrugged her shoulders, allowing it to slip to the floor, leaving her in her undergarments. Also exposing the scars on her back to the man in there with her. She reached for the outfit and dropped it over her head then fastened it up with haste.

Turning back to him, she said, "And shoes?"

"You have some."

"These are not maid shoes."

Irritation flashed, but there was a pair for her shortly. She slipped them on and smoothed her hands down the dress. *Nothing more than playing hostess. I can get through this.*

They had set up food outside, and as she carried the drinks out, she breathed a bit easier when her gaze landed on Phillip, who sat near Trace. General Harrington was there as well, but she'd expected that.

They discussed the sale of Hawk's Cove and she did as she had been instructed — served the men and kept her mouth shut.

There was no way to ignore how Trace's gaze followed her whenever she was in sight, and the struggle not to react was hard. Walking back inside, she stiffened when the general smacked her on the ass.

"Keep your fucking hands off her," Trace growled.

"Remember your place."

Leona whirled around in time to see Trace launch himself up and out of his chair to hit the general square and take him down. She couldn't even find it in her to scream. In her peripheral vision she noticed Phillip getting up, but she couldn't take her gaze from Trace and the general rolling around before her.

Flashbacks of Trace fighting with his brothers came to mind, but this was much more deadly, the consequences more severe.

She felt the staff gather beside her but she still didn't look away. Two of the larger men stepped forward.

"No," she said. "This is between them. We do not interfere." The men listened to her.

She regretted her words moments later when the general rose up over Trace, hands around his neck, choking him. They were so close Leona could not see space between them. They continued to fight and tussle. Time slowed for her until the loud retort of a gun shattered her world.

"Trace!" She leaped toward him but was caught up by Phillip, who had returned at some point.

"Give him time to get to his feet."

"But he was shot." Or so she thought because it looked like the general had the upper hand.

General Harrington's body was heaved to the side and Trace exhaled sharply before he got up. Phillip released Leona right away and she ran to the man she loved. He caught her and yanked her close. Mouth slanting over hers, he kissed her.

Digging her grip into the collar of his shirt, she held Trace as tight as she could. Tears slid unchecked down her face.

He peppered her with kisses until he finally put them nose to nose.

"I love you, Leona. I want you to be my wife."

"Yes."

"Do not ever do anything like that again."

"Your life for mine is acceptable, Trace Morgan."

"Not to me, kitten. Never to me."

She moved her hands up to his jaw, held him and kissed him. "What about the rest of his men?"

"I don't care," he said without looking away from her.

"Should we not be worried about them?"

"No. I have to explain this to Falcon then you and I are going to bed."

She dropped her gaze. "Trace, it's the middle of the day. And there are people around."

"Then they can leave. I don't fucking care. You and me, kitten. Give me a few minutes to talk to our son." One more kiss and he stepped away.

Trying to control her embarrassment at how loudly he'd announced he was taking her to bed, she finally looked up and gasped. The general's men were all on their knees before a group of men she'd not thought she would see again. Lucien, Jackson, Conar and Rafe stood there beside Phillip.

Jackson stepped around them and held out his arms. She flew into them and held him.

"I am so sorry, lass."

"Thank you for coming."

He tipped her chin up. "You are my daughter. I will do anything for you."

"Thank you, Papa." She hugged him again and looked to the others there. "How? I thought you were not coming until later."

Lucien shook his head. "My wife said if we did not get on the same ship as you did, she would. We know she would have, so we did. We just did not disembark until after you had."

"Thank you all."

"You are family."

"Kitten?"

She melted at that familiar endearment. Brushing a kiss over Jackson's cheek, she hurried up the steps to Trace's side. Falcon looked at them both then scampered down to where the other men stood.

Trace swept her up in his arms and carried her inside, not stopping for anything until he got to his bedroom and placed her down. Bracing himself over her with his body, he kissed her until she trembled.

"I will always love you, kitten." Another kiss. "I'm going to sell this place and you are right, it's time for us to take flight, but I do not want to go without you."

Skimming her hands up his torso, being careful of any injuries he may still have, Leona smiled. "By your side forever, Trey."

He claimed her mouth once more as her world shrank to the two of them, only.

Epilogue

A cottage along the English coast

"Are you sure?" Trace demanded, dashing up the stairs to the bedroom he shared with his wife. Bursting in, he hurried to the large chest of drawers and grabbed the ring sitting there.

"Of course I am, boyo. I know what an arriving carriage sounds like. Plus, those two hounds of hers are running up."

Dashing back downstairs, he skidded to a halt beside Jackson as the carriage rocked to a stop before the door. He patted the dogs on the head before they streaked inside to shake off the rain and settle by the fire.

"I will go somewhere else," Jackson said.

Trace didn't take his gaze off the carriage door. Leona stepped out and his heart leaped up in his throat.

Hurrying to her side, he kissed her.

"Hello, Trace," she mumbled when he allowed her up for air.

Rain sluiced down around them but he didn't give a damn.

"I missed you, kitten." He ran his hand along her swollen belly. "Both of you."

"We missed you too. I did pick something up on the way."

"Hello, Papa."

"Falcon!" He hugged his son and went back to his wife, helping her inside the cottage. After she had said hello to Jackson and Falcon went with him, it was just the two of them before the fire.

"How is Ciara?"

"Ciara is well. Another son. They named him Henry."

"I am sure they are thrilled. Lucien will become even more arrogant."

She leaned against him and he wrapped his arms tight around her.

Picking up her left hand, Trace slid the ring on Leona's finger.

"What is this?"

"The ring I should have given you when we wed."

"I do not need a ring, Trey. I have you and Falcon."

"I needed you to have it." He turned the ring, showing her the hawk in flight with their names on either side of the wings.

She kissed his hand and placed it back against her stomach. "Love you," she muttered before she fell asleep.

He held her there until he too, drifted off to sleep. He still wasn't a huge fan of her being out of his sight, not with what had happened on the island, but she seemed to have recovered from that. She was focused on the fact that their family would soon be growing by another one—or more, depending on what she carried within her belly.

Trace had loved this woman since the first time he saw her and would far beyond the day he took his last breath. She was his everything.

Want to see more from this author? Here's a taster for you to enjoy!

S.W.A.L.K.: Cross My Heart
Aliyah Burke

Excerpt

Washington, D.C.

"Come on, sweetcheeks. Don't be like that. This is your lucky night."

Cyn tucked a curl behind her ear, opening her mouth to inform this man—and that was a term she used loosely—just how wrong he was just as two men, both taller than her, appeared at her side.

The man, Jack, she recalled his name being, eyed them both up and down with challenge. She fought to hide her snort.

"You know," she remarked as if his life weren't in danger, "you should probably just walk away now."

Jack puffed up and sent another scathing look at the two males beside her. "These your men? You one of those broads who enjoys more than one dick at a time?"

"Oh," she said with a smile, "these aren't my dates. But you'll wish they were."

He snorted. "Who are they then?"

"My brothers."

The words barely had time to leave her mouth before her two brothers each took one of the obnoxious man's arms and backed him away from her. Not the slightest bit polite about doing it either. Rolling her eyes, she turned back to the pool game she'd been keeping an eye on and sucked on the straw while watching the woman there set up the man she was playing against.

"How do you do it, Cynzia?"

One shoulder up in a shrug, she waited until the woman sank her latest shot before glancing back to her brothers. They were triplets, the three of them—she was not only the youngest but the only girl—and it tended to make her brothers a bit overprotective.

Michael, the eldest, wrapped his arm around her, and she sank into him. She was also the shortest, not having gotten the height the boys had from their father, Giovanni Cassano. She was closer to their mother's height.

"What are you doing here, Cyn?" This time the question was posed by the middle brother, Dante. "Why aren't you home with Mom?"

Pushing her now empty drink at her brother, she turned to be able to see them both. "I'm not in diapers. I'm twenty-three, same as the two of you. I am allowed to go out to bars."

Michael growled low in his throat. "And get picked up by assholes like the one we just had to chase off? You should be smarter than that."

That dig hurt and pricked her normally laid-back temper.

"One, I wasn't getting picked up. He was hitting on me, and I was about to tell him to fuck off when you two walked over."

"You didn't tell us where you were going," Dante snapped.

"Of course I didn't. I needed to get away from the smothering. You two are far worse than Mom and Dad, and let's face it, between Dad and our uncles, I didn't think anyone would be able to be worse. But you two have surpassed them with flying colors." They both grinned. She scowled. "Not something to be proud of. I came here to get away from everyone."

"We followed you." Michael pointed out the obvious.

He had always been so literal. A lot like their mom, Jaydee. Very blunt and took statements as they were given. He didn't have the time or the care to try to see if there were hidden meanings in the words coming out of someone's mouth.

Cyn flattened her lips and took several deep breaths. It wasn't like she didn't love her brothers. She did, and she would die for them in a heartbeat. However, she also wanted to do things without them. Like find a man and have sex. Lots and lots of it.

"Why did you follow me, Michael?"

"You're our sister."

His tone told her everything. He found nothing wrong with his behavior.

"I am, yes. And I love you both. But you have to stop following me everywhere. I'm capable of taking care of myself. I want to go out and not see you boys there behind me, scaring away a guy I may want to talk with."

Dante crossed his arms. Michael ran his gaze over her.

"You want us away because you are looking for sex."

May the good Lord just let the floor open up and swallow her because she was mortified. Her siblings weren't quiet, and Michael's statement had gotten more than a few males' attention.

She ignored the flush scampering over her face and held up her hands. "Stop it. Right now, both of you. You're trying to get me to leave, well, fine. I'm leaving." They both stepped forward, but she shook her head. "No. I'm leaving by myself. I'm going to a different bar and I don't want to see you until morning. We'll meet at the hotel for breakfast. We'll talk, laugh, and I will go with you to the airport to get you on a plane to head back home and let me enjoy my trip."

"You'll be without protection," Dante protested.

"I don't need it. I grew up in the same house as you did. We have the same parents. The same uncles. All of whom taught us self-defense. Not to mention Aunt Bailey." She took a deep breath. She wasn't a schoolgirl who was in danger. She knew how to take care of herself. "I'm leaving now. And I'll show you I can survive by myself. I'll even kiss a guy on my way out, and you'll see, it will be okay."

Pushing up on her toes, she kissed Michael's cheek then Dante's. She walked to the door after putting her empty, which she had taken back from her brother, down on the bar. As she neared the exit, three men walked in that took her breath away. All of them were fit, and she would bet her life they were military. Having grown up in her household, it was easy to pick them out.

It was the man in the middle, though, who made her heart beat all the faster. Darkly tanned skin, short black hair and a body she would love to touch. He turned toward her as he looked around the establishment and his lips quirked up in the left corner of his mouth. Those blue eyes mesmerized her, and she nearly tripped over her own feet.

Standing before him, before she could talk her way out of what she was about to do, she smiled. He replied in kind.

Now or never.

She slid her arm around his neck and once again stood on her toes. This time, instead of the cheek as she'd done with her brothers, she went for his mouth, to touch those bow-shaped lips.

Seconds later his hand palmed the nape of her neck, holding her close in a proprietary motion as his other hand pressed against the small of her back. His tongue dipped inside her mouth and teased hers.

Cyn scrambled to get her senses back enough to pull away. She didn't want to, even as she did. The din of the bar faded into obscurity, and all she could focus on were this man and the harsh pounding in her chest combined with the way her lungs struggled for air.

Forcing her legs to move, she ducked by the men there and walked out of the bar.

Holy shit.

"The hell, man? How do you pull that shit off?"

Lucas Hoch shrugged as his two friends continued to razz him. He, personally, had done a one-eighty to follow that woman — who'd just walked up and kissed him — with his eyes as she exited.

His entire body trembled with the slow to depart tingles along his skin, every nerve hyper aware.

"It's crap is what it is," Trey, best friend and fellow Marine said, clapping Lucas on the back.

"Agreed," Alberti, other best friend and fellow Marine, added. "We're just as hot as you. I would say hotter but she went to you."

Yeah, she did.

And he craved more. A fucking ton more.

I have to find her. No way in hell do I let this woman get away.

"Be right back." He ducked off before they could say a word. Those two would have plenty of words to say as well.

Outside the crowd out to enjoy the nightlife was growing. Grateful for his height, he scanned first left then right.

God, he could still taste her, the harsh taste of alcohol hidden beneath what he knew was her and her alone. A sample he craved more of, needed to indulge in. And one he wasn't willing to allow another to taste. Ever.

Then there was her soft skin and curves beneath his hand and pressed into him as they'd kissed. He'd forgotten everything but her.

Lucas checked both directions once more and found her, by a lamppost talking on the phone. He was on his way far before he was conscious of his action.

She had a shoulder against the pole, and her ankles crossed. Unlike some of the people walking the streets, she was aware.

Sharp eyes locked onto him despite the fact that she didn't move. With a calm he didn't feel he stared at her as she ended her call and pushed the phone in her front pocket.

Lucas moved until the toes of his boots touched the tips of her heeled footwear. Even with the ugly light from the streetlamps, she was stunning.

Smooth skin the color of coffee with two splashes of cream. Maybe three. High cheekbones, incredible full lips he wanted to taste again.

He placed a hand over her head on the pole she was against. Her tight red shirt drew his eyes directly to her breasts, which teased a hint of flesh.

"You can't just kiss me like that and vanish."

Her smile gutted him.

She ran her gaze over him. "You look like a man who can take care of himself."

He licked his lips, preening when she followed the move with these golden-brown eyes. Then she met his gaze again.

"I used to think so but then this stunning sexy woman walked out of a crowd and kissed me so that I forgot my own name."

"What name would that be?"

He bent closer, still keeping an eye on their surroundings. "Lucas. Corporal Lucas Hoch. United States Marine Corps."

"Pleased to meet you, Corporal Hoch."

Closer still.

"Lucas." He inhaled and was surrounded by a floral citrus scent. "Or Luc."

All she did was smile.

He wanted her name. "And you are?"

She looked past him, and her grin grew. "Leaving."

What? No, he wanted to keep her with him. "Name?"

"You want to know that bad you'll figure it out. But I will be at the Wall tomorrow around three."

This hadn't gone his way.

She pushed up and brushed her mouth to the corner of his mouth. "'Night, Marine."

As she walked away, her fingers trailed along his midsection, like she couldn't stop herself from touching him. Gut tight, he turned and watched her walk off.

Time lost all meaning, but he did know when his friends settled on either side of him. Both crossed their arms as all three of them stared off in the same direction.

"I'm going to marry that woman, boys. That right there is the future, one and only, Mrs. Lucas Hoch."

Alberti snorted. "Marriage? You're twenty-five. Why are you thinking about marriage?"

He pushed his hands in his pockets. "I wasn't. Until she walked into my life." Lucas couldn't stop the smile from turning up his lips. Hell, he'd never felt this way in his entire life. And none of it mattered. She was his. His heart belonged to her.

"I'm heading back to the hotel. I have to get some sleep. I'm meeting her tomorrow."

"What's the first name of your Mrs. Hoch?" Trey asked.

"No clue. She wouldn't tell me."

As expected, his friends laughed. "Let me get this straight. You're hung up on some broad because she kissed you for all of a second in a bar. Now you're ready to marry her and don't even know her name."

He nodded. "Correct, Alberti." Lucas rocked back on his heels. "'Night." Without waiting for them to say anything else, he walked off. They would be fine without him, but he wasn't going to get plastered now. No way was he going to meet her again nursing a hangover.

Lucas didn't expect them to follow him back to the hotel, but he'd just stepped out of the shower and had dressed for sleep when they both walked in. Scowling.

"I thought you two were going to go get drunk."

They both flipped him off. "Fuck you, Luc. You know we're a trio. Plus if you're in here moping about your woman, we can't bring back any whores."

"Trey, no whores even if I wasn't moping, which I'm not." He sat on the couch where he was going to be sleeping. "You want strange pussy, you go to their place, we never bring them back here. I thought you learned that in Hong Kong."

Trey flushed at the memory. "Fuck you."

Lucas laughed and lay back, pulling the blanket up. "No thanks. Didn't want you then, want you even less now. 'Night, guys."

He was up early in the morning and got his workout in. While his friends still crashed, he ate breakfast then made his way through the nation's capital. Three was far away, but he didn't have any intention of missing her.

His entire body hummed at the prospect of seeing her again. And soon.

About the Author

USA Today Bestselling author Aliyah Burke is an avid reader and is never far from pen and paper (or the computer). She is happily married to a career military man. They are owned by six Borzoi. She spends her days at the day job, writing, and working with her dogs.

Aliyah loves to hear from readers. You can find her contact information, website details and author profile page at https://www.totallybound.com

Home of Erotic Romance

Sign up for our newsletter and find out about all our romance book releases, eBook sales and promotions, sneak peeks and FREE romance books!